Ronan O'Brien

Ronan O'Brien is a solicitor who specialises in the area of criminal law. He is originally from Dublin but now lives in County Kildare. This is his first book.

Confessions of a Fallen Angel

Ronan O'Brien

SCEPTRE

First published in Great Britain in 2008 by Sceptre
An imprint of Hodder & Stoughton
An Hachette Livre UK Company

2

A CIP catalogue record for this title is available from the British Library

ISBN 978 0 340 95245 0

Typeset in Caslon Book by Palimpsest Book Production Limited,
Grangemouth, Stirlingshire

Printed and bound by Clays Ltd, St Ives plc

Hodder & Stoughton policy is to use papers that are natural, renewable
and recyclable products and made from wood grown in sustainable forests.
The logging and manufacturing processes are expected to conform to the
environmental regulations of the country of origin.

Hodder & Stoughton Ltd
338 Euston Road
London NW1 3BH

www.hodder.co.uk

For Aoife O'Brien
(1971–1988)
Thanks for looking out for me.

I
Owen

Dying was the easy bit. It was during my life after death that things started to go wrong. A conspiracy of coincidences perhaps or else maybe some higher power was having a laugh at my expense. But when I returned from the other side I brought something fearful back with me.

I died for the first time on the day after my tenth birthday. I was Ian Rush at the time, the 1984 European Golden Boot Winner for the thirty-two league goals that he scored for Liverpool Football Club. Owen Collins was Ronnie Whelan, Andy Kavanagh was Liam Brady and Mark Croke was Mark Croke, an annoying little fucker who owned the only leather football amongst the lot of us so we had to let him play. Our pitch was St Peter's car park; St Peter's being the local Catholic church in Rathgorman on the north side of Dublin where I grew up. Deano Maguire and Robbie Campbell were also playing that day and there were others as well whose names have become shrouded in the mists of time, like extras in a dream sequence. Although maybe that's kind of appropriate because the whole dying thing did feel a lot like a dream. After a certain point, it wasn't frightening anymore and it certainly wasn't painful. Nor was it a dream, of course. It was just something that happened to me and nothing has been quite the same ever since, so it's probably where I should begin my story.

Liverpool Football Club was far and away the biggest thing in my life around that time. I remember dropping about a million unsubtle hints to let my parents know that I wanted a Liverpool jersey for my tenth birthday and my ma had countered my pleas with equal enthusiasm. She loved to subject me to the usual bleeding heart – 'We can't afford to put shoes on our feet and you're looking for a football jumper that costs *how much*?' – routine. But that was all just a part of my ma winding me up. She was brilliant at it. On the morning of my birthday, she presented me with a small wrapped box and yet another variation of the Monty Python 'I was raised in a hole in the road' sketch. I pulled off the wrapping paper to reveal a box of Lyons tea bags.

'Ah, lovely, make us a cup o tea would ya love? I'm parched!' she said. And then as she walked away from me, she threw off her dressing gown to reveal a red footballer's jersey about ten sizes too small for her with the number nine printed across the back in white.

'MAAA, you'll stretch it!' I said. She turned around, grabbed the box of tea from my hands and started kicking it around the kitchen like a football. I took her on at her own game even though she was fouling me something terrible. My brother Jack stared at us from his high chair with his mouth open and an expression on his face like we had gone mad. Then he put his fingers in his mouth and started giggling. When my father walked into the kitchen to see what all the shouting was about, my mother had one hand on my face pushing me away while she attempted to pick up the 'ball' with the other.

'REFEREE!' I tried shouting at my da, but by then I was laughing so hard that a wheezy 'Ref!' was all I could squeeze out. I took a blast of my inhaler to help me get my breath back. My mother looked at me guiltily while my father seemed to have no idea where to look. After a few seconds, he came over and ruffled my hair a bit.

'Happy birthday, son!' he said. 'Hope you like your present.'

Now you're probably thinking that the formative years of my life unfolded like one big long ice-cream commercial – smiley happy faces everywhere and endless sunny days, and I do have a few memories that fall in with that picture. But then I went and fucked it all up by killing my best friend. But that wasn't for another two years or so after my own death, which, as I've already said, really wasn't all that bad. It was quite pleasant, in fact. Dying for me wasn't wholly unlike the first time I got intoxicated or the first time that I made love, in that while it felt very strange at the time, I realised afterwards that it couldn't feel any other way.

It was 26 February 1988, the day after my tenth birthday, and a kiddie version of the FA Cup final was taking place in the icy grounds of St Peter's. It was Liverpool versus Arsenal and even better than the real thing as far as we were concerned. Even better because we were playing in it. I would say that I was playing as a striker but no positions had been allocated except for the goal-keepers. In fact, apart from the two goalies, every kid present would have described himself as a striker. Tactics were non-existent and there wasn't a whole lot of passing going on either. We all followed the ball around like Benny Hill chasing after scantily clad women and the result was that the game play resembled a giant moving huddle of people and flailing limbs.

On this particular day, I remember at one point the ball emerged from the scrum of bodies and rolled in my direction. I was the nearest one to it but not for long because the other kids were already charging after it. I started running in order to get there first. My intention had been to hoof the ball as hard as I could towards the goalpost coats at the other end of the car park, but just as I pulled back the trigger, I slipped on an icy patch of ground and went sprawling head over heels on to my arse. The other kids were almost upon me now but still I hadn't given up. I tried to kick the ball from a horizontal position on the ground but I couldn't get any satisfying contact on it because it had rolled to a stop near my midriff.

Mark Croke was the first of the other kids to reach me. I was still lying on my side on the ground with the ball beside me but he didn't even slow down as he approached me. Instead he blasted the ball at point-blank range straight into my stomach. It rebounded away from me and so when the rest of the pack arrived, the focus was on an area a couple of yards in front of me. The game continued but the damage had been done. I watched Robbie and Deano hacking at the ball from different directions. Nobody was paying me the slightest bit of attention. Then I caught Owen's eye and I think he saw the frightened look on my face because he stopped following the ball and walked over to me.

'Are ya aw righ?' he asked.

I had manoeuvred myself on to my knees but I was unable to speak. It was more the fact that I was unable to breathe that worried me though. I was winded and having an asthma attack at the same time. I reached into the pocket of my tracksuit bottoms and pulled out my inhaler. I put it to my lips and fired off two quick puffs but when I pulled it away from my mouth, I could see the gaseous medicine drifting out of my mouth like a smoke ring. That wasn't supposed to happen but I wasn't capable of sucking it into me. My throat had closed to the size of a pinhole, making it almost impossible to pull any air at all into my lungs.

The seconds ticked by nonchalantly while I grabbed my stomach and my throat and fought my losing battle with suffocation. Oxygen was all around me but I couldn't take a breath. I felt like my own body was trying to kill me. My face went from white to red to blue like an animated *Les Misérables* poster. When I got to the blue stage, Owen was roaring at the others to go for help. The game had stopped and I was vaguely aware of the puzzled looks on some of the other kids' faces. I lay down on the ground in the foetal position and I managed to suck a few tiny breaths into my panicked lungs. But it wasn't enough. It wasn't nearly enough. Everything started to go grey and at the same time I started to relax and feel a little better. Breathing didn't seem that important anymore and a sense of calm washed over me. I've read since that terminally-ill people often show a slight improvement in their condition just before checking out of their bodies and there's a theory that this is owing to the mind readying itself for the next life. I don't know about that but what I do know is that even though I had drifted into unconsciousness, some small part of me remained fully switched on and that part was no longer trapped within the confines of my body.

Time seemed to collapse in on itself and I felt as if I was floating in black velvet space. I didn't see any dead relatives or tunnels of white light but I do remember a tremendous feeling of well-being that found its way into every cell in my body, if I even had a body anymore. It wasn't clear to me whether I did or not but it wasn't a concern either. I felt like an astronaut floating away from my space capsule, just waiting for my air to run out. But there was no panic. I was beyond that. What I did feel, more than anything else, was a kind of relief. It wasn't wholly unlike the feeling that I some-times got after waking from a troubled dream. I suppose it's quite possible that at the time of death the brain floods itself with endor-phins, and hence the druggy, chilled-out state of mind in the final seconds of electrical activity in the brain. Maybe that's all it was. Or maybe it was something else. Because there was something else.

There was knowledge. Or maybe it was just the feeling of knowl-edge, but it was such a powerful feeling that I can't help thinking that it was something more than merely a final burst of activity in a dying brain. I felt as if I could reach out with my mind and pull in any piece of information that I cared to imagine. My thoughts were no longer bookended by my experiences. Everything from a cure for cancer to next season's FA Cup winner was within my grasp. I could feel it. And it was all so simple. I just had to think of a subject and then I realised that there was absolutely nothing that I didn't know about it.

As a sort of experiment, I thought about Michael Collins, the famous patriot. When I had lived inside my body, all I really knew about Michael Collins was what my father had told me – he was the greatest Irishman who had ever lived but then he got stabbed in the back by de Valera. And because I was just a dumb kid, I had always imagined that Dev had murdered him with a big knife. But now I realised my mistake and a whole lot more besides. I knew exactly what my father had meant and I knew who had really killed Michael Collins. I even knew stuff that the historians didn't. I knew stuff that nobody knew. For example, I knew that when he was twelve years old, Michael Collins was playing in a field behind his house one day when he came across a huge brown rabbit that was dying of myxomatosis. The young Collins ran back to his house and got a pair of heavy rusty shears from the barn. He then returned to the rabbit which hadn't moved at all but he knew that it was still alive because he could see its heart beating through the fur at about a thousand beats per minute. The creature stared at the boy through sad black eyes that were leaking gooey stuff, a symptom of the myxomatosis. Collins stared back for a few seconds and then he chopped off the animal's ears with the shears. The rabbit went crazy and started rolling around on the ground while blood poured out of the holes where its ears had been. The boy felt bad then because the animal was obviously in such distress, so he raised the shears above his head and bashed its skull in with a single blow. Then he picked it up by its hind legs and threw it down a rabbit hole in order to conceal what he had done.

It has taken me a minute or two to impart that dark little piece of trivia but when I was floating outside of my body, it took literally no time at all for the information to be fed to me. The knowledge was just there in the same way as when I had a body, my fingers were just there, or my brain was just there, but now the possibilities seemed endless. My only regret is that when I was in that magic place, I thought about the past and not the future. And I may well have been about to consider the future were it not for a nagging sense of doubt that somehow sneaked into my soul through the back door. And then I realised that I had forgotten something; I had forgotten to say my last words. Obviously whatever I had said before I was winded would have been my last words, but I didn't want something like *kick it up, kick it up* to be my parting phrase to humanity. I wanted something else, even if it was just a simple goodbye. I don't know why that seemed so important to me but it did. It wasn't as if I was Julius Caesar or Obi-Wan Kenobi or anyone the world would actually miss. But I knew that I had to go back all the same. I wasn't ready to die. I had to turn out the lights and say goodnight properly to this world before I could think about the next.

After that I became aware of a sensation that felt like there was a baby elephant jumping up and down on my stomach while simultaneously trying to suck my face off with its trunk. I opened my eyes and there was a gaunt-looking skinhead pushing up and down on my belly with both hands. He was wearing a grey overcoat that had seen better decades and he had scrawny hands that reminded me of chicken feet. After a few seconds he stopped and plunged his mouth over mine. He tasted like cigarettes.

'Breathe, goddammit!' he yelled, as if for the benefit of an invisible TV camera. I suspect that he had learned everything that he knew about CPR from watching bad hospital dramas on TV.

It's no use, Doctor, we're losing him.

Keep trying, goddammit! No kid has ever died on my watch and I'm sure as hell not gonna lose one now.

That last bit of dialogue only happened in my head but it made me groan aloud nonetheless. I had come back *for this*! I didn't have the strength to push the skinhead off me but just as he was lunging towards me for another bout of tonsil tennis, I turned my face away and breathed in a great big gulp of air like a swimmer breaking through the surface of the water. There were cheers from my team-mates and one or two of them even started applauding. I thought for a minute that the skinhead was going to stand up and take a bow.

You were wonderful, Doctor.

Just doing my job, Nurse. Just doing my job.

I stayed on the ground and shot a couple of puffs of my inhaler into me. People were starting to drift away. The excitement was over now that I hadn't died. When I turned my head around again, I saw the skinhead walking away towards Rathgorman Village, his overcoat billowing around him like Batman's cape. I never even said thank you.

Owen crouched on the ground beside me and asked me if I was going to be okay. I wasn't sure; I was still very shaken. A lot had happened in the space of a minute. I thought about how I had returned to utter my final words and now I found myself with absolutely nothing to say. I felt like the biggest fool on the planet because I knew that the door had closed behind me and there was no way back. Not that day. A couple of fat tears rolled down my cheeks and fell to the ground. I should have felt even worse at that point because there I was crying like a big girl's blouse in front of my friends. But I didn't care about that. I was still thinking about the place of infinite knowledge and the incredible sense of peace that I had felt there. I reached out and I took hold of one of Owen's hands. I wanted to make him understand but I couldn't find the right words. Owen construed my gesture as an unspoken request to be pulled up and so he stood up and then hauled me to my feet. After that he walked me home. I didn't say much on the short journey. I think I was still in shock.

What did ya do today, son?

Ah, ya know, the usual . . . played football, died, turned into a sort of all-knowing God for a little while.

But now that I was back, I felt trapped within my own body. Trapped and stupid. Unbelievably stupid. All that knowledge and I didn't even bring back a set of winning lottery numbers.

But I had brought back something. I just didn't know it yet.

As a kid, I had never felt the desire to go too far outside Dublin, apart from maybe Disneyland. I felt as if I had everything that I needed right there within a two-mile radius. Most importantly, I had my mates. My best friend was a kid named Owen Collins. Everybody loved him because he was such a natural entertainer and he certainly made my life a hell of a lot more interesting. I had other mates as well. Andy Kavanagh, Deano Maguire and Robbie Campbell are the ones that I remember the most. The five of us were like North Dublin's answer to the *Famous Five*, minus Timmy the dog. There was a dog as well, by the way. He was my dog and I called him Smellyhead which seemed like the obvious name for him when I found him. He was an abandoned mongrel, a cross between a border collie and the Cookie Monster, my ma used to say. He was so smart that he made Lassie look like one of those toy wooden dogs on four wheels that pre-PlayStation poor kids used to play with. And he was so much fun. Maybe I should have called him Peter Pan because he never grew up. He just wanted to play all the time, even when he was an old-age pensioner in dog years.

Robbie Campbell's appalling mother reversed over him coming out of her driveway one hazy summer day and that was the end of poor old Smellyhead. My da had to scrape him off the path with a shovel and dump him in a black plastic refuse sack. I didn't watch that, I couldn't, but I could still see it in my mind's eye. And so to try and compensate in some small way for the shame of being shovelled off the pavement like a lump of furry excrement, I buried my poor squashed dog in the graveyard on the hill behind the terraced house where I grew up. It seemed like the decent thing to do. I remember asking my ma whether I'd meet Smellyhead in heaven one day. She said that if Smellyhead was my heaven, then he'd be there. She was pretty cool, my ma.

My parents' house didn't have a back garden but even if there had have been acres of oak trees and rose bushes surrounding our house, I still would have buried my dog in Rathgorman Cemetery. Smellyhead loved that graveyard. I used to take him for walks up there and he was in his element, digging craters in freshly laid graves and pissing on headstones. The sanctity of the burial ground doesn't hold all that much significance for boys on the cusp of adolescence or for dogs that only want to play. For me, Rathgorman Cemetery was a carnival of dreams where every ride was free.

Maybe that makes me weird; I don't know. But the best fun I've ever had with my clothes on was when I was a kid playing with my mates in the graveyard on the hill behind our house.

My favourite game was one where four of us pretended that we had escaped from a chain gang, and we had to hide out in the graveyard because the cops were swarming all over the town looking for us. One of us would play the crooked sheriff who wanted the rest of us dead because we were going to tell the newspapers all about how corrupt he was. Andy Kavanagh's little sister always begged us to let her play, so we would make her bring us chocolate biscuits that she would steal from her house and then we would wolf them down like we hadn't eaten in days.

By the age of twelve, I was just starting to discover girls although it would be a couple of years yet before they discovered me. Robbie boasted that he had lost his virginity when he was ten. He said that he had shagged his fourteen-year-old next-door neighbour one night on top of one of the grassy graves in the ancient part of the cemetery. We all knew that he was lying but none of us had the balls to contradict him because Robbie was the only teenager among us. None of us except Owen, that is. Owen told him that he was so full of shit that it was coming out of his ears.

Although we spent a lot of time playing in the cemetery, I was always careful never to be caught there after the sun went down. I had this idea in my mind that the ghosts of the dead came out at night and sat on top of their graves chatting to each other. I pictured them drinking ghostly cups of tea and gossiping about the newly dead and the dreadful boys from the neighbourhood who had been running back and forth over their graves all day long.

'What age is that young Andrew Kavanagh fella?' Mrs Creavy who used to work in the post office would say with that look on her face where you just knew that the next words out of her mouth were going to be dripping with bile.

'He must be twelve or thirteen by now,' old Mrs Gleeson, the former lollypop lady, would pipe up. 'I heard him talking about starting secondary school in September.'

'Starting secondary school! That fella should be starting a prison sentence.'

Then Paddy McKenna who fell off the motorway flyover when he was drunk would make his voice heard. 'Isn't it nice to have the bit of aul company during the day all the same though, isn't it?'

Nobody ever came to lay flowers on Paddy's grave. He lived on the streets and he died on the streets.

'Nice? You think it's nice to have brats desecrating my final resting place with their language and their filth and their . . . their God only knows what else. Ya can feck off with your "nice" ya senile aul parasite, ya.'

That's what Eugene Ingles, the former headmaster, would say. Old itchy balls Ingles had died in mysterious circumstances shortly after the cops started investigating him for alleged sexual assault. I say 'alleged' just to be politically correct because even the dogs in the street knew all about his locker-room antics. Talk about asking the cat to look after the canary! The official line was that he died of a heart attack but unofficially the word was that he had chased a bottle of sleeping tablets with a bottle of vodka. Whatever the case, my friends and I made a point of pissing on his grave every time we were in the vicinity and felt the urge to relieve ourselves. Owen said that Jingle Balls had stuck his mickey into Owen's big brother's mouth and now Owen's brother had to see a doctor that crazy people go to.

Owen himself was a great kid. He once swiped an arm from a shop dummy that he found in a skip in town and we planted it in one of the new graves with the fingers reaching towards the sky as if in a desperate accusatory plea of *Why? Why have you buried me alive?*

Maybe we were intoxicated by the waves of testosterone surging through our bodies for the first time, or maybe we were just incurable brats, but that summer when I was twelve years old is one that I will never forget for all kinds of reasons, but mostly for just one. Two weeks before he was due to start as a student at Rathgorman College, Owen Collins drowned in the canal.

I have spent most of my life trying to forget about Owen's death and so some of the details might be a bit foggy, but I suspect that if I try hard enough then I can penetrate that fog like a laser beam. He had been underwater for over five minutes by the time they managed to pull him out and all attempts to resuscitate him failed. His face had turned so pale that he didn't even look like Owen anymore. His lips were a horrible shade of blue that no lips should ever be the colour of, and there was green slime on his forehead and in his hair. And his eyes ... his eyes were what frightened me most, because they were still open, paralysed in an expression of utter horror and disbelief that Death had come looking for him when he had only just begun to live.

There must have been dozens of reasons why swimming at the

canal lock was a bad idea. Robbie Campbell's appalling mother said that the creature from the black lagoon lived under the lock and ate small boys for breakfast. Then she pinched both my cheeks and said that I was so cute that she could just eat me up herself. Compared to that experience, the creature from the black lagoon didn't seem all that scary and its breath could definitely not have smelled any worse. Mrs Campbell's breath smelled worse than Smellyhead's and he spent half of his life licking his genitals. Her first name was Phyllis but when Robbie wasn't around, we always referred to her as Syphilis. I only ever went into Robbie's house to steal cigarettes from his mother's handbag and it made absolutely no difference whatever that plague of a woman said to me, the response in my mind was always – *You killed my dog you vile, disgusting bitch.*

But it wasn't Syphilis Campbell who killed my best friend Owen Collins.

It was me.

Technically speaking, it was an accident, but I have no interest in hiding behind technicalities. The really horrible part of it all was that I could see it coming. I knew that it was going to happen and that intuitive knowledge is something that I believe came back with me from the other side. I know that the gift of foresight might sound kind of cool, but I use the word 'gift' in the loosest possible sense because really it is a curse. Hindsight may be a wonderful thing but believe me, foresight can be a real pain in the arse. I've never gotten true and accurate premonitions of, say, me being the biggest rock star on the planet, or the highest-paid footballer or even more modest aspirations, such as seeing an older version of me enjoying a picnic with a gorgeous wife and kids. That might be nice. Certainly easy enough to cope with at the very least. But I don't have any of those Mary Poppins-type intuitions. Instead I have these really fucked-up recurring dreams that only end when somebody close to me is dead.

It started with the dreams about Owen but it's been more or less the same formula every time. Nightmares that initially haunt me once or twice a week before gradually intensifying until I am having the same dream every night. My dreams about Owen didn't unfold in slow motion or through a soft focus lens in the way that dreams are usually portrayed in films. On the contrary, the bits that I was allowed to see were projected into my brain with perfect clarity, and they were always the same. The problem was that there was a curtain drawn over certain aspects of the future and it was the resultant blind spot that turned me into a killer.

I saw everything through my own eyes in the dream and so I couldn't see myself but I was definitely there. I spoke to no one and no one spoke to me. An invisible observer, observing everything. There was a furniture removal lorry in the background and two or three removal men were carrying furniture out of a Georgian house and stacking it into the lorry. There was something written on the side of the van that I could never quite make out even though everything else in the dream was painfully vivid. The day itself looked like a scorcher. On the bridge over the canal, the traffic was horrible and I could see agitated motorists slowly cooking in their cars amidst a tide of exhaust fumes and blaring horns. On the canal bank, Deano was trying to remove Andy's shorts and Andy was bashing him with what looked like a burst football and screaming that a queer bastard was trying to rape him. Meanwhile, Robbie was leaping from the black wooden lock beams into the canal itself. His technique was to jump high into the air and then, with his hands pressed tight against his thighs and his feet pointed downwards, he would shoot into the water feet first like a torpedo, hardly making a splash.

Owen was the last to get into the water. I could see the sun glinting off a sign nailed to the lock over the exact spot where he jumped in. His eyes were closed when he entered the water but when they pulled him up on to the bank they were wide open, horribly wide open. And at that point I would always wake up struggling to catch my breath and I would have to take a blast of my inhaler before I could breathe properly again. As I sat up in bed while waiting for the asthma medicine to kick in, the horror of my dream sometimes left me physically shaking. I managed to relax a little by telling myself that it was only a dream. Except it wasn't only a dream. It was reality waiting to happen.

Did I believe in it? Sure I did. At the age of twelve, I'd already spent half my life believing in Santa Claus and the tooth fairy, so premonitions in my sleep didn't exactly require a major leap of faith. But its authenticity as a genuine premonition seemed unlikely to say the least, mainly because Owen was a good swimmer and the canal lock was small. It wasn't more than twenty square feet and maybe seven or eight feet deep. And as there were no currents or undertows in the canal, it seemed inconceivable that anyone who knew how to swim could possibly drown there. And yet I was having these dreams about Owen that were so vivid, they were almost like memories.

I didn't tell anyone about the dreams. My mother would have

given me the standard it's-only-a-dream platitudes, and if I had have told Owen that he had a starring role in my dreams every night, he would have just told me to stop being such a dorkface. So for a long time, I just stuck my head in the sand and did my best to carry on as normal. But then out of the blue I was presented with an opportunity for a pre-emptive counter-strike and I jumped at the chance to do something.

It was at a point when the dreams were at their most intense. Over a period of weeks, they had gradually become more and more frequent until I had reached a stage where I could hardly close my eyes without seeing Owen's lifeless body lying on the canal bank. But during the daytime, it was business as usual. I was on my summer holidays and my friends and I had no problem filling the hours with a variety of different activities, some of which were even legal. On one particular day, Andy, Owen and myself were having a few smokes up behind the Connors' gravestone in the cemetery. The Connors' gravestone is roughly the size of a double decker bus so discretion was more or less guaranteed. Owen was the champion smoker out of all of us because he could do perfect smoke rings. We chain-smoked four or five fags each and then headed for home. I said goodbye to my friends outside Silvio's Takeaway and then I walked the rest of the way on my own. I was almost home when I came across an abandoned shopping trolley lying on its side on the foot-path like the skeleton of a primitive vehicle. Instead of just walking around it, I stopped and pulled it upright on to its four wheels. The ghost of an idea was forming in my head and before I could talk myself out of it, I turned around and started wheeling the trolley back along the path in the direction from where I had come.

The plan was a simple one. Every time I closed my eyes and thought about the canal, the images from my dream flashed through my mind with frightening clarity. I could identify the exact spot where I saw Owen flailing around because it was directly underneath a small metallic plaque nailed to the horizontal beam that spanned the lock. The plaque said NO SWIMMING but it might as well have said NO SKYDIVING for all the difference it made to us. In any case, I figured that if I dumped the trolley at that exact spot under the sign, then in that location at least, the depth of the water would be reduced by a couple of feet because a person could quite easily stand on the trolley and keep his or her head above the surface of the water.

With this in mind, I pushed the trolley all the way to the canal and then I pushed it right over the edge and into the water. It went straight to the bottom with hardly a splash and came to rest almost directly under the NO SWIMMING sign. I was delighted with myself because I was sure that it was a really great idea that might even save my best friend's life. As I turned around to make my getaway, a hatchet-faced old biddy was standing directly in my path.

'I've called the police and they're on their way,' she said to me through teeth that looked like corn kernels.

'Eh, why?' I replied.

'You know very well why. I saw what you did with that trolley. You stole it and then you dumped it in the canal.'

'I was just gettin it outta the way cos it was makin the canal bank look untidy.'

'You're a thief and a vandal and a hooligan and I'm making a citizen's arrest and holding on to you until the guards get here.'

I realised at that point that the woman was quite clearly mad. I turned on my heel and legged it and by the time I reached my front door, I had practically forgotten all about her.

I slept well that night, untroubled by dreams of any description. I pulled back my curtains the following morning and the sun's warm rays came flooding into my room. It was a beautiful day. I watched television for an hour or so and then Owen knocked on the door.

'Well, gidday, Charlene!' he said in a bad Australian accent by way of greeting. We were all avid *Neighbours* fans at the time. We goofed around for a bit and then we decided to call to Deano Maguire's house. His da was a merchant seaman who was never at home and his ma was a large woman with greasy skin. As we approached the house, Mrs Maguire came waddling down the driveway towards us carrying an empty shopping bag.

'Howya, lads,' she said. 'Dean is inside if ya want to ring the bell.'

I presume that Dean would have remained inside whether we wanted to ring the bell or not but even I wasn't cheeky enough to raise this point with her.

'Thanks, Mrs Maguire,' said Owen. 'We'll keep an eye on him for ya until ya get back.'

'Will ya now?' she replied. 'And who's gonna keep an eye on you?'

'Colonel Groucho!'

Inside the house, Deano made us a couple of SodaStream drinks which we drank while watching a video of an R18 film called *Breathless*. We fast-forwarded most of it searching for dirty bits but there wasn't anything to get excited about. In the corner, Colonel Groucho's cage had a white hood over it to keep him quiet but he still let out the occasional squawk. I was thinking about how great it would be if we watched a pornographic film and then Colonel Groucho started repeating what he had heard during a sex scene. But everything changed when Andy and Robbie called to the door and said that they were going swimming.

The bottom seemed to fall out of my stomach like a plunging elevator because suddenly all of the main players from my dream were present and they were talking about going swimming in the canal. Owen and Deano both said that they would get their shorts and go along. Neither of them sounded hugely enthusiastic about the idea but that was just a part of being cool. I could tell that they were dying to go really.

'Wha about you, are ya comin?' Andy asked me.

'Nah, it's just the way I'm standin,' I replied on auto-pilot.

'Ya look like you've seen a ghost or somethin,' said Owen.

'Yeah well, it's prob'ly just the shock o seein Robbie without his make-up on.'

'Are ya aw righ?' chipped in Deano.

'I'm not feelin the Mae West, to be honest, so I think I'm gonna skip the swimmin.'

'Sure, come along anyway,' said Owen. 'Ya might change your mind.'

And with that, the five of us left Deano's house and made our way to the canal, stopping off on the way at Owen and Andy's houses so that they could pick up towels and shorts. I felt like I was sleepwalking. But as soon as I saw the removal lorry, I knew that my dreams and reality were about to collide. The lorry was parked exactly where I expected it to be parked. It was big, red and unmissable with RAPID REMOVALS painted down the side in two-feet-high black letters. That's what I hadn't been able to make out in the dream, but now déjà vu was screaming at me from all sides. There was a smell as well, a smell that had been teasing my nostrils ever since I had woken up that morning, except now it was hitting me full on like invisible smelling salts shoved under my nose. Only it didn't smell like smelling salts. It smelled more like a sweet coppery kind of a smell and it made me want to throw up. I felt as if there was a black hole opening up in my stomach and my insides had disappeared into it, leaving me hollow and ready to collapse.

When we arrived at the lock, the boys threw their towels on the ground and started pulling their clothes off. Owen was walking along beside me at the back of the group and so he was the last to start undressing. I looked at the bridge where the cars were stacked end to end as I knew they would be. The drivers all looked so vexed, wishing they could be somewhere else, anywhere else, as I did. I envied their ignorance of the impending tragedy and their consequent clean hands in the whole affair.

I heard a splash and I looked to the canal where Deano was already in the water. Robbie yelled something at me that I didn't hear properly. I wouldn't have replied in any case. My voice felt as if it had died in my chest.

Andy told Owen to hurry up and get his kit off.

'Tha's wha ya said last night,' shouted Robbie. I think that Robbie fancied himself as a razor-sharp wit but the extent of his one-liners didn't really stretch beyond the use of the phrase 'that's what you said last night' at every possible opportunity. In any case, the high spirits of my friends prevented them from even noticing that I seemed to have lost all power of speech and movement.

When he went to hide his clothes, Andy found an old burst football in the tall grass to one side of the lock. He threw it at Deano and then he threw himself into the canal after it. Owen was still sitting on the ground fumbling with one of the knotted laces of his big white runner boots. The other three were already in the water by that stage. I remember hoping that Owen wouldn't get the knot untied and go home alive instead. But in the end he just yanked the boot off his foot with the lace still tied. At that point, I was chanting three words over and over in my mind – *Please be okay, please be okay, please be okay*. But it wasn't okay. It most definitely wasn't okay.

The really shitty thing is that I could have saved him, I know I could have. I could have saved him in a hundred different ways. When he had one boot off and was still working on getting the other one off, I could have just walked up to him and punched him hard in the face. I still would have lost my best friend, but he would have mooched off home alive with just a bloody nose or a black eye and I would have been so happy for him, even though he might not have spoken to me ever again.

I could have told him that I'd just remembered that Lara Sheahan had told me to tell him to meet her by the rope swing at that exact time. That would have sent him running. Owen had been chasing after Lara for the previous six months which is about the equivalent of a lifetime at that age.

Or maybe if I had just taken him aside and pleaded with him not to go swimming, he might have come with me to the dead fields for a smoke instead. He would have seen the fear and the anguish in my eyes and that might have been enough.

But I didn't even do that. Instead, I just stood there and watched my best friend run towards the canal and leap off the bank feet first into the canal. He hit the water almost exactly under the NO SWIMMING sign and when his head didn't pop up again a few seconds later, I knew that he was in trouble. The seconds ticked by and I found myself thinking about the time two years previously when the breath had been robbed from my lungs. On that occasion, there had been people all around me but Owen had been the first to notice my difficulty and the first to try and help me. And now the tables were reversed, but instead of rushing to his aid I just stood there rooted to the spot with my eyes closed. He was my friend and that was how I repaid him.

It was Andy who first drew attention to Owen's arms thrashing the water while his head was still below the surface. Another vital few seconds elapsed as the boys tried to figure out if Owen really was in trouble or just messing around. Deano's head disappeared beneath the surface while the rest of us just stared in disbelief at a pair of arms flailing around the surface of the water. Then Deano reappeared and he screamed at us that Owen's foot was trapped and that he was drowning. Andy and Robbie both took deep breaths and followed Deano underwater. I walked forward towards the bank of the canal for a better view of my best friend's death. His head was close enough to the surface for me to see his pale face as he fought the murky water like a beacon bobbing crazily. Further down in the water, I could just about make out the milky white bodies and brightly coloured shorts of Deano and Andy and Robbie as they tried to free Owen from the iron cage that had swallowed his foot.

Then a shoal of bubbles rose to the surface and I knew that he had exhaled his last breath and was now breathing in water. His arms went limp and sank slowly back into the water.

A couple of seconds later, the surface of the water exploded upwards and belched out a supermarket trolley that Andy and Deano had managed to throw on to the bank. Owen's foot was stuck in the part of the trolley that could be adapted into a child's seat. But with the trolley now out of the water, he had been turned upside down with the top half of his body pointing downwards in the water. Robbie came up beneath Owen and pushed him on to the bank. I hadn't seen any supermarket trolley in my dream but in real life it was unmissable, lying sideways on the bank of the canal.

I grabbed my best friend by the arm and pulled him further up on to the safety of the bank. That was the pathetic extent of my efforts to save his life. Andy jumped out of the water and began giving him mouth to mouth while Deano started shouting for help at the top of his lungs. I took a step backwards and felt someone rush by me at the same time. It was one of the men who worked with the removal company. RAPID REMOVALS was printed on the back of his red overalls and he seemed to know what he was doing. He alternated between pumping Owen's chest with both hands and administering the kiss of life and I thought about the skinhead who had once upon a time performed a similar act on me. On that occasion I had returned from wherever I had been so it certainly wasn't impossible to believe that Owen would suddenly start coughing and spluttering and then everyone would start clapping and smiling with relief. That's what would have happened on TV but real life had other ideas. People started coming out of nowhere to see what was going on. Some motorists had even abandoned their cars in an effort to try and help. Nosey bastards mostly. I remember one guy in a grey suit saying that he had called an ambulance on his car phone. The removal man kept pumping away but Owen just lay on the bank growing colder and colder. He completely missed his cue to start coughing up the water in his lungs and instead he just lay there on the bank, stubbornly dead. I felt a warmth on my cheeks before I realised that tears were streaming down my face.

'Well I hope you're good and happy with yourself, that's all I can say.'

I turned around and I saw the poisonous old bag who had attempted a citizen's arrest on me the night before.

'This is all *your* fault,' she added in case I was a bit slow and hadn't already figured that out for myself.

'I know,' I said, and then I turned around and walked away.

II

Angela

My mother died two years after my best friend and she was buried one field across from him. My ma was the funniest person that I have ever met in my life and I would give anything to see her once more, even for just a few minutes. She taught me a lot of things but most of all she taught me kindness and now I can't even remember what she looked like. I have a clearer memory of the face of the mother from *Little House on the Prairie* than I do of my own mother and I know what a terrible admission that is but it's true. And I didn't even like *Little House on the Prairie*; I hated it.

I keep a picture of her in my wallet but when I try and picture her face, the best that I can come up with is to visualise my wallet photo of her in my mind's eye. But that's not remembering her, that's just remembering the picture in my wallet. And if I start from scratch with an oval shape and try to build on that, then the features inside the shape just seem to dissolve into each other, as if the image were being sucked down a plughole. I feel pretty bad about that because I loved her so much and I'll miss her every day for the rest of my life.

I had barely made it into my teens when cancer took her away from me, and just about the only good thing that can be said about that is that I didn't see it coming. Not in my dreams anyway. But for those of us that were left behind, far and away the worst aspect of my mother's death was a woman named Doreen. Doreen was a lot of things and unfortunately for my little brother Jack and I, one of those was that she was our new stepmother, and it's important not to forget the *step*, because Doreen walked all over everybody in her slut-red high-heeled shoes. She looked like a tired old hooker, which in itself I probably could have coped with, but she had a tongue sharper than a truckload of razor blades; every time she opened her mouth, she made me want to strangle her. But I will concede that it's at least possible that part of the reason why we never saw eye to eye was my fault because I was an out-of-control rebel without a clue for most of my teens. But Doreen must take some blame as well, because she was a walking talking bitch. She still is, I'm sure, but I don't see her anymore and that suits me fine.

I have no idea what my da thought he was doing getting mixed up with the likes of Doreen. There was one night (well, maybe more than one!) when I got careless and he caught me coming home off my face on vodka and glue, so maybe he saw me heading off the rails like a demonic steam train and decided that I needed a strong maternal influence to get me back on track. Or maybe he was just lonely. Whatever the reason, dragon woman had moved herself into my ma's old bedroom within a year of the funeral. Doreen and my da never actually got married because of a messy divorce. Doreen's of course. It wasn't messy in the legal sense, it was messy in the sense that Doreen's ex-husband was very likely to mess her face up even worse than it looked already if she was dumb enough to even think about asking him for a divorce. That's because her ex-husband was well aware that a divorce settlement would be expensive, and Joe Furey would rather chop off his own genitals before he would pay a penny of maintenance money to Doreen. Although he was little more than a small-time thug when he turfed my stepmother out into the street, it didn't take long before Doreen's ex had graduated into the criminal big leagues. Once he ditched the dead wood that was Doreen, he expanded his enterprise from bag snatching and petty cons to having his finger in every poisonous pie in the city – money lending, forgery, credit-card fraud, prostitution, drug dealing – you name it, and my stepmother's ex had a hand in it.

The way I see it, Joe Furey knocked up Battleship Doreen one night in a haze of beer goggles; he married her out of a misguided sense of doing the right thing, and then a few years later when he came to his senses, he dumped her in a refuge for battered women. Rumour has it that he drove her to the front gates and then threw her out of the car without even bothering to stop first. And believe it or not, I can appreciate how he felt at the time.

The manner in which she snagged my father is so unsettling and disgusting that it makes me sick to my stomach. Basically, my da was visiting my ma in the graveyard one day when Doreen came up to him and started some bullshit chit-chat about how she had spied him visiting his dearly departed wife on many previous occasions, and how if he needed to talk to someone she would only be too glad to be a shoulder to cry on because she knew what it felt like to lose someone special and blah, blah, blah, blah, *blah*. In his heightened state of vulnerability, my da fell for this bullshit bollox hook, line and sinker. Next thing he knows, she's dragged him off to the local boozer for a medicinal drink and six or seven pints later, my da was crying his eyes out with the loneliness of it all, and vampire Doreen was cuddling up to him saying 'there, there' while she gave him a shoulder massage with one hand and a crotch massage with the other.

And that's pretty much how it happened. I know all this by the way because it happened in a pub where my best mate Damo was working at the time. But Doreen had snared my da before they even set foot inside the pub. What kind of sick, twisted fuck goes to the local cemetery to try and score? My stepmother, that's who. I can't think of any other possible reason for her to be there. Unless she was visiting the spot where she had buried her humanity. But using God only knows what as bait, she very gently impaled my dumb old da on her hook and then simply reeled him in. And after a couple of months of living with Doreen, my da didn't look much like my da anymore. He acquired a permanently furrowed brow and to everyone's surprise, he started reading the Bible every day and going to mass on Sundays. With the loss of my mum and then Doreen arriving on the scene, I would have expected him to lose his faith but the more things deteriorated at home, the harder he prayed.

He must have been praying to the wrong God though because after my mum's death, things went from bad to worse at home and they didn't start improving again until we got rid of the local gang-ster's moll and her idiot offspring. When Doreen and Joe Furey were together, they spawned a lizard-like creature that they named Johnny. So when my da got together with dear old Doreen, it was a package deal and Johnny Rotten came too. And so without even being consulted, I suddenly had a stepbrother from the planet

Arsehole. He was six months older than me and he believed that this gave him a God-given right to take and break every one of my worthless treasures. I think that my da in his idealistic innocence had hoped that Johnny and I would become best buddies, always looking out for each other. But things didn't quite work out that way. My stepbrother took after his mother in a number of ways: he was as thick as a box of Mars bars and he had a face that could curdle cream. But that in itself could perhaps be forgiven if it wasn't for the fact that he was also downright mean.

Personally, I could cope with the fact that after my ma's death, bad people moved into our house and very soon after that it never felt quite like home again. I could cope with that because I felt responsible for my best friend's death and so I couldn't help thinking that what goes around comes around and therefore I had brought all this on myself. In a fucked-up kind of way, I wanted to be tortured and so I was fully prepared to take my medicine and swap my ma for the likes of Doreen and Johnny Rotten. But Jack didn't deserve any of that. Jack deserved to grow up in TV land where everything was sugar-coated. If we couldn't have our ma, then Jack deserved someone like Julie Andrews for a mother but instead he got Doreen. And so I turned my back on drugs and shoplifting and joyriding and I was there for him. I was there for him when he learned to ride his first bike. I was there for him when he dislocated his elbow after falling off a rope swing and I carried him all the way to Dr Cassidy's surgery. And when some bullies threw his bag on top of a bus shelter one day on his way home from school, I waited at the gates for them the next day and when they emerged, I beat seven shades of crap out of them. They never even looked sideways at him after that.

I'm not claiming to be some sort of saint though and I'll be the first to admit that once girls started to show an interest in me, I very quickly forgot all about my little brother. I was almost sixteen before I had my first real girlfriend and that made me something of a slow starter by the standards my mates had been setting. Her name was Lucy and she used to wear a pink coat which I thought made her look like a pixie. She was a cutie and I could make her laugh a lot so I thought that I was in love. I thought that we would be together for ever but it wasn't meant to be. In fact, fuck that annoying cliché; maybe it *was* meant to be but we'll never know because she dumped me for Deano Maguire four weeks later. The bottom line was that my first big romance left me in Dumpsville and it hurt like a bastard.

Well, for about a month, anyway, and then I was going out with somebody else. My second big romance was with Jo, Andy Kavanagh's little sister. She was hardly recognisable anymore as the little girl who had brought us stolen biscuits when we were hiding out in the dead fields behind my house. Jo the teenager could chew gum and look bored better than anyone else I had ever met. That's what did it for me in fact. She just looked so damn cool all the time. And then one day I saw her blow a bubble the size of a human head and that was it, I wanted her to be the mother of my children. And I know all about the unwritten rule that you don't mess around with any of your friends' sisters, but Andy was already out of the picture by that stage. He got packed off to a reform school after being caught breaking into a house in Rathmines and we lost contact after that. As I was falling for Jo, he fell in love with heroin and it wasn't long before that was all he cared about.

But back in my own slightly more innocent existence, my da suggested one day that I bring my girlfriend around for tea and stupidly I agreed, thinking that it would make a nice change from our usual dates, which generally consisted of either the back row of the cinema or else knacker-drinking in a field. So that's how Jo ended up sitting down to a meal one evening with the civil war that now passed for my family. Right from the moment we walked through the front door, the evening was a horrible ordeal. I had of course warned my guest that my stepmother and stepbrother were poisonous creatures exhumed from the tomb of a putrid vampire, but Jo had simply assumed that I had been exaggerating because of a natural resentment of these strangers that had been thrust upon me. And so she really had no idea of what she was letting herself in for.

I blame myself to an extent because I should have known better but I fooled myself into believing that it would be all right because I thought that I could still feel my ma's presence in the house, and I know that she would have loved to meet my first real girlfriend. My ma would have made a big fuss of Jo. She would have cooked something really special and even organised some delicious treat for dessert, even if it was just bread plates with sliced peaches on them that looked like big orange smiles. She would have made Jo feel like she was in a place where she was welcome and where she belonged. But best of all, she would have made us laugh in a hundred different ways. She would have forced us to play charades and then she would have taken the floor and made a holy show of herself, and of course I could never let on that I was embarrassed because that would only have made her a million times worse.

'Who's that skinny little young one standin in the hall like a lost sheep? If it's money she's after, tell her to clear off out of it and come in for your tea.'

'That's Jo, Doreen. I told ya three days ago tha she would be eatin with us this evenin.' That was the perfectly reasonable response I volunteered in a discussion with Doreen just inside the kitchen while Jo was taking off her coat.

'WHAT? Ya never told me any such thing ya little liar. Do ya think it's a mission for the homeless I'm runnin here? Is that it? Open all hours for you to arrive in whenever ya feel like it and bringin every stray dog off the street with ya to be fed.'

'My da thought it was a good idea. He suggested it. And she's not homeless or a stray dog, *she's my girlfriend, okay?*'

Bad start. Very bad start. And we hadn't even got to the introductions yet.

'Don't you raise your voice to me, you ingrateful little swine. I've been slavin away over tha cooker all evenin while you're off runnin around with God only knows who and doin God only knows wha.'

I couldn't resist it.

'I think you'll find, Doreen, tha the word is "*un*grateful".'

I knew how to push her buttons all right and I stuck my knife in every chance I got. Mostly it was just little things that pissed her off, but whenever she pissed me off, or to put it another way, whenever we were in the same room, then the gloves were well and truly off and because dear old Dore wasn't exactly the sharpest knife in the drawer and because I was such a smartarse, I would always get the last word in. Had I been an adult, I'm sure I would have been rewarded for this with the quiet admiration and respect of my peers, but as I was still just a kid, I usually received a good smack in the mouth or a clip around the ear instead. It was still worth it. Every time.

My favourite technique to drive Doreen crazy was simply to say her name in every sentence out of my mouth, and before long, she would always want to strangle me. When I was a kid, it sounded massively disrespectful for any child to address an adult on first-name terms. But there was no substitute for 'Doreen' and I knew it. Ex-Missus Furey? Auntie Dore? Ma? I don't think so. So it was always 'Doreen' to her face, and any one of a million appropriate put-downs behind her back.

My second favourite torture-Doreen technique was to go out of my way to correct her grammar every chance I got. And believe me, I got plenty of chances and I pounced on them all. Now you may well consider it particularly cruel to use a person's lack of education as a stick to beat them with, so I'll offer three consider-ations by way of a defence: firstly, we're talking about Doreen here; secondly, I was just a kid with enough chips on each shoulder to fill a casino; and thirdly, eh, we're talking about Doreen here.

I walked out of the kitchen while my stepmother was still in mid-rant and I took Jo into the TV room in our house. We sat on the couch together and turned on the TV. *Blockbusters* was on. We waited until some snooty looking English girl said 'Can I have a "P" please, Bob?' and then we changed the channel. *Blockbusters* was crap. Jack stuck his head around the door, shamelessly checking out my girlfriend. Jo said hi but he didn't answer. Instead he burst into a fit of giggles and scampered off again, having been temporarily trapped in the body of a shy person.

Then my da came into the room and after the introductions had been made, he said that dinner was on the table and we moved to the kitchen. As we walked in the door, Doreen was banging on the ceiling with the handle of a brush. This was her way of summoning Johnny Rotten to mealtimes. A minute later he appeared. He smelled of stale sweat and cum which was normal for him as he was a DIY sex maniac. He didn't offer to shake hands with Jo and I'm sure she was relieved. He always was an ugly fucker, but at that time his face was so ravaged by acne that it would have put anyone off their food. His skin looked like the surface of the sun and to make matters worse, he had tried to grow stubble to conceal his spots but his stubble was so sparse that you could count the individual hairs, and each one seemed to be like an arrow with a big greasy pimple at the end of it.

I tried to turn the spotlight on to Jack. 'Did I tell ya Jack's a great little speller? Champion o the world.'

'Yeah?' said Jo.

'Oh yeah. Can ya spell "indigestible" for us, Jack?'

I remember that I was being especially nice to Jack at the time because the previous day, he had arrived home from school with a wooden pencil box that he had won in a spelling competition.

'Prob'ly made in Taiwan by blind orphans,' had been Doreen's reaction, so naturally I overcompensated by heaping praise on Jack, telling Jo about how the people from the Oxford English Dictionary had been on the phone the previous night wanting to verify the spelling of a few words with my little brother. I probably made it sound as if the kid had just walked away with the Nobel Prize but Jo went along with it.

Doreen banged down plates of mystery meat in front of us all.

Nobody said grace and nobody waited until everybody had been served before eating. My da did his best but he was paddling a sinking canoe.

'Jack, don't be eatin with your mouth open. It's not polite.'

Jack wasn't too concerned about table manners though. Instead he just gazed at Jo with a permanent beam on his face.

'Do ya have any kids yourself, Jo?' was my da's attempt at ice-breaking humour.

'I'm expectin my first in July,' she replied, seeing his gag and raising it.

My father almost choked on a piece of broccoli before realising that she wasn't serious. Then Doreen entered and plonked herself down at the table.

'Jack wet the bed again last night. I spent half o today washin sheets and the other half cookin.'

That was her opening offering of conversation at the dinner table. My little brother's impossibly cute smile died like a rose in a bucket of acid. There was a horrible silence for a second or two and then I hit back on his behalf.

'How's tha menopause thing workin out for ya, Doreen?'

That prompted Johnny Rotten to pipe up.

'Shut up you, ya greasy pus bag.'

Talk about the pot calling the kettle black!

My father intervened before things got out of control. A wise move considering that most of us had knives in our hands.

For most of my teenage years I attended Rathgorman College or Ratser's as it was commonly and more appropriately known. Although I use the term 'attended' loosely because I was rarely present, so let's just say that I was enrolled there. The school itself and the facilities weren't too bad but the problem with Ratser's was that most of its teachers had obviously been hired on the basis that no one else would have them, because the staff consisted of a motley crew of alcoholics and sadistic pricks.

I did pretty much as I pleased after my mum died and attending Ratser's barely featured on my list of things to do. A further disincentive to attend school was the fact that it was ridiculously easy to get away with not going. Apart from a few sporadic half-hearted roll calls, there was no one checking up on me. And besides, I was a smart kid who looked as if butter wouldn't melt in my mouth and that practically gave me powers of invisibility.

And so because I didn't bother much with school, I had lots of free time on my hands. Snooker halls and amusement arcades and all of the other usual hideouts for truants were not for me. Instead, the embarrassing truth is that I spent a big chunk of my adolescence hidden away in a corner of the local library like a giant nerd. Bunking off school in order to read books in a library never struck me as being strange at the time. I loved the smell of the place and the feeling of security I got from the walls of books. Occasionally other kids ventured in after 4 p.m. but they were always of the geek variety. I gave them dirty looks in case they mistook me for one of their own.

The main librarian was definitely my favourite thing about the local library. Her name was Mrs Horricks and we were firm friends almost from the first time we met. She wore reading glasses on a string around her neck and she looked to me like someone who had been born old. I found it impossible to imagine her as a little girl or even as a teenager. Old age seemed to embrace her like a warm blanket and she seemed very comfortable with it. She used to bring me tea and chocolate biscuits, and even soup from a flask sometimes. I told her that I was working on a project for the Young Scientists' Exhibition and she seemed happy enough with this explanation for my continued attendance.

'Well, aren't you the clever one! Rathgorman's very own little Einstein!' she would say. And then for the best part of a year, it was always: 'How's the project coming along, Professor?' to which I would reply whilst munching on a chocolate biscuit – 'Comin along nicely, Mrs H., very nicely indeed.'

Despite the fact that she never actually saw me writing anything, or the fact that there was apparently no end in sight to my famous project, she never once asked me a single awkward question. It was as if there was an understanding between us that our conversations would not stray into topics that concerned life outside the library walls. Occasionally she would sort of mention the subject of my bunking off, but it was always in such a roundabout way that she practically went via China, and she always seemed to get lost along the way.

'Have you read that *Catcher in the Rye,* dearie?'

'I certainly have, Mrs H. and I loved it. Two thumbs up! What did you think?'

'Oh well, it's been a few years now but yes, that Holden Caulfield was just too good to forget. I mean, he was a bit of a rogue as well, that's for sure, getting thrown out of school like that. He must have had his poor parents driven demented.'

'But he didn't believe in school and instead he stood by the things that he did believe in, which is ten times more important, don't ya think?'

'It's good to believe in things, love, just make sure the cat doesn't run out of lives; that's all I'm saying.'

And just like that, my favourite old lady would come out with statements that were almost brilliant, but a shade wide of the mark somehow, rendering them completely meaningless.

'Eh, I think I know what you're sayin, Mrs H., I do, but I think much better with a mug o tea in me hand, if ya know what *I'm* sayin?'

Of course, she should have kicked my arse back to school in a heartbeat but she didn't because we were best mates. Although I would never, ever have admitted that to anyone at the time, not even to myself. I'd had a best mate once before who was now worm food, and so I was adamant that I didn't want to be anyone's best friend ever again. Not even Jo's and so, perhaps inevitably, I ended up breaking her heart.

I didn't have any money at the time and so for Jo's sixteenth birthday, I made her a papier-mâché heart which I then painted red and presented to her with our initials written on it. I know it was a bit sappy but she said it was the best present that anyone had ever given her and then she gave me a big hug and an even bigger kiss. Later that evening, she told me for the first time that she loved me. Instead of reciprocating, I shamefully made up some rubbish excuse and ran home. The next day, I dumped her by letter saying that I thought we should take a break because I felt that we were getting too serious, which was almost the truth.

Jo didn't respond to my letter at all but a few days later, I received a padded envelope in the post. When I pulled open the flap, I had to hold my nose because the stench was so bad. Fearing the worst, I took it outside and emptied the contents on to the footpath. My papier-mâché heart fell to the ground looking as if it had been stamped on and then liberally smeared with dog shit. That was Jo's non-verbal response to our break-up that said it all really. I ran into her a couple of times after that but she always turned her face away and never spoke to me again. She had a sort of stubborn dignity about her that made me respect her even more. One of the hardest things I've ever had to do was to let her go but I convinced myself that if I didn't let Jo or anyone else get too close to me, then there would be no chance of a recurrence of the type of dreams that I'd had about Owen.

But there was a fatal flaw in my logic. I had not accounted for the fact that I had about as much control over my situation as a tennis ball does when a cat is toying with it. I was no more than a plaything of some unseen and immensely powerful otherworldly force that would not be denied its fun, and certainly not because of my pathetically ineffective countermeasures. And so it wasn't long before the nightmares started to come again and there wasn't a single thing that I could do about it.

Before that happened, though, I tried to bury my broken heart under the weight of all the stories in Rathgorman's library. My break-up with Jo by itself was enough to keep my conscience churning on a steady spin cycle but on top of all that grief, my head was still seriously wrecked from trying to come to terms with Owen's death and then my ma's. But the books didn't care about any of that. There was no judgement in them and so I completely immersed myself in their stories. I heard it said in a film once that we read to know that we are not alone and I think that whoever came up with that idea was definitely on to something, because in the library I never felt lonely.

I certainly never felt lonely whenever Mrs Horricks was around. As the months rolled by, we became closer and closer pals. She wasn't in the best of health though, that much was obvious. She had arthritis in both her hips and there was something wrong with her heart which meant that she had to take a handful of tablets with every meal. She sat down beside me one day with two steaming cups of tea and a packet of chocolate HobNobs and I could tell straightaway that something was up.

'Well, Professor,' she said after some small talk about what I was currently reading, 'I'm afraid I have some bad news.'

I sort of guessed what was coming but I braced myself for the worst.

'The fact is, I'm not getting younger and I haven't been feeling too well lately so I think it's about time that I retired.'

'Are ya serious?'

'Yes, dear.'

Mixed emotions were racing through me at that point. Obviously I didn't want her to go but the woman really shouldn't have been working at her age and so I couldn't protest too much, simply for my own selfish reasons.

'Wow, that is bad news. When are ya leavin?'

'I'll be leaving at the end of next week.'

My head dropped as I tried not to show how upset I was.

'But I want you to come and visit me at home whenever you feel like it because sure I'm only living down the road. And believe it or not, the thing that I'll miss most about this place is you.'

'I'll miss you too,' I said in a little lost voice.

'But listen, sweetie, it's not really goodbye so don't be sad. It's goodbye to my life as a librarian, of course, but we're still going to see each other.'

'Course we are,' I said, not feeling half as confident as I pretended to be. In fact on the inside, I was completely devastated that one of the last remaining people on this planet who I felt close to seemed to be drifting out of my life.

I abruptly excused myself and went to the toilet because I didn't want anyone to see me cry. When I returned to my desk, I took up the copy of *Howards End* that I had been reading but I could no longer concentrate on the words on the page. I kept spying Mrs Horricks out of the corner of my eye. I noticed that she was having trouble reshelving a load of books. Without a second thought, I got up and commandeered her trolley along with an offer to help. She gratefully accepted and I had all the books back on the shelves in double-quick time. She didn't even need to show me the ropes as I already knew exactly where everything was supposed to go. As I left the library later that evening, Mrs Horricks slipped a tenner into my pocket and insisted that I buy myself something nice. I tried to refuse but she wasn't taking no for an answer and so I took the money and I bought myself half a litre of vodka and a big bottle of coke. Later that evening, I made a very impressive dent in the bottle of vodka before I finally passed out. Thankfully I was already at home in my bed because I've noticed that it's quite hard to get a taxi when you're on your own and lying unconscious on a footpath or in a doorway somewhere.

That same night, Mrs Horricks appeared in my dreams for the first time. As had been the case with my nightmares about Owen, these latest dreams unfolded in an outdoors setting. I could see Mrs Horricks standing on a patch of grass and chatting to someone but I couldn't hear what was being said because, maddeningly, the people were too far away. My dreams about Owen had been beamed into my brain in vivid technicolour with accompanying stereo surround sound that captured every splash of water and every terrified cry for help. But this time it was different. This was more like some bullshit foreign film where the camera was positioned a hundred yards away from the main actors and then very slowly zoomed in on them.

By the time Mrs Horricks filled the screen in my mind, it was clear that something was very wrong indeed. I could see her looking behind her and I knew instinctively that she was looking for somewhere to sit down before she collapsed. There was nowhere within easy reach, though, and her need was such that she tried to sit on the grass. I'm guessing that you've never seen an arthritic woman of retirement age trying to sit on the ground and that's because it's a major ordeal for an elderly person to attempt such a feat. Almost impossible, in fact, without considerable assistance from a helper but whoever Mrs Horricks had been talking to didn't seem to be offering any help at all. In fact he just ran off as soon as she showed the first signs of being in difficulty. Judging by the look of horror on her face, I figured that the scumbag must have been trying to rob her. But I could never get a proper look at him because in the dream he had his back to me and the focus was always on the pained expression of my librarian friend.

As she was trying to get to a sitting position her manoeuvre turned into a sort of controlled fall. When she reached the ground, she lay on her side, gasping for breaths that would not come quickly enough while the blood drained from her face. Her fingers became like talons that clawed and dug into the grass in a desperate attempt to pull herself free from the clutches of Death. But it was a battle that she could never win. The last thing that I would see before waking up was the look in her eyes as she lay motionless on the ground. It reminded me of what I had seen in Owen's eyes when they pulled him from the canal – it was the look of someone who, when they least expected it, has found themselves staring Death in the face, right before being pulled into his clammy eternal embrace.

I never told Mrs Horricks about my nightmares in which she was the star. I thought about telling her, but I didn't want to upset her and even if she did believe me sufficiently to take the threat seriously, there wasn't a whole lot that she could do about it. And so I said nothing. But even after she had worked her last day in the library, I still kept a very close eye on her. In fact, I called around to her house almost daily offering to do odd jobs and any chores that she could think of and there was no shortage of work for me to be getting on with because her house was falling into disrepair. She always gave me money for my trouble which I always tried to refuse but ended up accepting simply because it made her happy to make me happy. And vice versa, of course. I doubt Mrs Horricks had expected to see so much of me when she had presented me with an open invitation to visit her, but she always looked hugely pleased to see me nonetheless and not just because of the cheap labour. Her husband, Frank, had died while still in his forties and they never had any children so I don't think it's overstating the case to say that Mrs Horricks regarded me as the son she never had.

The library had been my favourite place in the world when Mrs Horricks was working there but things went rapidly downhill after she left. Her replacement was a lunatic from Northern Ireland who had watery eyes and thinning hair that appeared to be rinsed in brake fluid. But his hair wasn't remotely as disturbing as his enormous Adam's apple which continually bobbed up and down as he talked. He reminded me of a turkey so in my mind I christened him Turkeyman. I knew that he and I were on a collision course after the very first time that I spoke to him. The library copy of Nabokov's *Lolita* was missing and so I approached Turkeyman and asked him whether the library would be replacing it anytime soon. He glared at me like I was a spoilt child demanding new toys because I was bored of the million toys that I already had.

'DA YOUUU THINK THAT THE GOOD PEOPLE WHO RUN THIS LIBRARY HAVE NAWTHIN BETHER TA BE DOIN THAN TA BE OWT SPENDIN MONEY ON PORNOGRAPHY FOR THE LIKES O YOUUU?'

Turkeyman had an incredibly annoying foghorn voice that was incapable of whispering, an unfortunate trait given his profession. Naturally I was taken aback by his unprovoked aggression and for once I was almost lost for words.

'Eh, wha?' was the best response that I could come up with.

'THUS HERE IS A LIBRARY, NAUT SOME KIND A ... CHILD-PORNOGRAPHY DISTRIBUUSHUN POINT.'

Now I really was lost for words.

'I'm lookin for *Lolita*, by Nabokov,' I said again, thinking that he simply must have misheard me.

'IS IT DEAF YOUUU THINK I AM?' he said in a voice that almost gave me whiplash. The fact was, he was talking so loudly that I had in fact decided that he was quite obviously deaf and he had apparently decided to make it his mission to try and make everybody else deaf as well.

'*Lolita* is not pornography; it's a recognised classic,' I told him in a loud, distinct voice, thinking that the batteries in his hearing aid must be knackered and so I was trying to make it easier for him to read my lips.

'DON'T YOUUU RAISE YOUR VOICE TA ME, SONNY, OR I'LL HAVE YOUUU BARRED FROM THIS LIBRARY SO QUICK, YOUR FEET WON'T TOUCH THE GROUND.'

Conversing with Turkeyman was like swimming in treacle and so I decided around that point that he might be mildly retarded because I couldn't understand how I wasn't getting through to him. I tried once more, punctuating each word with a small pause in an effort to make myself understood.

'Not – pornography, a – recognised – classic,' I said.

'RECOGNISED BY PEEDAPHILES MEBBE. I WASN'T BORN YESTERDAY, SONNY, SO DON'T YOUUU BE THINKIN YA CAN COME IN HERE AN PULL THE WOOL OVER MY EYES.'

I threw my hands in the air in exasperation and stormed out. Clearly I was wasting my time. I stood a better chance of getting intelligent conversation from Colonel Groucho than I did from Turkeyman.

I blame my stepbrother Johnny Rotten for what happened after that because, well, because it was completely his fault. I was in the middle of reading *Moby Dick* when that loathsome little pukemonster stole into my room one day in my absence and proceeded to rip out half of the pages of the book. He then drew childish-looking nudey pictures on what was left of it. On the cover, he mutilated the title with black biro so that the book became *Mouldy Dick* and he complemented this with a badly drawn penis that had wavy smell lines emanating from it.

When I discovered the violation, naturally I went ballistic. Unfortunately for me, though, Johnny Rotten's legs were a crucial six inches longer than mine at the time with the result that I had come off the worst in all of our previous scraps. My problem was that I was all heart and no technique, which meant that I was usually left with more than my fair share of shiners and bloody noses. And because the code of the street was like the catechism to me, I would never grass on anyone, not even on Johnny Rotten for his multitude of sins against me.

But after my stepbrother's assault on my library book, my diminutive status did not prevent me from exacting a bittersweet revenge. Without hesitating, I went straight for the thing that he loved the most. I charged into his empty bedroom, seized Luke Skywalker from his locker and ripped apart the packaging that entombed him. In doing so, I exposed his molecules to fresh air for the first time since he had left the factory, thereby shattering his prized status as a collectible. But I didn't just leave it at that. Amongst other things in the locker drawer, there was a thick black marker. I grabbed it and then I reached under the mattress and pulled out one of Johnny's lingerie catalogues. I ripped out a centrefold spread of some doll wearing a lacy red bra and knickers and then, enclosed in a large speech bubble, I wrote on the page – 'FWOAAAAAHH! WORTH COMING OUT FOR!'

I stuck the picture over Johnny's locker after stealing a small piece of Blu-tack from the back of a poster of Jean Luc Picard and then I positioned Luke on top of the locker in such a way that it looked as if the speech bubble was coming out of his mouth. And then for the grand finalé, I took the tiny light-sabre accessory and I placed it in Luke's two hands in a way that suggested he was clutching his own monster penis.

I had no regrets at that point. Regrets came later after I made the huge mistake of trying to return the library book. I think that a showdown with Turkeyman would probably have happened sooner or later but it all came to a head when he nabbed me re-shelving a considerably shortened version of Herman Melville's classic, now illustrated with cartoon breasts and hairy cocks. This might sound incredibly stupid, but in all that time I spent at the library, I had never bothered getting myself a library card. Mostly I just read whatever I wanted to read in the library itself, and whenever I did want to take a book out, I just popped it into my bag and off I went. No hassle and Mrs Horricks certainly didn't mind. I always returned books when I was finished, of course, and there was never any problem, and that's why I thought that I could return my version of *Moby Dick* with the minimum of fuss. But I hadn't reckoned on Turkeyman.

As soon as I walked into the library on that fateful day, I got the feeling straight away that something wasn't quite right. The first sensation that usually hit me upon entering the library was the musty smell of old books. But not on that day. On that day, I smelled something different and my mouth filled with a metallic taste as if I had been sucking on a penny. As I placed *Moby Dick* back on the shelf, I was still trying to determine the source of the unusual odour but then Turkeyman intervened and I forgot all about it.

'DON'T YOUUU MOVE ANOTHER MUSCLE, MISHTER, BECAUSE I'VE BEEN WATCHIN YOUUU, AND I KNOW EXACTLY WHAT YOU'RE UP TA, YOU LITTLE SHITE,' he said in his best Belfast accent. I could barely understand what the fucker was saying but as he was attempting to lift me off the ground by my earlobe at the same time, I knew that he wasn't merely exchanging pleasantries.

'GIMMEE DHAT,' he roared, and I figured that he was referring to the ruined book that I'd been returning. I gave it to him and he looked at his hand as if I'd just taken a shit in it. Then he slammed me up against a stack of shelves and kept his forearm at my throat whilst flicking through the book. Judging by his next reaction, I started thinking that, just maybe, Johnny Rotten had inadvertently defiled a first-edition handwritten version of the Bible signed by Jesus himself, because Turkeyman's face went from a pasty grey colour to lobster red in the time that it takes to say Oliver Cromwell.

'WHAT THE … OH JESHUS, I'LL KICK YOUR SKINNY WEE ARSE UP AND DOWN THE COUNTRY FOR THIS, YOU WEE BASTARD YA.'

Then he started speaking again, only this time he punctuated every word by giving me a good solid whack on the head with the book as if I was some kind of monstrously unholy tent peg that needed to be shown who was boss.

'THUS (whack) IS (whack) WHAT (whack) HAWPENS (whack) TO (whack) DEGENERATES (whack) WITH (whack) NOOO (whack) RESPECT (whack) FOR (whack) OTHER (whack) PEOPLE'S (whack) PROPERTY (whack).'

On the final word, he belted me extra hard and whatever way he was holding the book, the pages flew out of the cover in a cluster and fluttered wildly across the room like a paper aeroplane shot down in flames.

'You're after wreckin tha book,' I said to him like a drowning man seeking salvation in apportioned blame. Turkeyman's face went from lobster red to bright purple. I could see a vein bulging in the centre of his forehead and I figured that he was probably just about one more smart comment away from having steam come out his ears. I threw in another cheeky remark just to see if I could make the fucker have a coronary.

'But here, listen, I'll say nothin about it if ya promise not to go wreckin any more books. Righ?' And with that I gave him a big wink.

55

He had caught me with the smoking gun in my hand and now, somehow, I was making it sound like I was doing him a favour. Turkeyman went apoplectic with pure rage. A rivulet of white spittle emerged from one corner of his mouth and trickled down his chin. He reminded me of the android in the film *Aliens*, which had leaked white blood when it was dying. But Turkeyman wasn't dying; instead he had murder in his eyes and I started to think that this time I might have gone too far. He shook me like a rag doll and then he clamped one of his oversized hands around my throat and started squeezing. The penny dropped; I had never had a reasonable conversation with this man because he was insane – completely and utterly off-his-tits bonkers, and now he was trying to kill me.

My survival instincts took over and one of my hands shot upwards, catching his hand by the wrist and dislodging it in the same manoeuvre.

'Fuck off, ya fuckin lunatic,' I barked, and then I placed both of my hands on his chest and gave him a good solid shove. Turkeyman clearly wasn't expecting this because he stumbled backwards a few steps and then crashed into a set of freestanding bookshelves. He backed into the shelves with such force that they started tipping backwards and because he was still leaning on them, they kept moving after the initial impact, becoming perilously close to toppling over. I didn't hesitate for a second. I raced around to throw my weight against the far side of the shelves. At that point, they paused in a deft balancing act upon two corners, teetering on the brink of either returning to their original position or else crossing the point of no return and crashing down on my side. I threw my entire weight against the shelves and initially it didn't seem to make any difference. They were so heavy and I was so light, it seemed as if they were determined to decide for themselves whether or not they would fall.

But then, slowly but surely, they started to move again back in the direction from where they had come, very gradually changing course like a lumbering giant. I felt like Superman lifting a bus off a crippled child and maybe a sudden surge of adrenaline did give me extra strength because I overdid it. The bookshelves returned to their original position and simply kept on going. I was unaware that Turkeyman, on the other side, had grabbed a shoulder-high shelf with two hands and was pulling for all that he was worth. The shelves were now moving away from me at a speed that no set of bookshelves should ever travel at. They reached the point of no return once again except this time they just kept on going. Books started to topple from their positions on to the floor. We both saw what was coming and desperately tried corrective measures, Turkeyman now pushing for all that he was worth while I tried in vain to gain some purchase on the shelves so that I could pull. There was a ripping sound as a small white sign that said 'Fiction M to R' came off in my hand and then a scream shattered the sacred silence reserved only for libraries and churches. The scream was compounded by the sound of hundreds of books raining down on the carpet. When the shelves finally came to rest, the sound of the crash was not as loud as it might have been because Turkeyman broke their fall.

I raced over to him but he wasn't moving. His whole body was buried beneath the bookcase and his head was the only part of him sticking out. A deep gash running from his left temple to the middle of his forehead had opened up and was starting to bleed heavily. The fucker was dead. I knew it. I had recently finished reading *Howards End* and the scene in that book where Mr Leonard Bast is killed by a bookcase that comes crashing down on him was foremost in my mind. Who would have thought that such a thing could happen in real life? I certainly didn't; not in a million fucking years. And yet that was exactly the situation in which I found myself.

I walked out of the library without looking left or right. I just wanted to get out of there and put some distance between me and my terrible crime. As soon as I was out the door, though, all of my emotions seemed to explode forth and I burst into tears. It was all too much for me. I was crying not because I was mourning the demise of Turkeyman but because I felt that a higher power was definitely fucking with me and there was nothing I could do about it.

There was only one place for me to go and I ran all the way there. Mrs Horricks lived about half a mile away and I was quite out of breath by the time I got to her house. I rang the doorbell repeatedly and when she didn't come shuffling down her hallway within a few seconds, I started banging on the front door with the heel of my hand.

'Mrs Horricks! Mrs Horricks! It's me,' I yelled. 'Open the door!'

I heard a faint call from around the back of the house and so I ran down the side passage. My favourite old lady was standing in her back garden with a pair of secateurs in her hand but she had stopped whatever she was doing and she stood facing me as I ran up to her.

'He's dead!' I panted. 'I fuckin killed him.' I had never used bad language in front of her before but these were exceptional circumstances.

'Who's dead?' she asked, her eyes growing wide with alarm.

'The librarian. The new one. I killed him. It was an accident but I think he's dead. There was blood comin out of his head and he wasn't movin. I'm so completely *fucked!* They're gonna send me to prison for this. What am I gonna do?'

Mrs Horricks didn't have an answer for me. Instead she just put one hand up to her mouth in shock and then she started shaking her head as if that could somehow make it all not true.

I started sobbing all over again and I was so caught up with my own woes that I failed to notice the effect that my anguished cries were having on Mrs Horricks. The colour drained from her face and all of the strength in her body seemed to go with it. It was only when she started looking around her for somewhere to sit down that I realised what was happening. And what was about to happen.

'My pills,' she whispered while placing one hand on her chest over her heart. 'They're in ... in my bag. In the ... kitchen. Be a good boy and get them quick.'

I was briefly torn between deciding whether I should stay with her or else try to find her pills but I opted for the latter course of action because I figured that she needed her tablets more than kind words at that point. I ran to the back door and seconds later I was in the kitchen that I had been in many times over the previous couple of weeks. But Mrs Horricks' handbag was nowhere to be seen. It wasn't on the kitchen table and it wasn't on the countertop anywhere. I looked on all the chairs and under the chair-cushions but there was no sign of it.

'*FUCK*!!!' I roared in desperation. Then I ran into the hallway and up the stairs two at a time. I burst into the old lady's bedroom in a frantic search for her bag. When I couldn't find it within around ten seconds, I ran downstairs again and back into the kitchen. I figured it had to be there somewhere. A black leather bag. I had seen it only about a million fucking times. I started opening cupboards looking for it and I eventually found it in the cupboard under the sink. I pulled it out and dumped the contents on to the floor. Four different pill bottles were among the contents scattered on the linoleum. I snatched them up as fast as I could and I ran back into the garden.

'GOT THEM!' I shouted as I ran over to where Mrs Horricks was now lying on the grass. I dropped to the ground beside her head and started unscrewing the cap from one of the bottles.

'Which ones do you need? Is it these?' I asked while shaking some small white tablets into my hand. There was no response from Mrs Horricks. She looked for all the world like she was sleeping and I tried to pretend to myself that this was indeed the case.

'Mrs Horricks? Are these the right tablets?'

When she didn't answer, I shook her shoulder gently and when she still didn't respond, I physically pulled open her mouth and dropped one of the tablets on to her tongue. That's where it stayed though because I couldn't make her swallow it. I couldn't get any reaction at all from her and I could feel the tears start to roll down my face as the finality of the situation started to sink in. One of the pill bottles was of the brown-glass variety and after giving the bottom of it a quick rub on my T-shirt, I held it right up to Mrs Horricks' lips. A few seconds later, I inspected it and there was no sign of any condensation at all on the glass. She wasn't breathing but I still refused to accept that she could be dead. I had spoken to her not five minutes ago so how could she possibly now be dead?

I felt as if I could hardly trust my own limbs as I stood up and walked back into the house. Using the phone in the hallway, I called for an ambulance. I gave Mrs Horricks' address to the emergency services but I hung up the phone when they asked for my name. I should have stayed with her until the ambulance men arrived but I was too ashamed of what I had done. Once again I had killed my best friend and the shock of that realisation was like a flesh-eating virus attacking my brain. I walked out the front door and strolled home in a daze. I never even said goodbye to Mrs Horricks.

The cops called to my house later that day and arrested me for assault and criminal damage. I was very surprised that I wasn't being arrested for a double homicide but I didn't ask any questions. They put me in handcuffs like I was some sort of mad-dog crazy man and then they walked me out of my house and into the patrol car waiting outside. I didn't even pretend to be any kind of hard man because the truth is I was scared shitless. The two cops who carted me off to the cop shop had a great laugh telling me all about their sergeant, who they said was an expert in various forms of torture that didn't leave any marks on the body. They said that if I didn't sign a statement confessing to everything then I would get a full demonstration. They probably didn't realise just how scared I was and so their efforts to scare me even more were pointless as I was already too terrified to speak. For the duration of the short journey to the station, I sat completely still in the back of the car while a feeling of numbness seeped into me like frostbite.

At the station, a skinny cop with a downy moustache asked me if I wanted to contact a solicitor. I mumbled something incomprehensible and when he asked me again, I said in a faraway voice that I didn't know any solicitors.

'Yeah, but do ya want one?' he asked. I shrugged my shoulders and he took this to mean no. That was fine with me. If it was even possible for me to be in any more trouble than I already was, then a fat solicitor's bill addressed to my dad would probably send me even deeper into the pile of shit that I was drowning in. The concept of free legal aid meant nothing to me and it wasn't explained to me at the time. Or maybe it was explained and it just went right over my head. All I really wanted was for that nightmare to end and to wake up at home in my own bed. But I couldn't manage to wake myself up. This particular nightmare was for real. I felt like a little kid lost in a busy department store where his mother is nowhere to be found. Everyone at the police station seemed to be over six feet tall and they all spoke in big bogger accents that I could just about understand.

The skinny cop started reading something to me from a form but I couldn't concentrate on what he was saying. When he was finished, he asked me if I had any questions. There was one name that I had heard mentioned a few times – Gerald McAllister – and so I inquired who that was. The cop said that that was the name of the librarian that I had assaulted.

'Is he dead?' I asked.

'Not yet anyway,' said the cop. He must have noticed how worried I looked because he added, 'A couple of stitches and some aspirin and he'll be fine, I'd say.'

The revelation that I hadn't killed Turkeyman after all gave me very little comfort. If anything, it merely made Mrs Horricks' death seem even more pointless.

After that, I was placed in a cell for what seemed like hours. There was no one else in the cell, which was a relief. A cop came to check on me about every fifteen minutes, presumably to see whether I had topped myself, and I have to admit, that was starting to seem like quite an attractive option. He asked me if I wanted anything and I told him that I wanted to go home. He just laughed and said 'I bet ya do' in his big bogman voice.

Eventually two cops arrived and escorted me to an interview room in a different part of the station. As I walked through the door, the first thing that I saw was my father sitting there waiting for me. The cops must have contacted him because I certainly didn't. He didn't look angry, though, just disappointed. Anger I could have coped with but this was worse. He could barely bring himself to look at me. The cops made him sign something allowing them to interview me and then they started firing questions at me. One of them asked the questions while the other wrote down my answers. The whole thing was being recorded by a video camera on to three VHS cassettes so I wondered why they were bothering to write down the questions and answers. I've learned since that the video was actually for my benefit so that the cops wouldn't be tempted to slap me around a bit. They wouldn't have dared try anything like that though with my da in the room. All of their questions were about what had happened at the library and I answered truthfully and to the best of my knowledge. They never even mentioned Mrs Horricks and so I didn't either.

The interview lasted about an hour, and when it was over my father signed the interview notes and then I was let out on bail. I was free again but I think I would have preferred to stay in the police cell rather than face my father's disappointment. He hardly said two words to me in the car on the short journey home. When we pulled into the driveway, Doreen was standing by the open front door and she looked all smiley and smug. All the effort she had invested in telling anyone who would listen that I would amount to nothing had apparently been proven right and consequently she looked like a four-word sentence personified, and the sentence was 'I told you so'. She reminded me of a four-letter word as well, but you can work that one out for yourself. I chose to ignore her and threw myself upon the mercy of my father once we were in the kitchen.

'Da, I didn't do this. It wasn't my fault.'

'Don't even speak to me, you. Do you have any idea how disgusted I am with you?' he replied.

'But it was an accident.'

'So ya did do it?'

'Nooo! I didn't! Or at least not the way tha they're sayin I did. I was just tryin to push the bookshelves the other way and they fell on him.'

'Wha the fuck were ya doin pushin over bookshelves in a library anyway? It doesn't sound like much of an accident to me.'

I gave up trying to persuade him of my innocence. Even in my own ears, my story was starting to sound a bit unlikely and I was growing tired of not being believed.

'Are ya tryin to punish me for somethin? Is that it?' he asked.

'No,' I said in a sad little voice.

'Well I'm just glad tha your mother isn't alive to see this,' he added. Anger rose up in me at the whole injustice of the situation and suddenly I was really pissed off.

'Well, I'm not, because she would have listened to my side of the story and she would have believed me.'

'Don't you go draggin your mother into this shameful mess.'

'You brought her up.'

With that, he raised his hand to give me a slap in the face. I was too quick for him though and I caught his arm by the wrist in mid-strike. We stared at each other for a few seconds in silence, eyeball to eyeball.

It was me who finally broke the deadlock.

'Da, listen to me, I swear to God it wasn't my fault. It was an accident, and for what it's worth I'm sorry, aw righ?'

He had no idea how sorry I was. Nobody did. My father looked at me for what seemed like a long time. I felt as if it was the first time that he had looked at me properly in months. He was starting to believe me. Two or three seconds passed in a further awkward silence while we both just looked at each other. The fight was gone out of both of us.

Then Doreen stuck her crowbar in.

'They say tha tha librarian is fightin for his life in hospital,' she said, barely suppressing a triumphant smirk. 'I'm just prayin to God that it's not murder you're charged with,' she added for good measure. She had no idea just how close she was to being spot on. I was willing her to say something about how I had brought shame on the family and then I could have thrown in a comment about her ex-husband's colourful criminal record. My da didn't say another word. He just walked out of the kitchen and then banged the front door, presumably on his way to the pub. I went upstairs and locked myself in my room where I cried silent tears into my pillow.

A couple of months later, I found myself in a courtroom for the very first time. The judge was a cantankerous old bastard who had a hard drinker's red nose and massive jowls. I remember thinking that if his entire body from the neck down got toasted in a fire, a plastic surgeon could probably have grafted the skin from his jowls to cover the whole of his body.

He opened his mouth to make some ruling and my heart sank. The fucker was from Northern Ireland! I was sure that after hearing the facts according to Turkeyman, Judge Jowls was going to put me away for this life and the next, but as it happened, I wasn't sentenced that day. My case was called, I said that I was pleading not guilty, and then I was given a date to come back and told to get myself a solicitor in the meantime.

I randomly picked a firm of solicitors from the yellow pages and, after making an appointment, I went to their offices for a consultation. The solicitor who saw me looked a bit like the actor Gregory Peck, apart from one small aspect of his appearance that seemed peculiar. It took me a few seconds to figure out what it was and then it hit me: his hair was a distinguished silver-grey colour but his bushy eyebrows were almost jet black.

He took me into his office and asked me if I'd like a cup of coffee. I told him that I'd love a cup and he said that he'd been hoping that I'd say no because they didn't have any coffee. I explained to him everything that had happened in the library and his brow furrowed as he digested this information. While he was in that earnest, thinking mode, his eyebrows reminded me of two slugs trying to stand up and so in my mind I christened him Slugger.

'These are the facts then,' he said to me. 'And facts can be stubborn things.'

I wasn't sure what he was talking about and so I didn't say anything.

'But facts without foundation are liable to collapse like a house of cards. Do you understand?'

'Eh, I think so.'

I had no idea.

'Facts, my young friend, are negotiable. You learn that quickly in the lawyer business.'

Well, that's just fucking great, I thought. But as I wasn't in the lawyer business or likely to be signing up for law school anytime soon, I really didn't give a shit.

'You say that this librarian assaulted you, and so in court we'll say that you acted in self-defence.'

'But I *did* act in self-defence.'

'Indeed,' replied Slugger, clearly not believing me. I should have just told him to go fuck himself at that point and found myself another solicitor, but I was too scared and inexperienced and so I ignored my better instincts.

'Was he a young man, this librarian? Was he big? Bigger than you maybe?'

'He was ... I dunno, about fifty maybe. And skinny.'

'Mmmm, that's not so good,' he replied and then he got up and started pacing around his office while stuffing tobacco into a pipe. This went on for about a minute and then he walked over to the door and opened it. He went to leave and then changed his mind, like he was Columbo or somebody.

'What we really need here is a credible independent witness who will back up your story.'

'It's not a story, it's the truth.'

He sat down again and asked me whether I could provide any witnesses who might have seen Turkeyman trying to strangle me. I couldn't. After the bookshelves had come crashing down, I had simply walked out the door without looking back. At the time, I had been vaguely aware of a few other people in the library staring at me like I was Jeffrey Dahmer or someone, but I was careful not to catch anyone's eye, thinking that to do so might fracture my magic cloak of invisibility that only worked if I didn't look at anyone. The upshot was that I only had my word for it that what had started out as an act of self-defence had somehow escalated into a very unfortunate accident.

Slugger nodded his head slowly and then he rocked back and

forth on his chair for a long time. The slugs on his face were trying to stand up again.

'The bottom line is this, Mister eh ...' He had clearly forgotten my name and when he realised that it wasn't forthcoming a second time, he tried to disguise the pause by clearing his throat. 'This librarian obviously didn't assault himself and you have already made admissions that you were present at the scene. Therefore we can hardly claim in court that it's a case of mistaken identity. So that only leaves us with the defence of self-defence which is no defence at all if the court decides that you used excessive force.'

'So wha's gonna happen to me?' I asked, anxious as always to wade through the bullshit. Slugger then launched into a sermon about the advantages of pleading guilty in my circumstances. I listened politely and then told him that there was no way I was pleading guilty to something that I didn't do. He didn't look too pleased with this response. He asked me whether I had taken any photos of my injuries after Turkeyman's assault on me. I hadn't, and now it was long past the time for thinking about that. He asked me if I knew anyone of good standing in the community who would come to court and give evidence of my previous good character but I couldn't think of anyone. I didn't know any priests and my teachers didn't know me because I had spent so much time bunking off. Mrs Horricks was no longer with us and my father didn't count because he was my father. So when that line of inquiry fizzled out, Slugger started fishing to see whether I just happened to be some sort of sporting superstar. I told him that I didn't like football or rugby or swimming. I especially didn't like swimming.

He asked me a few more perfunctory questions after that and

then he stopped talking altogether and gazed out the window. There was a pregnant pause that miscarried and so I gathered that our consultation was over.

When the date of my court case finally came around, I found myself wearing a horrendous stripy suit that was at least two inches too short at the cuffs and the trouser ends. Doreen had borrowed it for me from her sister's husband – a borderline midget who works in the social welfare office. She had presented it to me the previous week like it was a family heirloom that had been passed down from one generation to the next. I thought she had to be joking. A chimpanzee in a circus clown act wouldn't have been seen dead in that suit. But she looked so serious that I just took it from her without even a whisper of protest, just a sort of a grunt that was supposed to mean thanks. My da sat smiling in the corner. He probably thought that he was observing some kind of bonding ceremony between Doreen and me and all his prayers had been answered. I rushed upstairs to my bedroom before someone suggested a group hug and I hid the suit at the back of my wardrobe. But when the day of my court hearing arrived, I was so anxious that I would have worn a tutu and wellies if there was the slightest chance that such an outfit might have kept me out of jail. And so desperation overcame my good sense and the suit came out of the wardrobe again.

My da took the bus into town with me and then we walked together to the courthouse. We arrived fifteen minutes early and my father had a smoke outside the main door while we waited. I didn't see Slugger anywhere but I assumed that he would be there for ten-thirty. Ten-thirty came and went and there was no sign of him. The judge came out and cases started to get called but still my lawyer was nowhere to be seen. Every time the door of the court opened, I turned around expecting to see him but he never arrived. Then when my case was finally called, a young barrister with a lisp stood up and said that he was representing me. Nice of him to tell me! I had noticed him sitting in the court but he looked about twelve, and so I had just assumed that he was some kind of student on a field trip. Not so! My boy barrister appeared to be all set to represent me and so I moved to the front of the court and the drama commenced.

The lawyer for the prosecution was so smooth that he may as well have been wearing ice skates and gliding across a frozen lake while I drowned beneath his feet. I'd never even laid eyes on him before but he seemed to have made it his personal mission to bury me. He got things rolling by calling one of the guards who had arrested me. The cop started banging on about how he had received an emergency call in relation to an assault at Rathgorman Public Library and had arrived first on the scene whereupon he immediately requested an ambulance for the injured party. It was all downhill after that. A doctor gave evidence of what she described as 'the extensive injuries suffered by Mr McAllister', and then a couple more cops gave evidence in relation to what had happened at the police station. One of them had a bag of exhibits with him. From the bag, he produced the mutilated copy of *Moby Dick*. I couldn't believe my eyes. I must be the only person in the history of the

State who has ever been prosecuted for damaging a library book. And I didn't even do it! But that didn't seem to count for anything.

The judge flicked through the graffiti-strewn pages and shook his head in disapproval. He looked at me like I was a great big dollop of dog shit that was stinking up his court. I shook my head at him as if to say it's nothing to do with me, Judge, but all I got in return was a frown that was more like a repressed snarl. I wouldn't exactly call it another premonition but I think that it was around that point when I began to realise that I was going to prison. And after Turkeyman's evidence, I was sure of it.

Turkeyman took the stand and told the court about how he had caught me vandalising a book and when confronted, he said that I had headbutted him and then deliberately pulled down a set of bookshelves on top of him. As he spoke, he stuck his chin out in what he probably considered to be a gesture of proud defiance. The upturned angle of his head made his potato-sized Adam's apple appear even more disturbing than usual. He swallowed hard a couple of times in order to give an air of authenticity to his bullshit, and when he did so, his Adam's apple looked like a small animal trying to escape. Towards the end of his evidence, he told the court that on my way out of the library I had spat on his broken body and called him 'a Loyalist baby-killing cunt'. What an imagination! Bravo Turkeyman! He turned out to be more than a match for me. He twisted the facts, and then he twisted his knife in me.

The prosecution star witness was an attention-starved old bollox who got into the box and testified that he had been in the library on the date in question and had witnessed the whole incident occur just as Turkeyman had described it. Turkeyman probably bought the old man's testimony in exchange for writing off a lifetime's worth of library fines. But whatever the deal, that senile old fuck earned every penny.

And so it came down to my word against the other side and as that made it two against one, the judge went with the majority and convicted me. This wasn't Judge Jowls anymore, by the way; it was some other ancient old relic. This one was like something out of an episode of *Doctor Who*. He had a voice that sounded as if he had a throat full of bubbling phlegm and every time he spoke, I wanted to scream at him 'WILL YOU CLEAR YOUR FUCKING THROAT?'

I didn't, though. I was too busy trying to numb myself to the proceedings through a form of self-hypnosis. That's a trick that I use sometimes in shitty situations whereby I pretend that the nightmare facing me is in fact happening to somebody else. For maximum effect, I concentrate really hard on imagining myself to be in a completely different place, and when it's working really well, my eyes glaze over and then close to half-mast.

At one point while one of the guards was giving evidence, the judge told me to wake up but I didn't even hear him because I had so successfully detached myself from reality. I was dragged back to the real world by the judge roaring at me to pay the court the respect that it deserved. Meanwhile, my twelve-year-old lawyer started apologising on my behalf and by way of explanation he told the court that my methadone treatment had been reduced to 60 mls per day. *My methadone treatment!* That dopey fucker was after mixing my file up with some junkie arsehole's case and he had hammered another nail into my coffin as a result.

I told the judge that I had no idea what my barrister was talking about but this only seemed to make matters worse and so I clammed up again. I got the distinct feeling that the judge was under the impression that I was bombed out of my brains and so when it came to the sentencing, the Honourable Judge Phlegm stuck the boot in at every opportunity. He called me a brazen young thug who hadn't shown the slightest remorse for my callous and cowardly actions. I didn't have any previous convictions but he didn't give a fuck. He went on to say that had I pleaded guilty he would have given me a six-month sentence, but in the circumstances he said that he had no hesitation whatsoever in imposing the maximum sentence that was available to him. Then he gave me twelve months like he was handing out goody bags. Prison officers appeared from nowhere and hauled me down to the cells and then later off to St Patrick's Institution for Young Offenders.

After arriving at St Pat's, I was searched and then placed in a cell on my own. I spent most of my first twelve hours in a bad way and so solitary confinement suited me fine. I was so depressed that I could hardly even speak. I was only eighteen years old, not quite a boy and not quite a man, and I had never been in trouble like this before, so to say that it was a big shock to my system would be putting it mildly.

The evening meal was already over by the time that I arrived on my first day in the place, but I didn't care. I couldn't have eaten anything anyway. A female prison officer came by my cell at some point and gave me ham sandwiches that were wrapped in a triangle of plastic. I asked if she would contact my solicitor because there had been a dreadful mistake. She told me that I could buy a phone card in the prison shop when it re-opened the next day and contact him myself. But she wasn't being a bitch about it. She was just following procedures and she smiled at me, just to prove that it was nothing personal.

I cried a lot that first night. Perfectly silent crying that was only apparent by my wet cheeks. I couldn't help thinking that if only I hadn't been such a smartarse to Turkeyman, then none of this would have happened. Doreen used to say to me, 'I am being harsh with you now because the world will be far harsher with you later on.' I never quite understood the logic of that statement and I always thought that it was just another excuse for her to be the queen bitch, but now I started to think that she might have been right after all.

I didn't see any of the other boys that night but I could sense their presence all around me. They called themselves *cons* as in convicts but they were really just kids. Most of us had a cell to ourselves although there were a few people sharing due to over-crowding. The cells themselves weren't all that bad. There were no vertical bars of the type that you always see in prison films. We all had rooms with four walls, one of which contained a heavy door with a square window in it that was strengthened with re-inforced glass. There was a steel toilet in one corner and a TV in the other. I didn't turn on the TV that first night; I had too much other stuff to think about.

Sleep came to me eventually just when I had given up all hope of ever nodding off. At eight the next morning, I was woken by a bell that sounded like a fire alarm. It was coming from somewhere outside in the corridor. I found myself wondering how we would know the building was on fire if the fire alarm rang out at the same time as the rise-and-shine bell was due to be sounded. Although mind you, an evacuation was out of the question, so it probably didn't matter too much anyway.

To my immense relief, when I had checked in the previous night, I had been presented with a pair of grey trousers and a grey sweatshirt so thankfully I didn't have to wear my dodgy suit again. A suit like that was liable to get me killed. I followed the crowd to the main dining hall where breakfast consisted of a choice of cereals, warm orange juice and cold toast. The toast was so lightly done that it didn't even deserve to be called toast. It tasted like slices of stale white bread that someone had breathed on for a few seconds. I sat on my own at the end of a long table and tried not to look scared. Nobody paid me much attention and that was fine with me.

After breakfast, I was told to report to a prison officer called Mr Jones who was in charge of looking after the new kids on the block. As soon as I saw him, he reminded me of a character who featured in an old joke that I had heard somewhere. In the joke, a woman sees an old man sitting on his porch smoking a cigarette and watching the world go by. She comments to him about how content he appears and she asks him the secret of his happiness. The old man tells her that he consumes half a bottle of whiskey and a line of coke with every single meal, and on top of that, he says that he shags two or three prostitutes every single night.

'Well fair play to ya,' says the woman. 'It hasn't stopped ya living a long life anyway, that's for sure.'

'I'm only twenty-six,' says the man.

That's sort of how Jonesey looked – twenty-six going on about sixty. But he didn't try to bully me with any heavy-handed bullshit. He gave me the choice of either continuing with school and sitting my final exams or else signing up for a trade workshop. I took the former option without hesitation because I thought that it would be less effort. Less effort for me anyway because I had always found academic work in the past to be easy enough once I put my mind to it. And in St Pat's, bunking off simply wasn't an option so I knew that I would have to attend class no matter what.

We had a two-hour lunch break every day between noon and 2 p.m. and then it was back for two more hours of lessons. 5:15 p.m. to 7:15 p.m. was our own time when we could do whatever we wanted, within reason. Visits from friends and family usually happened around this time of the day. Visits took place in a separate grey building that was filled with long benches and long tables in what I considered to be a bullshit-free zone. In the yard, little men talked big and big men acted even bigger, but in the visitors' hall, I saw plenty of so-called hard men with tears welling up in their eyes as their mothers walked out the door. My da visited me twice a week and although he never said very much, I looked forward to seeing him all the same. Jack visited me around once a month and that was fine with me. He was just a kid and I didn't want him to have insider knowledge of prison life before he was even ten years old. Doreen and Johnny Rotten didn't visit me at all and that was fine with me also. In fact, as things turned out, I never saw either of them ever again.

My da usually visited on Mondays and Thursdays but there was one Thursday when he didn't show up. He didn't appear on the Friday either, or over the weekend. He re-appeared the following Monday and he had Jack with him. Almost overnight, my poor father appeared to have developed lines around his eyes that had nothing to do with laughter and so I immediately assumed that something terrible had happened.

'How's Doreen?' I asked early on in the conversation, because my intuition was telling me that she was the reason for my da's long face.

'She's gone,' he replied. He took off his glasses and closed his eyes tightly while pinching the bridge of his nose.

'Gone where?'

'Just gone.'

I didn't learn the details of how she left until much later after my release. The story was that Joe Furey had been shot twice in the head at point-blank range as he emerged from a city centre casino very early one morning. At the time of his death, he was still technically married to Doreen and so she inherited all of his assets, making her a very wealthy woman practically overnight. Before my da was even aware of his common-law wife's windfall, she arranged a nice little surprise for him. She went into a travel agent's and booked two round-the-world plane tickets with a departure date the same week. The surprise for my da was that he wasn't going. Doreen didn't even have the courtesy to tell him to his face that she was leaving him. Instead she just left him a note on the kitchen table like he was the milkman or something and then she fucked off for ever, taking Johnny Rotten with her.

But back in the visitors' hall at St Pat's, Jack tactfully changed the subject to talk about an indoor soccer tournament that he was involved in and there was no further discussion about my step-mother. I never found out what became of her. I remember one time she told me that someday I would weep bitter tears over her grave. I didn't believe her at the time. I was right not to. Looking back now, I feel that the Doreen days are best forgotten about as an unfortunate period in my life but sometimes it's not so easy to forget. There is no statute of limitations for the resentment that I feel for that woman.

There was a very small library at St Pat's which I sniffed out on about my second day in the place. All of the books had been donated and so it was probably no coincidence that most of them were rubbish. But I went ahead and read as many as I could anyway. It was my way of escaping without ever leaving the compound.

I spent my first week at St Pat's telling whoever would listen that there had been a serious miscarriage of justice and that I was an innocent man. By and large, I did get a lot of attentive ears whenever I told my story but I didn't get an ounce of sympathy. I told the story well though. I could do a good impersonation of Turkeyman and Judge Phlegm and whenever I got to the part about the bookshelves falling over, the boys always laughed. I learned very quickly that my comrades in chains didn't give a shit about whether I was innocent or not; they just wanted a laugh and once this fact registered with me, my story became exaggerated beyond all recognition. And somewhere along the way, I came to be regarded as a funny guy. I knew that funny guys didn't get beaten up all that much and so I embraced my new-found joker status.

It was while I was in St Pat's that I first met Norman Valentine. I met him during my second week in the place but I spotted him across the dining hall on my very first morning there. He was hard to miss as he was well over six feet tall with spiky blond hair and a face that looked as if it had been hacked out of rock with a chisel. There was a creepy-looking gap between his front teeth and most of the time he wore one big gold earring like a pirate and a chain so chunky that you could have used it to pull a double-decker bus out of a swamp. The St Pat's grapevine told me that he was doing a three-year stretch for stabbing a bouncer in the stomach. Apparently he had been refused entry into a twenty-threes' nightclub and he reacted by pulling out a blade and carving up the doorman. This made him something of a folk hero in the eyes of some of the other inmates, but I wasn't impressed. I just thought that he was a psychopath.

We spoke for the first time in the yard at lunchtime one day when I was in the middle of doing my funny-man routine for a couple of teenage joyriders. I was midway through my Turkeyman story when I realised that Norman was standing behind me, leaning against a wall and listening. I turned to acknowledge him and I noticed that he appeared to be leering at me. An air of violence seemed to emanate from him like a bad smell.

'Aw righ?' I said with a slight nod of my head. He ignored me and so I carried on with my story. As I've already said, the latest version of my story had evolved into something that bore only the vaguest whiff of truth about it and the version that I had been spouting that day in the yard went something like this: I had been returning a couple of erotica books to the photographic section of the library when Turkeyman challenged me about having damaged them. He couldn't get the inside cover of one of the books open because the pages were stuck together with baby batter.

'OH SCHWEET DIVINE JESHUS,' he said. 'YOU'LL NAUT CHECK OUT ANOTHER SINGLE BOOK FROM THISH LIBRARY UNTIL YOU'VE PAID IN FULL FOR THISH ONE THAT YOU'RE AFTER DAMAGIN.'

At that point, the fantasy version of myself grabbed the rubber stamp from his hand and date-stamped his forehead while saying, 'Check out your head, motherfucker,' and then I headbutted him right where I had stamped him. After that, I had me jumping over the counter and kicking the crap out of him for twenty minutes or so until the cops arrived. It took five or six cops to pull me off him and in the struggle to get me into the police car, I managed to give one of them a bloody nose and another a black eye.

I found that by and large, teenage boys would believe just about anything that an entertaining liar was prepared to dish up to them. They wanted to believe me. Norman was different though. He wanted a role model about as much as he wanted a gangrenous penis. I told my story all the way up as far as Judge Phlegm sending me down for the maximum sentence while frothing gleefully at the mouth like a rabid Rottweiller. The other boys laughed at this but not Norman. He gave me a slow hand-clap instead. I turned around and glared at him, very much aware that the balance of power had already shifted.

'And then wha happened?' asked Norman in a mock serious tone. 'No, no, let me guess. Ya jumped out o the witness box, ran over to the judge and stabbed him in the throat with his own pen?'

I paused for a beat and then I spoke in a voice that I didn't recognise as my own.

'Are you talkin to me?'

My smartarse mouth seemed itching to get me into more trouble and suddenly I found myself playing the role of the tough guy. I'd practically advertised to the two joyriders that I was a stone-cold killer so now I had to prove to them that I really did have balls of concrete. Except that was going to be difficult considering that I probably looked about as dangerous as a bag of marsh-mallows.

'Who the fuck else would I be talkin to?' asked Norman, who looked as if he was just starting to enjoy himself.

'So whaddya want?' I asked, in a voice that had suddenly risen by about an octave.

'I want ya to know, that *I* know, tha you're talkin *shite*.'

'Are you callin me a liar?'

'Yeah,' he replied without the slightest hesitation.

'Well tha's totally out of order for a start,' I said, trying to sound indignant but not overly hostile. 'Why would I make all this shit up? If ya don't believe me, ya can just phone up Rathgorman library and ask them whether their chief librarian has come off the life-support machine yet.'

A flicker of hesitation passed across Norman's face and when he spoke again, it was in a different tone. 'Are you from Rathgorman?'

'Yeah,' I replied, sensing that I might not be about to get killed after all.

'Well whaddya know!' said Norman, flashing a big toothy grin at me. '*I'm* from Rathgorman.'

'Yeah?'

'Yeah!'

'Whereabouts?'

'The Glenpark estate.'

'Aw yeah. I know it well. Me stepmother Doreen Bolger used to live there.'

The Glenpark estate was like Mountjoy Prison without the high walls.

'Not Joe Furey's missus?'

'Yeah. Ex-missus. He fucked her out of a movin car so she left him and started goin out with me da after me ma died.'

'Tha's just fuckin mad, tha is.'

'Yeah well, Joe Furey is fuckin mad.'

'No, I mean it's mad like tha we're both from the same place and we both know the same people and all.'

'Too righ, man. Small world and tha.'

'Fuckin tiny. I prob'ly shagged your sister ya know!'

Norman exploded into hollow laughter at this and slapped me on the arm. I smiled and nodded my head at him as if to say 'good one!'

'So wha are ya doin in a shit hole like this?' he asked me.

'Ah, ya know ... time,' I replied. Norman flashed another big toothy grin at me. I think I was growing on him.

'How long are ya in for?'

'Twelve months. I really did fuck up tha librarian pretty bad ya know,' I added in a further unnecessary show of machismo. 'Wha are you in for?'

Instead of just answering the question, Norman lunged at me with an imaginary knife and succeeded in punching me in the guts. I drew back into a fighting stance and tried to look at least a little bit dangerous.

'I stabbed this cunt who was wreckin me buzz.'

I cleared my throat and spat on the ground to one side of me. 'Nice one!' I said. Somewhere in the inner depths of my brain, a voice screamed 'Who are you and what have you done to the nice kid who used to bunk off school to read *Catcher in the Rye* in the local library?' But those days were gone. Long gone. This was all about survival, and there was a brand-new set of rules that I was learning fast.

'So were ya in school or wha?' asked Norman.

'I was in Ratser's but I got pulled out to come here. Fuck it, I'm glad,' I lied. 'It was a shit hole anyway.'

It turned out that Norman had been in the year ahead of me at school but he had been kicked out at the end of first year for threatening one of the teachers with a knife and so our paths had never crossed. I told him that I had been on the verge of being expelled myself a couple of times and that Banjo, the headmaster, had it in for me ever since I took a dump on the bonnet of his car. Big whoppers of lies seemed to spew out of me every time I opened my mouth but Norman no longer questioned my credibility now that he had established that we were practically from the same tribe. We swapped stories about various teachers in Ratser's and Norman fired out the names of some of his cronies. I didn't know any of them but I recognised some of the family names because of their notoriety and so I gave the impression that I was at least a nodding acquaintance of each of his buddies.

I spat on the ground again because it was something that I had observed the other kids doing at least once every two minutes. I noticed that two fingers on Norman's right hand were stained yellow from nicotine and so I asked him if he had any smokes.

'Wha do I look like? A fuckin cigarette machine?' he replied. I didn't tell him what I thought he looked like.

He went on to tell me that he had opted to learn a trade at St Pat's and so they had stuck him in the chippie program. He spent most of his time making bird tables and dog kennels, although he later confided in me that his pet project was a hand-carved crucifix that concealed a home made dagger. It was quite ingenious really.

Once Norman took me under his wing, *nobody* fucked with me. All I had to do was nod at him every time that I saw him and be seen to show him a certain respect. In return, Norman would always greet me with the phrase 'Aw righ, buddy!' It really wasn't so bad. If anybody was giving me a hard time about anything, then all I had to do was mention to Norman that so and so was a cunt. Norman would ask me why, and the problem would just sort itself out after that. I gave him a couple of boxes of cigarettes as payback from time to time and he continued to call me his buddy.

Before the end of my first month in St Pat's, I had filled out an application form for an appeal and filed it with the staff in the general office on the compound. I picked the name of another lawyer at random from the Golden Pages and then I wrote to him asking if he would handle my appeal. My new solicitor came to visit me about a week later and he agreed to represent me. It took around another five months after that before my appeal came around and I found myself back in court once again. This time, though, it was very different. There was a different judge for a start and I had a lawyer who showed up and fought my case tooth and nail. Also, and perhaps most crucial of all, the senile old bollox who had previously testified against me was no longer around to give evidence because he had died in the meantime. Hallelujah!

Most of the same bullshit evidence was spewed up all over again but because it was no longer two against one, the judge said that there wasn't enough evidence to convict me beyond a reasonable doubt and he overturned my conviction. I was released back into the wild later the same day.

One thing I learned during my time in a young offenders' institution is that the biggest searchlight in jail is not the one that occasionally lumbers across the exercise yard at night; it's the one inside a prisoner's mind that illuminates his shortcomings and is fuelled by guilt. While it's true that there are all sorts of training courses that inmates take during their detention, I could never kid myself that prison is anything more than a gigantic waste of time and it was my unwavering certainty of this fact that made my own imprisonment even more punishing.

St Pat's didn't reform me because there was nothing wrong with me in the first place. My crime was that I was a stupid kid who was in the wrong place at the wrong time. In fact, if this was an autobiography, then the story of my life would be that of an idiot who always seems to be in the wrong place at the wrong time and it could be the shortest autobiography ever written: 'I came, I saw, I fucked it up.' The End. But I'm not claiming to be any sort of a special case. From what I could see during my short time behind bars, prison doesn't reform anyone. Just the opposite, in fact.

I'm reminded of a restaurant scene in the film *Carlito's Way* featuring Al Pacino and Penelope Ann Miller. During the scene, she asks him what it was like in prison and he tells her that prison didn't reform him; he just ran out of wind. And there's an even better restaurant scene involving Pacino in the film *Heat* where he asks De Niro's character if he wants to return to prison and De Niro says he's never going back.

The only thing that I was sure of upon my release was that I was never going back. And I could say this with a degree of certainty not because I had been reformed, but because I knew in my heart and soul that I didn't belong in prison. Now there are certain liberal-minded people out there who would argue that nobody really *belongs* in prison but it's a safe bet that none of those people have ever met Norman Valentine. Norman belongs in prison in much the same way that Hitler belongs in hell. But even Norman counted down the days to his release. We all did. I constantly wrecked my own head with endless plans about what I was going to do on my first day out, and what I was going to do on my second day out and so on. I read in the prison library about Nelson Mandela who had been incarcerated for twenty-seven years and, upon his release, became President of South Africa. I didn't have any aspirations as grand as that, however. All I wanted was to live as normal a life as possible and my ambitions didn't really extend much further than that.

But there was one thing that I really wanted to do. I spent lots and lots of sleepless nights thinking about it while I was in St Pat's and I did it on the day I was released. My da didn't come to collect me from the prison because he didn't know that I had won my appeal. I would have told him that there was a chance I would be getting out but I wasn't sure myself and I didn't want to get his hopes up. Before I left, the warden called me in for a little 'make sure you keep your nose clean' chat that he had probably given a thousand times before. But he was a decent sort really. I told him that there was no one coming to pick me up and so he gave me twenty pounds and told me to get a taxi home. Sound man. And he let me keep the prison-issue trousers and sweatshirt that I was wearing, so thankfully I didn't have to change back into the suit that I had arrived in.

I got a bus into town and then another one to Rathgorman Village. Once there, I got off the bus and walked straight across the road and into Rosie's Flower Shop. I wasn't really sure what flowers to buy but in the end I bought one red rose and I spent the rest of my money on a bunch of lilies. Then I walked up the hill to the cemetery. My mum's grave had a black granite head-stone with gold writing engraved on it. It described her as a *Loving Wife and Mother* and even though she wasn't particularly religious, my da had decided to put a quote from the Bible on her stone. It read: 'Thou hast made us for thyself o Lord, and our hearts cannot rest till we're together.' The bed of her grave was covered with little green and white stones. I kissed the rose and placed it near where her head would be. I didn't say any prayers but instead I talked to her in my mind and I never doubted that she could hear me.

After I had said all that I wanted to say to my mum, I walked across the field until I found Owen's final resting place. He didn't have any of the little stones that were on my mum's grave and so weeds were sprouting through the soil over where he lay. I got down on my knees and I pulled all of them out by the roots, even a big thistle that I first had to hammer into submission with a stone. After all the weeds were lying in a pile on the path, I smoothed the soil with my bare hands. I wasn't going to put any flowers on Owen's grave because he would have considered that gay, but then I changed my mind and placed one lily at the foot of his grave. I didn't have as much to say to him and so I just said hello and told him about what had been going on with me, although wherever he was, I felt that he probably already knew. But I think he appreciated me stopping by all the same and clearing away the weeds. It was the least I could do.

After saying goodbye to Owen, I made my way to the more recent graves at the bottom of the hill. I found what I was looking for easily enough. She didn't have a headstone yet, just a wooden cross with *Angela Horricks* and the date she died written on it in black paint. I never knew before that moment that her first name had been Angela. I liked it. It suited her. For the first time I could imagine her as a little girl playing outside while her mother called her name. I knew that when she had been the age that I was at that moment, she would have been a beautiful young woman because she had an inner beauty that shone through, and so she was beautiful all her life.

I placed the lilies in the centre of her grave and then I got down on my knees and I apologised to the woman. I told her how sorry I was for killing her with my selfishness, and for being too stupid to prevent her death even though I had seen it happening in my dreams loads of times. I apologised for not finding her pills in time and for not going to her funeral or even acknowledging her in the slightest after she had died in case I got blamed for her death. I kept on apologising until tears were dropping off my chin and falling on to her grave. In all the time that we had known each other, she had shown me nothing but kindness and I paid her back by killing her and then disowning her.

Before I finally managed to pick myself up and walk home, I made a vow that in the future, I would never, ever hurt somebody I loved in the way that I had hurt Mrs Horricks. And at the time I absolutely meant it with every ounce of fibre in my being. But it wasn't enough. Love wasn't enough and it turned out to be another promise that I wasn't able to keep.

III
Ashling

I was nineteen the year they let me out of St Pat's and my brother Jack was nearly eleven. My father died that same year and I said my goodbyes in the only way that I knew how: I went to the pub and poured drink down my throat until I passed out. His death was quick enough at the end and people said that he didn't suffer, but of course he suffered. He suffered every single day that he spent on this planet after he met Doreen, so much so that when it came near the end, it was obvious that he had lost the will to live. Neither Doreen nor Johnny Rotten showed their faces at the funeral and I was glad.

In the days after that, Jack and I were left rattling around in our big empty house. I'm fully aware that suddenly finding myself wholly responsible for the welfare of another human being ought to have made me grow up fast but it didn't really work out that way. Jack was a little kid and I was a big kid and every day that we made it the whole way through without burning down or blowing up the house felt like some kind of miracle. I did the best I could to be his ma and da and of course I failed miserably. While my brother was at school, I sat around the house drinking booze and waiting for the adults to arrive home. Of course, they never did. In fact, the only people who called to the door were a man and a woman from social services who insisted that Jack be taken into care and that's what happened. It was only for a few weeks, though, until my uncle Gerry could formally adopt him. I felt terrible about that whole situation because Jack was all that I had left of my immediate family and so his departure was like a bucket of black coffee for me. I made a pledge to myself that I would never drink again after that and I stayed good on that promise for quite a long time.

When money started to become a problem, I decided that I needed to get a job but I didn't have a clue what kind of job I wanted. I started buying an evening newspaper every day and scanning the jobs section but there was very little that I could apply for as I had no experience in anything really, and I had a criminal record which didn't help. I certainly didn't have any qualifications or skills, and probably not much talent either. My stepmother Doreen always used to tell me that my only talent was for causing trouble. And when my initial job-hunting efforts came to nothing, I started to wonder if she might have been right after all.

But with practice I learned how to be a better liar at interviews and not long after that, I got a job as a barman. An added attraction was the fact that my old friend Damien Halpin was already working in this particular pub. Damo is a big lad, well over six feet in height and not scrawny either, but he is a sheep in wolf's clothing. I never would have stuck with the job for so long if it hadn't been for Damo, and I don't know whether to thank him or to throttle him for that.

The pub in question is a local one in Rathgorman and it's officially called The Jolly Roger except nobody calls it that. To the locals, it has always been known as Happy's because names always get shortened around here and Happy's is a shortening of the nick-name, The Happy Fuck. The place is owned by Roger Sparrow who is supposedly the eponymous Jolly Roger, but the reality is that Roger is about as jolly as a scrotum full of cancer. And he probably does have cancer as well. He certainly doesn't look healthy anyway, that's for sure. Roger installed his cousin behind the bar not long after I started working there. Her name was Mary although everyone called her Scary Mary because she had breasts that you could suffocate a rhino with and an arse that looked as if someone had tried to stuff a waterbed into a pair of jeans. We tried to contain her to one corner of the bar as it was almost impossible to pass her behind the counter.

It was Damo alone who kept me sane. He was the one that I could shoot the breeze with and the one who regularly reminded me that fucked-up is not normal. The job itself wouldn't have been so bad if it wasn't for the customers. The place seemed to have magical magnetic qualities for all the local great unwashed. They would sit at the bar all day delivering clichés with a gravitas that was more laughable than pitiable. On Tuesday nights Roger hired the services of DJ Derek to inject a bit of white noise into the atmosphere for a couple of hours. DJ Derek only played the kind of shit that would make your ears bleed, and consequently a lot of the Happy's regulars stayed at home on Tuesday nights.

But the truth is that most of the Happy's regulars shouldn't have been allowed out at all. Or certainly, the ones connected with Norman Valentine ought to have been locked up. That's the same Norman Valentine with whom I did time in St Pat's, but I never felt as if that meant that there was a special bond between us or anything. Norman doesn't have a special bond with anyone and that's because Norman is as mean as a bag of snakes. He still called me his buddy, though, and I still smiled and fed his ego with bullshit. But my attitude to Norman has always been dictated by fear and never respect.

Norman's cronies feared him as much as anyone but they were the loudest in pretending not to. Fozzie, Benny Binchy, Skidmark, Bernie, Spanner and Madser were Norman's crew. He also had a dog called Big Mickey that frequently accompanied him to the pub. The gang spent most of their lives sitting around a table in the corner discussing everything and nothing. And whenever there was trouble, Norman and his mates were usually considerate enough to take it outside. Not because they were afraid of getting barred, mind you; I think they were just worried that they might have enjoyed their pints less with some guy's head leaking blood all over the carpet while his wife or girlfriend ran around screaming like a banshee.

And in case you think that I'm wildly exaggerating, let me give you just one example of Norman at his worst. Frank Worrall, aka Lefty, was a guy who used to come in about once or twice a week and read the *Racing Post* at the bar when he wasn't moaning about how the world had gone to shit. He was a couple of years older than me and he had a prosthetic leg from just above the knee on his right leg. One night, Lefty was in Happy's when he somehow got talking to Tanya Cox who was propping up the bar waiting for Norman to arrive. Tanya used to come into the bar all the time and I liked her. She had all the latest information about who was doing what to whom and I paid her back for the lowdown by turning a blind eye whenever she off-loaded her five-finger discount goods inside the pub. On this particular night, Lefty was only about half a shandy away from passing out and he started getting all emotional and teary in the course of dumping his life story on Tanya. Maybe he was genuinely distraught or maybe he just wanted to stick his nose down her cleavage, but whatever the reason, he ended up with his face in her tits while Tanya stroked his hair like his head was a pussycat. That poor dumb fucker simply had no idea that Tanya was one of Norman's women. If he had have known, he wouldn't even have looked sideways at her. But he didn't know and I never got the chance to warn him.

After a while, Norman came in, saw the cosy little scene at the bar, and promptly dragged Lefty outside by the hair. I was already dialling 999 before they were fully out the door. By the time the ambulance men arrived, they found Lefty beaten unconscious by his own artificial leg. I haven't seen him since; I don't think anyone has.

Roger attempted to justify Norman's continued destructive presence by saying that he and his cronies spent a lot of money at Happy's and that was true, but they undoubtedly scared away a lot of money as well. Norman loved scaring people like pensioners love bingo. He used to carry a huge knife with him everywhere and one of his favourite gags was to stand up and whip out his blade before announcing to the whole pub in a menacing tone: 'I'm just goin for a quick slash.' Then he would give the air a few quick stabs before carrying on his merry way to the jacks.

But most of his antics were considerably less good-humoured

than that. Sometimes he would position himself at the bar beside some random punter who was buying a drink and whatever that person ordered, Norman would say 'Only fags drink tha.' The smart punters just ignored him and walked away but the not so smart ones ended up in a brawl that they could not possibly win because firstly, Norman kept a big fuck-off knife concealed somewhere about his person and secondly, his crew were never more than two steps behind him and they were more than willing to jump in at the first opportunity.

And so even though I worked there for seven years, I would be the first to admit that Happy's is a drinking hole for cockroaches. If Dublin was a big old house, then Rathgorman would be the outhouse, and Happy's would be the toilet bowl; a filthy, hoary old toilet with a rusty chain that doesn't work and a build-up of human waste slopping over the brim. Desperation has a smell and The Jolly Roger reeks of it, but it's amazing what you can get used to.

Perhaps the most amazing thing of all is that in the midst of the tide of detritus that gravitated towards Happy's, I met the great love of my life. She had a certain grace about her and a sort of serene beauty that, when I discovered it, was like opening the curtains on a winter morning and finding that a perfect blanket of snow has appeared overnight as if by magic. She was a thing to be amazed by and I can feel her presence on every single page as I write. Her name was Ashling. She never founded a charity, never painted any pictures that are hanging on a wall somewhere, never won any medals for bravery or discovered a cure for a terminal disease, but she was greater than any philanthropist, artist, soldier or Nobel prize-winning scientist who has ever lived. She was great because she was kind. She was great because she was humble, gentle and full of laughter. She was the sweetest, loveliest girl I've ever known and she could make me smile just by scratching her face. She didn't deserve to die, but that counted for nothing. Our lives are not what we deserve.

I met her in Happy's on a night when I wasn't working. It was Damo's birthday and a bunch of us were heading out clubbing with him just as soon as he finished his shift. On that particular night, I was sitting with a group of Damo's mates and we were discussing ways to seduce women. The conversation was dominated by a guy named Colin who claimed that he regularly gatecrashed the afters of weddings in order to hook up with babes. He referred to this technique as 'Colin-isation' and said that the romance of the occasion sent single girls into a man-mad frenzy and so it was a surefire winner every time. When someone questioned him about how he managed to get away with crashing the wedding, he said the secret was simply to bring a camera in order to look more like an authentic wedding guest.

Colin's bullshit was reasonably entertaining but it was bullshit nonetheless and after a while, my concentration started to wander. My attention was drawn by the sound of glass breaking and when I looked in that direction, I could see that a guy wearing a rucksack had knocked over a drink on a table occupied by three women in their early twenties. Either he failed to realise what he was after doing, or he chose to pretend that it was nothing to do with him, because he proceeded to the bar without offering even the slightest hint of an apology.

I focused on the three girls at the table where the drink had been spilled. Two of them had their backs to me and the third had her cheek almost resting on the table while she groped underneath it for something. Then her head disappeared underneath the table as she presumably went on a search and rescue mission for her bag on the floor. One of her mates ran to the bar in order to get a cloth to dry the saturated table. She should have got a mop though because things in the spilled-drinks department were going to get worse before they got better. From my vantage point, I was in a perfect place to witness the scene in front of me and I was hooked on the unfolding drama. What happened next was that an ice cube floating on the spilt drink on the girls' tabletop found its way to the edge and then over it went. It never reached the floor though because instead it slipped down the collar of the top worn by the girl that was still trying to rescue her bag from the miniature water- fall cascading down the side of the table. With the sudden cold, sharp shock, the crouching girl jerked upright, banging her head loudly on the underside of the table and knocking over all the remaining glasses.

The first word that I ever heard out of Ashling's mouth was 'FUUUUUUUUK!' I was a little concerned at that point that she might have seriously hurt herself but I needn't have worried. A second later, she was sitting fully upright, rubbing the top of her injured head and smiling that amazing smile of hers. She looked too beautiful for words. Dark-brown, shoulder-length hair. Vanilla- skinned with big dark eyes. Full lips like tiny pink cushions open

just wide enough to reveal the curve of her teeth. And an unbelievably cute little snub nose. Effortlessly gorgeous. She caught my
gaze and returned it for a fraction of a second too long. The fuse
was lit.

A minute later, she got up and went to the bar and suddenly
that seemed like a very good idea to me as well. I asked the guys
at my table whether anybody wanted a drink, but somebody had
just come back from the bar after having bought a round and so
nobody wanted one.

'Sit the fuck down, will ya, ya tightarse!' said one of the lads,
and I have to admit that it did look bad, offering to buy a round
when everybody still had a full pint in front of them.

'Ah, give him a break, will ya? Sure he's not even drinkin,' said
Colin, and it was true. The pledge that I had made when my little
brother was taken into care remained intact.

I mumbled something about going to buy some crisps and then
I set about chatting up the most beautiful girl ever to set foot inside
Happy's.

I stood beside her at the bar with no clue whatsoever of the
right words to say. Time was of the essence, though, because she
was only going to be standing beside me for as long as it took to
get another drink. I had to say something and quickly, but every
suggestion that my mind could throw up sounded pathetically lame.

'Hey,' I said eventually, sounding like a lobotomised baboon.
Cyrano de Bergerac has got nothing to worry about.

'Hi,' replied Ashling while staring at the bar.

'How's the head?'

She turned and looked directly at me. One look into those big brown eyes of hers and that was it; my heart no longer belonged to me. She looked slightly embarrassed for a second and then she smiled at me; the kind of smile that can melt rocks.

'Oh, I'll survive, thanks,' she said rubbing the back of her head with one hand. 'That guy knocked over my pint and he didn't even apologise! I can't believe that someone could be so rude.'

'Tha's people for ya. Listen, why don't I buy ya a drink just to prove tha there are still nice people left in the world?'

'Oh no, I'm fine, really. You don't have to do that.'

'No, I'd like to. No strings attached. Wha are ya havin?'

'No, honestly, thanks anyway but I'm fine.'

'Okay, well, how about this, you let me buy ya a drink and in return, I'll let ya talk to me while ya drink it.'

'Why would I want to do that?'

'Because ... because I like ya so much.'

'Yeah? How do you know that I'm not a complete bitch?'

'Because if you were a complete bitch, then I wouldn't like ya so much.'

Damo arrived on the scene at that point and gave me a wry smile.

'Ah yes, barman,' I said to him in a fake posh accent as I threw Ashling a wink. 'One of these pig-swilling ruffians has knocked over the beverage of this fair maiden and because she is now refusing to let me buy her a drink, I demand two of your finest ales on the house. Immediately!'

'Yes, my Lord. Right away,' said my wingman, playing his part in my little seduction scene. Damo knew without my telling him that I would have a pint of alcohol-free lager and Ashling had a bottle of Corona in her hand so it wasn't hard to guess what she was drinking. I stole a look at her while my colleague was getting the drinks and she looked suitably impressed.

'How am I doin?' I whispered to her.

'Very ... original,' she replied and then she gave me another of her knockout smiles. She had a magic smile; a smile that you couldn't help smiling back at.

'One for you, your majesty,' said Damo placing a pint in front of me. 'And one for the lady. Courtesy of Roger, the inn-keeping swine.'

'Good work, Batman!' said Ashling. 'Back in a sec,' she added and then she brushed past me on her way to have a word with her friends. Her touch was like the finest silk and it proved to my head what my heart already knew: I was in love. Personally I've always thought about falling in love in bowling-alley terms. As soon as you meet someone new, within a few seconds I think that sub-consciously you identify the reasons why you could never have a relationship with that person. But on the one per cent of occasions when your subconscious is not so sure, then your conscious mind moves into gear and gives that person a second look. And from that moment on, your interest in the potential partner is like a bowling ball rolling very slowly down a bowling lane towards the pins. As you become aware of what you consider to be various unattractive traits of the chasee, the bowling ball veers more and more off-centre, but when what you regard as a really good quality emerges, then the ball moves the other way back towards the centre of the lane. And when two soulmates find each other, then the ball gathers speed until it is hurtling faster and faster down the centre of the lane where eventually it smashes the pins into oblivion. Strike!

With Ashling, my bowling ball was in the dead-centre position all the way. She was 'the one' that people are always talking about. I felt it the second that I first laid eyes on her and it stirred something so powerful in me that throughout the days that followed, I found that I was quite incapable of thinking about anything apart from her. Before I met Ashling, I had a crap job and a crap life, and after I got together with her, I still had a crap job but it didn't matter anymore because suddenly I had a great life.

When she rejoined me at the bar, we started chatting and she told me that she was a nurse working in the Mater Hospital. To be honest, I can't remember an exact transcript of the conversation that followed but I know that once we started talking, I found it very easy to just be myself with her. I remember feeling dangerously close to blurting out something like 'I love you' and blowing the whole deal. But fortunately I didn't and the conversation flowed along beautifully.

I mentioned in passing that I had gone to Rathgorman College and Ashling said that that was right beside where she lived. It turned out that she had grown up just two streets across from the house where I grew up but she hadn't gone to school locally and so a lot of her friends weren't from Rathgorman. Her parents had sent her to a posh convent school in town, one known locally as the Virgin Megastore. I remember saying to her how unfortunate it was that we had spent most of our lives living within the same square mile and yet we were only meeting then for the first time. Ashling's response was, 'It could have been worse, we might never have met at all.'

She was right of course, but knowing as I do now the way things turned out, I wish we had gotten to spend more time together. I wish I had met her earlier. If only we could have met when we were five or six, I would have swept her right off her little pink bicycle. But I'm not complaining. The years that we did have together were like a gift from the gods.

When we finished our drinks, Ashling said that she had to get back to her friends. I asked her if she would like to have another drink with me some time. She flashed her wicked smile at me and said that she would love to. I resisted the urge to look over my shoulder in order to see who she might really be talking to. This was too good to be true and I was sure that there had to be a catch somewhere because I figured that a girl like Ashling was probably only single for about ten minutes every five years. But there was no catch. She gave me her number and I phoned her two nights later to arrange our first date.

I had been on dates before, of course, but this felt completely different. Ashling was not like any other girl that I had been out with. The girls I had been with previously always seemed a tiny bit too big or too small, or too needy or too moany, or just too damn shallow. But Ashling was none of those things. She was great because she didn't try to be anyone other than herself and that person was funny and charming and decent. And what made her really great was the fact that she didn't know how great she was.

I agonised over where to take her on our first date. I considered taking her to a nice restaurant in order to impress her but I wasn't used to eating in restaurants and so I was worried that it might backfire when I didn't know what cutlery to use or what wine to order. I considered bringing her to the cinema which was sort of the easy option because I could let the film do the entertaining instead of trying to be entertaining myself. But the purpose of the date was for us to get to know each other better and the cinema would only get in the way of that. I was tempted just to arrange to meet her in the pub but I already knew how special she was from our short meeting in Happy's and so I wanted our first date to be memorable. I wanted to do something out of the ordinary that would elevate me in her mind above all the other arseholes who wanted to take her out on a date.

The slam-dunk winner of a solution came in the form of my uncle Gerry. As I've said, Jack had gone to live with Gerry soon after my father died and I used to visit him there fairly regularly. I called over the day after I met Ashling for the first time and while I was shooting the breeze with Gerry, he asked me if I was fond of the U2. I remember that he called them *the* U2 as opposed to just U2 but I didn't bother correcting him.

'Sure, yeah,' I replied, with no clue what was coming next. He then pulled out two tickets to see the band playing at Slane the following night, and he gave them to me. Gerry said that he had been doing some work on The Edge's parents' house and they had given him four tickets for the concert. I could not believe it! Tickets for that gig were harder to get than golden tickets for Willy Wonka's chocolate factory and, while I wouldn't claim to be the biggest U2 fan in the world, Ashling had more or less told me the previous night that *she* was the biggest U2 fan in the world and she had been unable to get a ticket for that gig despite all her best efforts. I couldn't keep the smile off my face. Gerry kept asking me if I was all right. I think he suspected that I might have been taking happy pills or some other type of drug.

The concert itself was, without doubt, one of the most memorable experiences of my life. It was an outdoor venue with the stage at the bottom of a hill, a natural amphitheatre. The sheer scale of everything took my breath away. The stage was massive; the electronic screens behind and above the stage were massive; the walls of speakers were massive; the band was massive and, of course, the crowd was massive. I had never seen so many people gathered together in one place before and it was a sight that I found to be slightly unnerving.

Ireland were playing a vital World Cup qualifying match against Holland that day and before the band came onstage, the second half of the game was shown on a huge screen. There were more people watching that screen than there were attending the actual match. Jason McAteer scored in the sixty-seventh minute and somehow we clung on against all the odds for an amazing victory. When the final whistle blew, the crowd went bananas with everyone jumping up and down and embracing each other. I might have been a bit shy but I didn't miss the opportunity to hug my beautiful date. At the time, it was hard to decide which felt sweeter: the victory against the Dutch or holding an angel like Ashling in my arms. But now that I'm older and wiser, I'm well aware that when that football match has long been forgotten about by everyone, including me, I'll still remember what it felt like to hold Ashling in my arms for the very first time. The best attempt I can make at describing it will still be hopelessly inadequate but for what it's worth, it felt like two halves of something that has been broken being put together again. We were soulmates who had found each other at last and once we had gotten past that initial first physical contact milestone, I never wanted to let her go.

Although she had gone to a posh school during her teenage years, Ashling had not had everything her own way in life. Far from it. Her only sibling was an older sister who had literally starved herself to death because she thought she was too fat. So although she appeared on the outside to be a remarkably well-balanced individual, I knew that there were scars in her heart that time would not heal. I read somewhere once that soulmates are simply two people who recognise the damage in each other but the truth is that there's a lot more to it than that. Sometimes, I used to joke with Ashling that we were like Elliot and E.T. because most of the time we thought the same thoughts and we felt the same emotions. Ashling would laugh and say that as long as she could be Elliot, she wouldn't argue with me.

As the time approached when Bono and the boys would appear onstage, my date took me by the hand and pulled me through the crowd until we were right by the barricade separating the mosh pit from the rest of the spectators. I noticed that she had a daisy chain tattooed around her left wrist and, right there, I found another thing to love about her. I hadn't spotted the tattoo in the pub because her watch had been covering it but now she wasn't wearing a watch. I didn't let go of her hand until the band came onstage and kicked things off with the song 'Elevation'. I remember looking behind me during that song and I could see a tide of eighty thousand people bouncing up and down in unison. The crowd had transmogrified into one heaving monster and the fact that I was a part of that really struck a chord with me. I couldn't remember the last time that I had been a part of something.

I think that might go some way towards explaining why it was at that moment that I felt better than I had done in years. Although this was beyond feeling good about oneself. This was more like a shot of one-hundred-per-cent-proof pure joy injected straight into my brain which caused my heart to swell inside my chest until I felt that it might burst inside of me. At that point, I had been carrying Owen's death around with me for over half my life and on top of that, I also felt responsible for the death of Mrs Horricks. But guilt is like a bag of bricks and the time had come to set down that particular bag. And so I did. I just let it go. I let it all go. And by the time the band had started playing the second song, 'Beautiful Day', there were tears rolling down my cheeks. Fortunately for me, though, I was standing behind Ashling and so she never saw me crying, and that was definitely a good thing. First dates involving tears rarely lead to second dates.

A few songs later, Bono introduced the song 'Kite' and as The Edge hit the opening licks on his guitar, I slipped my arms around Ashling's waist. By the time the song had ended, there was a bond between us that would never be broken.

After the concert, we got a bus from Slane back into the city centre. We were both feeling very tired but very happy at the same time. I bought us some chips on O' Connell Street and we started walking in the direction of Rathgorman, hoping to flag a taxi on the way. Our first date had been going for about ten hours at that stage and I still hadn't kissed Ashling. Everything up to that point had gone better than I could ever have dared to hope and so I was worried about ruining the mood with a very uncool fumbled first kiss in which I ended up accidentally kissing her eye or the tip of her nose. Back then, it just wasn't normal for me to have a great day or a great anything without something getting fucked-up at least a little bit. I decided to try not to think about it and just to go with the flow although the more I tried not to think about kissing her, the harder it became.

'Have ya got two euro for a hostel?' said a man with grey stubble who stopped in front of us. He had a filthy-looking dog that panted contentedly and didn't seem to mind the fact that its master's breath smelled like rotting cabbage. I instinctively took a step backwards.

'No, sorry, I haven't got any change,' I lied.

'Ya can have the rest of these though if ya like?' said Ashling, and with that she gave the man her chips.

'Nice one,' he said, grabbing the chips, and then he shoved a clump of them into his mouth.

'Bandit, come on!' he roared at the dog and then he was gone.

'Tha was very decent o ya,' I said to Ashling.

'Well ya know, I thought what would a hostel want two euro for? And so I figured it would be better if I just gave him some food.'

As she said this, she pulled a tissue out from under her sleeve and used it to wipe her fingers. I filed this away in my brain as something to think about later, but it was definitely one more curious thing that I liked about her.

'I usually just give guys like tha twenty or fifty euros; whatever's in me wallet, ya know? But you've opened me eyes and so from now on, I think I'm gonna just take them out for a meal instead,' I said.

'Really? Well how about if I dress up like a homeless person, will you take me out for a meal?' said Ashling and my heart started to beat a little bit faster because I knew that she wouldn't even be joking about that unless she wanted a second date with me.

'Who told ya about me homeless person fetish?' I asked.

'You did!' she shouted and then she ran away because a downpour of rain had started and everything was getting soaked. I watched her running off in front of me for a few seconds and then I left my chips on a wall and went running after her. When I caught up with her, she was sitting on a bench in a bus-stop shelter and smiling that seductive smile of hers. I sat down beside her on the bench and then I reached over and held her hand. She looked me in the eye without saying anything. We both knew what was going to happen next. There would never be a better moment. I leaned over and kissed her on the lips and if we had have been actors in a movie, the camera would have panned upwards at that point to capture fireworks exploding in the sky. I didn't need any fireworks or orchestral symphonies to complete the moment though, because for me it was perfect exactly the way it was.

After that night, it felt as if everything I did was only to fill in time between bouts of thinking about Ashling. Time seemed to crawl by when I wasn't with her. It's my experience that time always appears to slow down at the beginning of a relationship but then as things develop, it goes by quicker and quicker; a bit like life itself. My friends had advised me that if I liked her then I should wait four or five days minimum before contacting her again. I phoned her when I got home that night after our first date. Ashling was such a complex person that I could have spent my whole life with her and on the day when we were reduced to feeding each other mashed carrots from a can be :ause we had no teeth left, I would still have been learning new things about her. Probably that she didn't like mashed carrots. Gradually we learned each other's stories and secrets and we fell madly in love; the kind of love that some people probably find nauseating. It was Ashling's idea to have our platinum wedding bands both inscribed with the same acronym – TTEOTWAB: Till the end of the world and beyond.

In those early days of our relationship though, I always thought that she was so perfect that there just had to be a catch. But there wasn't one. Five months and two days after our very first meeting, we were engaged and nine months after that we were married. And every day that I spent on this planet in the company of Ashling, I experienced the same sense of euphoria that I had tasted on our first date. I experienced something that in its simplest form can only be described as true love.

My wife and I only had one argument in all the time we were together. It happened one night before we were married and it was about her ex. Before I came along, Ashling used to go out with a guy called Stephen Dowling. He's a southsider and he's a real asshole. I met him only once but I could tell straight away that he was a dick because he was wearing a black leather jacket and boots that had little chains on the side of them. I was in the cinema on Parnell Street at the time and it was before the film had even started. Ashling had gone to the bathroom while I queued up to get popcorn. There were two parallel queues for snacks and for possibly the first and last time in my life, my queue was moving fastest. In fact, I was almost at the front when I saw someone pulling out of the queue beside the one I was in and walking towards me. I moved back a step in order to let the person pass, but instead of walking through the queue, he simply stopped right in front of me and started queueing ahead of me. I couldn't believe the balls on the fucker.

'Asshole,' I muttered underneath my breath. The guy in the leather jacket turned around and stood opposite me. He had attitude seeping out of every pore in his ugly face. I stared right back at him almost hoping that he would try something. I was angry now and that gave me an uncharacteristic boldness. He spoke first.

'Got a problem, pal?'

'Nothin I can't handle.'

'Wha the fuck is tha supposed to mean?'

'Which word did ya not understand?'

Then Ashling returned and addressed my new nemesis.

'Stephen!' she said to him.

'Howya, Ashling,' he replied.

I was left standing there with a stupid-looking expression on my face. I couldn't believe that a reptile like that was on first name terms with my girlfriend.

'Next!' said one of the people serving behind the counter. I walked forward and ordered a large popcorn and two large diet cokes. When I returned, Ashling introduced me to her ex-boyfriend. Her *ex-boyfriend*!

'Aw righ, bud,' said the guy, holding out his hand for me to shake. He had apparently failed to notice that I was carrying a large popcorn and two large cokes, making a handshake quite impossible. I ignored his outstretched hand and gave him the tiniest nod that I could possibly give. I didn't say a word though. Ashling and he chatted for another minute or so while I stood there looking pissed off. Then he left and it was just Ashling and me again.

'That was my ex, Stephen. Jesus, I can't believe I ran into him. He hasn't changed a bit.'

'Well someone should tell him to change those fuckin boots.'

'You didn't like his boots?'

'No I didn't. Only saps wear boots like tha.'

'What were you talkin about before I came over?'

'Nothin much.'

'Do you know him?'

'I know he's a fuckin asshole.'

'What?'

'You heard me.'

And so began my first ever argument with Ashling. She defended her ex while I verbally attacked him and in that way I let someone else come between us. Whether her ex-boyfriend was an asshole or not, it really didn't matter. He was the past and I was the present and the future. But the truth is that it was me who was the asshole that night and for that I am more sorry than you will ever know.

Sometimes I did wonder though why Ashling was with me. On the one occasion when I asked her what she saw in me, she wouldn't give me a straight answer. When I pressed her on it, she said that if someone loves you then all you have to do is let them.

On one of our early dates, Ashling called over to my place and we watched a video of *Carlito's Way*. Most couples probably have a song that they regard as theirs but we didn't have that. We had a film and *Carlito's Way* was that film.

'Aaaaaay, Carleeeeeto! I kill eem for you Carleeeeeto. I fockin kill eem myself.'

Al Pacino plays Carlito in the film but his onscreen girlfriend never calls him by that name. Instead she calls him Charlie and that became Ashling's pet name for me. She called me that more often than she used my real name. She was the only person in the world who has ever called me Charlie and I think it was for that reason that I grew to love the name. I didn't really have a pet name for her. I called her Ash quite a lot I suppose and sometimes, just to wind her up, I would call her Ashtray, or if she was looking a bit peaky – Ashen-face.

She still believed in love and it was beautiful. By the time I met her, I'd already had all the romance kicked out of me but with Ashling everything was like the first time all over again. She was my brown-eyed girl, like the one in that Van Morrison song, except that she wasn't like anyone else because she was so uniquely special. When she laughed, she looked like an angel and when she cried, you just wanted to hold her so tightly, and never let go. She was the great love of my life. She was my hundred miles-per-hour ten-pin strike. She was my life.

I'm sure that some people reading this are probably thinking that whenever I get back to planet Earth, I should realise that a fire that burns so brightly will eventually burn out. And if you're thinking that then I'm just glad that I'm me and not you. I heard someone say once that love is like people's mothers: everyone thinks that theirs is the best. But ours *was* the best. Everyone who knew us said so.

But fuck it; it's not a competition or anything. I was just opening the door on my marriage a few inches wider in case you wanted to peek inside. And I know that I've probably gone overboard and made Ashling out to be some kind of saint when the truth is, she wasn't perfect. She could be childish and moody and occasionally she could be brutally intolerant of idiots to the point of being unreasonable. She could hardly pass by a mirror without checking herself out and she was always late for everything. But still I loved her in spite of all that. I loved her *because* of all that. I knew that sometimes she drooled while she slept and that she cut her toenails on the sofa while watching TV and that she always burned toast and then left little black crumbs in the tub of butter. I knew all of those things and more but it made absolutely no difference to the way I felt about her. Those were the things that made her human and it was knowing those things that made her mine.

When the time felt right for me to propose, I bought her an engagement ring that I really couldn't afford. It was a solitaire diamond on a platinum ring and I got it in a jewellers on O' Connell Street called McDowell's – The Happy Ring House. I've always loved the name of that place simply because it doesn't make much sense. On the night itself, I took Ashling to a fancy Italian restaurant in town. My wife was a brilliant person to eat Italian food with because she could translate the names of all the different pastas into phrases like 'that's the one shaped like a dicky bow' or 'that's the one that looks like little pillows'. I don't know how she remembered stuff like that but she did.

We stared into each other's eyes between courses and we flirted with each other like it was our first date. There were photographs of actors all over the walls of this particular restaurant and there were candles inside red glass shells on each of the tables. I played a shepherd once in a school nativity play when I was about eight and Ashling had once played the part of a policeman in a school production of *Pinocchio* but our photos were nowhere to be seen on any of the walls. I pretended to be disgusted by this oversight and I let on to be on the verge of reading the riot act to the manager when Ashling found a way to calm me down. On her paper napkin, she drew a stick man and a stick woman holding hands. They had dots for eyes and huge semi-circular smiles that made them look very happy indeed. She wrote our names underneath the stick couple and hung it on the wall, the top of the napkin pushed under the lower edge of a framed photo of some fat man that I didn't recognise.

We left the napkin hanging there throughout the rest of our meal and then I paid the bill and we got up to leave. Ashling wanted to leave her drawing of us on the wall as a sort of testament to our visit but I had a better idea. I waited until we had left the restaurant before announcing that I had left my cigarettes on the table. I ran back inside and snatched the napkin from the wall. I wrote a quick message on it and then I took the ring box from my trouser pocket where it had been all evening. The sensation of it pressing against my leg provided continued and necessary reassurance that I hadn't lost it. I removed the ring from its small velvet cube and then I wrapped it up in the napkin and stuck it into my pocket.

'Can you hear my teeth rattling?' said Ashling when I went back outside. I listened until I could and then I gave her a big hug.

'Are they still rattlin?' I said as I held her.

'No, but they'll start again as soon as you let me go.'

'I'm never gonna let ya go,' I said, and then I did. She gave me a quick kiss on the lips and then rubbed her nose against mine, Eskimo-style. We started walking towards St Stephen's Green, arm in arm. It was freezing out but the cold air had a sort of magical feel to it. It made the dirty old town smell fresh and clean. We walked into Stephen's Green and sat on a bench so that we could gaze at the stars. The only problem was that we couldn't see any. Ashling said that this was because of light pollution and that was why stars were rarely visible over a big city. I said that if that was the effect of light pollution then I wouldn't want to live somewhere where there was heavy pollution. Ashling laughed and snuggled into me. A minute later, she thanked me for a perfect evening.

'The next time you're pissed off with me about somethin, I want ya to remember this night and then whatever it is you're pissed off about will just melt away.'

'I'll never be pissed off you. Never,' she said.

'Can I have tha in writin?'

'I'll give you a kiss instead,' she said and our kiss turned into a snog.

'Thank you for loving me,' said Ashling a few minutes later, giving me a little squeeze. Her modesty and her kindness blew me away.

'Thank you for lettin me,' I replied.

'Let's go home and get warm.'

'Hang on ... there's somethin I have to give ya first,' I said and with that I produced the folded napkin from my pocket.

'What's this?'

'Open it.'

'Is that our picture from the restaurant?'

'Open it!'

She slowly unfolded the paper napkin until the ring in the middle of it was revealed. I could feel her body stiffening beside me. She sat upright and looked at me in disbelief.

'Oh my God!' she said, looking at the ring once more. 'It's absolutely beautiful.'

'Look at the napkin,' I said and she did. I had drawn a speech bubble coming out of the stick man's mouth with two words inside of it – MARRY ME! Her eyes widened even more but still she didn't speak. And so just in case she was in any doubt at all about what I was asking, I got down on one knee in the middle of St Stephen's Green and proposed to her properly. Her eyes filled up with tears and she nodded her head.

'Is tha a yes then?' I asked, because obviously I wanted to be sure. Ashling nodded her head again and smiled at me. Shock had temporarily robbed her of the power of speech. I stood up and slipped the engagement ring on to her finger. Ashling stood up and threw her arms around my neck and then she started kissing my face all over. It dawned on me around then that she had said yes and so I picked her up and ran around the duck pond in the middle of the park, whooping like a madman all the way. There weren't many people around but Ashling was mortified all the same. I didn't care though. That was, without a doubt, the greatest moment of my life. I have endured the broadest possible range of emotions that can be weathered by the human heart and that night in Stephen's Green is the happiest that I have ever been or ever will be.

We jumped in a taxi and headed back to my place. We didn't tell the taxi driver that we'd just got engaged. It was still our moment and neither of us felt like sharing it with the world just yet. Instead we clung to each other in the back seat and smiled knowing smiles at each other. I still had one more surprise up my sleeve though. I had gotten up early that day and purchased seventy-six red roses in Smithfield market – one for each year that Ashling and I would be together if we lived to be a hundred. Before I had gone out that evening, I had distributed the flowers all over the house. I put a big bunch of them in a vase inside the front door but after that I went a bit mad and I stuck individual roses in random nooks and crannies in nearly every room. It looked a bit strange but Ashling loved it and that was all that mattered. After I opened the front door and the smell of the flowers greeted us, she let out a sort of a squeal and then she threw her arms around me once again. I loved that sound she made whenever I surprised her. I loved so many things about her. The reality is that I could fill every single one of these pages just writing and writing about all the things that I loved about my wife, and I still wouldn't even get halfway finished. But I'll spare us both the pain of that.

After Mrs Horricks, years went by and my dreams were untroubled by psychic phenomena of any kind. I dared to start to think again that the future is unchartered territory; a place where we make our own destiny. But once again I was spectacularly wrong. For a third time, some unknown force played a wicked game with me and then laughed in my face.

I think that there has to be such a thing as destiny, a power infinitely greater than the force which keeps the world spinning through space in its perpetual orbit around the sun; a power that moves each of us through our lives as if we were mere pawns in a board game. We fill our lives with endless amounts of things we don't need and it's all to distract ourselves from the fact that the rug can so easily be pulled out from us at any time. And there's absolutely nothing that we can do about it. We're at the mercy of the gods and the gods have no mercy.

But I tried my best not to think about any of that stuff because I knew that I would only end up wrecking my own head. And so I got on with things and I tried really hard to live my life purely in the present tense. To a certain extent I think I succeeded, but then the dreams started coming again and the future gatecrashed my reality. I could smell it; I could hear it; I could taste it; I could just about see it; and it looked like the end of my world.

After I got engaged to Ashling, I sold the house that I had grown up in and I split the proceeds with Jack. I didn't feel in any way sentimental about the sale because the house had stopped feeling like home after Doreen and Johnny Rotten arrived. Even though he was still a teenager, Jack didn't piss away his half of the house money on alcohol or something worse; instead he bought himself a one-bedroom apartment and paid his own way through college. He did an electronics course in Bolton Street and I'm extremely proud of him. But no matter what he did I'd still be proud of him. It's no secret that someday he intends to marry Fiona, his childhood sweetheart, and they're made for each other. He's a lucky man and he knows it. He knows it because I keep reminding him.

As for me, Ashling and I bought a three-bedroom house in Rathgorman and I carried on working at Happy's. The address of the new place was 22 Sullivan Street. It was a bit cramped and the kitchen smelled a bit funny but as far as my wife and I were concerned, it was our dream home. She didn't move in until after the wedding though because her parents are a bit old-fashioned and unfortunately, that's about the nicest thing that I can say about them.

An added bonus of our new house was the fact that Ashling's parents had moved, by then, to the other side of the city, almost far enough away. I never really got on with them which was regrettable, especially as I did my level best to demonstrate to them that their daughter's happiness was more important to me than my own. I was a perfectly considerate husband in every way, but they were blind to this. They couldn't see beyond the fact that around the time their daughter had been preparing to go to Nursing College,

I had been preparing to go into juvenile detention. The fact that my conviction had been overturned on appeal didn't seem to register with them. In their eyes, I will always be the scumbag who ruined their beautiful daughter.

I had a sneaking suspicion that Ashling could have been adopted because she was so obviously different in every way to her parents. Her mother is so uptight that you couldn't pull a needle out of her arse with a tractor. Before I married her daughter, the old boiler never missed an opportunity to point out my short-comings to Ashling behind my back, and after we were married, she didn't even have the courtesy to wait until I was out of the room. But I continued to keep my mouth shut and smile inanely whenever Betty was around because I knew that my wife would be upset if I told her mother to go fuck herself. And I loved Ashling way too much to upset her where it could possibly be avoided.

Ashling's father is more hip-replacement than hip but he doesn't have any malevolence in him. He also doesn't have a spark of the vitality that his daughter had in abundance. He's a keen gardener, or, at any rate, he just loves to trim his hedges. That's all he seems to do, in fact. Or at least that's all he did whenever I was in the vicinity. He has a handshake like a limp dick and that just about sums him up, really. Everyone calls him Willy, except Betty who never refers to him as anything other than William. I like to think of him as Slick Willy, a dead man walking and a man who appears to be in constant danger of being swallowed by his trousers.

But Ashling's parents play no part in this story except allowing me to further delay telling you about how my reason for living suddenly ceased to exist.

My wife and I had been married only eleven months when the dreams started coming again.

Those dreams were dominated by rain; relentless rain that hammered the ground before bouncing a couple of inches back into the air again. And there was Ashling, standing in the middle of the road in the middle of the rain. She was wearing a long black coat, the collar of which she held tightly closed around her throat but she was still getting soaked. The road seemed to be on a hill that wasn't particularly steep, and it curved around to the right as a person went up the slope. Ashling was facing up the hill, looking into the driving rain for some reason that wasn't clear. It was hard to make out very much at all in my dream. It was all so dark. My wife was almost invisible in her black coat. She looked like a ghostly white face suspended in the midst of the tempest.

I didn't hear the car in my dream but Ashling seemed to because she spun around and held out her arm as if the palm of her hand could somehow magically stop the car. I don't know if the driver even braked. Maybe at the last second. The initial impact would have broken both of her legs and as the car continued through her, she crashed on to the windscreen before being flipped right over the roof and on to a gravel verge by the side of the road. There was a horrible screech as car tyres fought the road for grip, and then there was just the sound of the rain again. Except it sounded different now. Quieter. The rain had done its worst and now it sounded almost peaceful.

In my dream I could see a single black high-heeled shoe lying on its side in a puddle near the centre of the road. It looked so out of place that it almost resembled something out of a Dali painting. I ignored the shoe and started walking towards Ashling. I wanted to run but I wasn't sure that I could. I was afraid because I knew that I was already too late. I just knew. Yet somehow I found the courage and I broke into a run, down the hill to the side of the road where my wife's broken body was drawing its final breath. I dropped to my knees and I turned her bloodied face towards me, and that's when I'd usually wake up.

My dreams about Ashling felt different to the ones that I'd had about Owen and Mrs Horricks. The recurring nightmares that I'd had as a child felt like they were being beamed directly on to a ghostly TV screen inside my head, one that only came alive when I was asleep. And as the fateful day came closer in real time, the signal seemed to become stronger and so the images became more frequent and clearer. But with Ashling, the signal was nothing like as strong as it had been, and so whereas my precognitive dreams about Owen had a kind of movie feel to them, my dreams about Mrs Horricks were less vivid, and my dreams concerning Ashling felt more like snapshots of the future seen through a door that was closing.

There were other differences as well. This latest set of nightmares were shorter and out of focus, and they weren't continuous. It was more like images being flashed in front of my eyes. If my dreams about Owen had a cinematic feel to them then my dreams about Ashling were more like watching the trailer before the film itself. Teasing, high-speed images that didn't really give all that much away, just enough to get my pulse racing and to cover me in a light sweat. It was as if I had my own personal bogeyman who would stand behind the film projector and present me with a private showing of snuff movies starring the people that I love the most.

I tried to dismiss my visions of Ashling's death as anxiety dreams brought about by a kind of delayed nervous reaction to what I had experienced around the time of Owen's death. And because I was in denial, my wife had no inkling of the exact nature of her demise until she experienced it firsthand. I can't deny that it's at least possible that things might have turned out differently if I had warned her, but I chose not to. Around that time she was working mostly double shifts at the hospital because she was trying to save up some extra cash for Christmas, and so I didn't see as much of her as I would have liked. Besides, I was almost constantly busy myself. I was working long shifts at Happy's six days a week and then on top of that, I was struggling through a Diploma in Business Studies during the day. The chronic laziness that I had wallowed in after my father died had become such a distant memory that it felt like a part of someone else's life. The Business Diploma had been my idea although the truth is that I simply wouldn't have bothered if Ashling had not come into my life. She made me want to be a better person.

When we did get to spend time together, we were both usually tired and consequently the last thing that I wanted to do was to further sap my wife's strength by dumping my crazy-sounding neuroses all over her. She knew that I had bad dreams of course; it was impossible to keep that from her. But when she asked, I would just tell her that I had already forgotten them. I didn't enjoy lying to her, but I wasn't ready to tell her the truth either.

Towards the end, the dreams intensified as they had done with Owen and Mrs Horricks and eventually it reached the stage where I was having the same dream at least once every night. Sometimes I would cry out in my sleep and wake up Ashling and other times I would wake up with my fist in my mouth, stifling a scream.

Another reason, perhaps, why my dreams about Ashling lacked any great detail was the fact that it was raining so heavily, and the rain gave everything a slightly blurry, inebriated kind of appearance. That alone should have triggered alarm bells in my brain because the subconscious mind doesn't normally trouble itself with details like the weather when it is programming our dreams. Have you ever in your life had a dream in which it was raining? It just doesn't happen. But in my dreams about Ashling, it rained so hard that if I was Noah, I would have been thinking that God was telling me to build another ark.

After about two months of this, I went to see Dr Cassidy who had been our family doctor for years. I knew as I sat in the waiting room that she wouldn't be able to help me but I think that what I really wanted was some reassurance that I wasn't going crazy. I told her that I was seeing my wife being killed night after night in a car accident. She asked me how things had been going with Ashling and I told her that I had never been happier and that everything was fine. Better than fine. Dr Cassidy then asked me if I was feeling stressed and I admitted that I was. I told her that of course I was stressed; I was being subjected to nightly visions of my wife's death. Who wouldn't be stressed under those circumstances? She leaned back in her chair and steepled her fingers under her chin. Then she jumped forward as if she had been stung on the arse, scribbled something on a pad and then she handed me a prescription for sleeping pills.

I tried to explain to her that there was more to this than meets the eye and that I really didn't think sleeping pills were going to fix it. I tried to explain to her that it wasn't just some bullshit anxiety dream and that I felt as if I had a third eye inside my head that could peek into the future whenever my subconscious mind was in the driving seat. She tried to calm me down a bit by telling me that she understood what I was going through, but her eyes told a different story. She thought that I was nuts: the plain and simple fruitcake variety. I persisted anyway and I begged her to help me. She said that abnormal psychology was outside her field but she offered to refer me to someone better equipped to deal with that sort of thing. It sounded like a waste of time but I didn't know what else to do, so I agreed. Dr Cassidy said that she would write to me in a day or so with details of my appointment with the psychologist or whoever she was dumping me on.

But as it happened, I never got around to seeing any head doctor.

December 10th, 2003.

It was the night of Ashling's Christmas party and some genius had decided on Johnny Fox's pub as the venue. There's a pub called the Fox and Hound on Dorset Street and for some fucked-up reason that I'll never properly be able to explain, I got it stuck in my head that this was where Ashling and her colleagues were headed. But I was totally wrong of course. Johnny Fox's pub is somewhere up in the Dublin Mountains and if I had have put my brain in that day when Ashling told me that she was going there, then who knows; I might have seen the winding approach road in my mind's eye, put two and two together and then found a way to convince her not to go. But I'll try to simply stick to the facts because otherwise I could very easily get drowned in a sea of what-ifs.

On the day in question, I woke up at around eleven, which is normal for me. For the first night in a long time, I had managed a full night without dreaming and so I felt great. I felt better than great. My first Christmas as a married man was fast approaching and watching Ashling sleeping beside me in our over-soft white bed was the best Christmas present that I could think of. She was wearing a T-shirt that showed Jack Nicholson made up as the Joker, and she looked irresistibly huggable. I reached over and put my arm around her, squeezing her gently without waking her. That morning she had got to bed at almost 5 a.m. after a late night/early morning shift at the hospital. She felt so warm even though the room was cold. She was like a giant hot water bottle. Heat just seemed to radiate from her.

As quietly as possible, I rolled out of bed and then I slipped into a T-shirt, tracksuit bottoms and my Reeboks and I went for a run to wake myself up properly. When I got back, I showered and then had toast and coffee in front of Sky News. After that I did a couple of hours of boring coursework. I didn't have any class to go to that day, but I did have a five-thousand-word essay to hand in by the end of the year, so I worked on that. In the run-up to Christmas, I was working extra-long shifts at Happy's and that day I was scheduled from 4 p.m. until about 1.30 a.m. Pain in the arse, but we needed the money.

Ashling on the other hand had that entire day off. At around 3 p.m., I brought her up a plate of scrambled eggs and toast on a tray. It was the only thing that I could cook properly so Ashling had always referred to that dish as my *legendary scrambled eggs*.

She was still asleep and I woke her with a kiss. Her sleepy brown eyes were like puppy dog eyes opening for the very first time. God how I loved to look into those eyes. Compassion, vibrancy, intelligence and humour.

'What time is it?' she croaked.

'Time for you to go to work. C'mon, c'mon, get up, you're late! Somebody phoned in sick so you got the call.'

'Arghhhhhh!' said Ashling, burying her head under the pillow.

'Sorry to be the bearer o bad news but hey, it's not so bad. You'll finish at midnight so ya can prob'ly still catch quite a lot o your Christmas party,' I said, laying it on with a shovel.

'ARGHHHHH!' she said even louder, this time from under the pillow.

'But the good news is tha I made ya breakfast!'

Breakfast however wasn't proving to be any consolation at all.

'You *have* to get me out of this, Charlie. Pleeeeeeeease!'

'If ya call in sick then ya can't go to the party tonight cos your boss will be there,' I said not very helpfully.

'NOOOOOooooo!' said Ashling as that realisation hit home. 'This can't be happening to me. It's *so* unfair.'

'Look at the bright side,' I said, 'all tha free drink would prob'ly just have given ya a monster hangover anyway, and now you'll be able to make me breakfast in bed tomorrow morning.'

She gave me the evil eye for a second and then went back to looking extremely sorry for herself. I decided that she had suffered enough and so I confessed that I was only winding her up. Her jaw dropped and she stared at me, mouth agape in a mixture of shock, happiness and vengeful mischief. The latter won out because she picked up half a slice of toast that was covered in scrambled egg, and then she pulled back the waistband of my tracksuit bottoms, slipped the toast inside, and then snapped the elastic closed again.

'Oh you are sooooooooo dead!' I said, dumping the tray on the ground and then fumbling down my trousers to retrieve fistfuls of toast and egg as I ran out the door. A few seconds later I was back, armed this time with a packet of ice cubes from the freezer.

'NOOOOOOOO!' screamed Ashling when she saw me coming, and then she squirmed to escape via the far side of the bed. I was too quick for her though. I jumped on top of the bed and managed to straddle her while at the same time pulling back the duvet and attempting to give her a bed bath using a bag of ice cubes instead of a sponge.

It's lucky that the cops didn't arrive because my wife's screams were nearly loud enough to wake the dead up in Rathgorman Cemetery. Eventually, she managed to wrestle the ice cubes from my hand and she threw them to the far side of the room. We had a lying-down hug for a few minutes until we both felt like grown-ups again and then she took me by the hand and led me into the bathroom where we made love in the shower.

Afterwards I got dressed again and then I ran out the door to go to work. Ashling was brushing her hair in the bathroom. I looked in as I passed the door. She was sitting on the edge of the bath with her head bowed and her hair hanging down in front of her face as she ran a brush through it, so conversation wasn't really possible. I went down the stairs and out the front door. There was no kiss goodbye.

Happy's was only about a ten-minute walk away and I always walked there and back. As I got closer, I could hear the leaves of the trees whispering as if passing secrets from branch to branch. There was a storm coming.

I met a regular called Dessie coming out of the pub just as I was going in.

'Looks like we're in for a little rain,' he said, glancing up at the troubled sky.

'I think ya might be right,' I replied, feigning interest. As a barman, I used to loathe punters who talked about the weather.

Inside Happy's, Damien, Roger and Scary Mary were already behind the bar and a quick glance around confirmed that most of Norman's gang was also in the house. I could see Big Mickey rolling around on the floor in front of the bar like a demented dervish. He looked as if he was trying to bite off his own bollox. Better his than mine I thought and then I went to work behind the bar just as I had done a thousand times before. Just another Friday night in the asylum.

By 6 p.m. I was working flat out in order to keep the drink flowing and yet still the punters were almost cutting each other's throats in order to get served quicker at the bar. Maybe it was the crush that sapped everyone's Christmas spirit, or maybe the Happy's regulars simply have no Christmas spirit but either way, the only evidence of the festive season were the Santa Claus hats that Roger made all the staff wear. Not very original but cheap and cheerful, as you'd expect from Roger. And definitely better than the previous year when he hired some kid to paint Christmassy pictures on the mirrors behind the bar. The kid said that he was an art student but his paintings were terrible. I had to spend about six weeks explaining to people why Rudolph the Red-Nosed Reindeer looked more like the Hound of the Baskervilles.

The Santa Claus hats did encourage plenty of slagging as you'd expect but Roger was adamant that we were to wear them for the full two weeks before Christmas. To be honest, I wasn't all that bothered about having to wear the hat although I felt a bit bad for Scary Mary because those hats were hot. The whole room was hot. And it was twice as bad behind the bar with all the running around and the steam from the dishwasher rising up every ten minutes. On more than one occasion, I spotted Scary Mary taking off her hat and mopping her sweaty face with it. Also, when she took off the hat, I could clearly see steam rising from the top of her head like she was a racehorse after running the Grand National. At the end of her shift, she must have smelled like a bucket of piss. Punters were opting to queue three deep at my end of the bar rather than one deep at her end because I think they were worried that she was going to drip into their pints.

Silky Mannix was in the pub along with his wife Gloria and their son Wayne. On that particular night, his wife was wearing a white leather skirt, white knee-length fuck-me-boots and so much make-up that she looked as if she might have to throw her head back just to open her eyes. Mutton dressed as mutton. She spent much of the early part of the night sitting at the bar and laughing shrilly and continuously for no apparent reason. I had a bad feeling that this might have been her way of flirting with me but I couldn't make her stop. Ignoring her just seemed to make her louder but I didn't know what else to do. She belched loudly in my direction at one point and then she threw a beer mat at me to get my attention.

'Get tha cute little arse over here, sweetheart. I need a large one and I think you're the man to see to me. I need a good seeing to,' she shouted before exploding once again into gales of empty laughter. Her son Wayne, incidentally, is the eldest of three Mannix kids. He has two sisters, Ulrika and Britney, and they are the sort of children who would make a paedophile lock the doors on his car if he saw them coming. Wayne isn't any better, just older and more ugly. And he has so much metal in his face that he looks as if someone attacked him with a nail gun.

On that particular night, Norman wasn't sitting with the rest of his crew. I spotted him in a corner chatting up a young slapper named Michelle O'Regan. He kept touching her upper arms as if he was reassuring her about something when in reality he was just slyly working his way into her pants. Meanwhile one of Norman's troops was starting to get rowdy. Benny Binchy is a weasel of a man who likes to pretend that he has heightened catlike reactions akin to some kind of ninja commando but the reality is a lot less impressive: his nerves are fucked.

Early on in the night, Benny got it into his head that, for no obvious reason, he was going to try and get everyone in the pub to be quiet so that the national anthem could be sung. But the more he tried to shush people, the louder they talked in order to drown him out, and naturally this pissed him off. Fozzie, another one of Norman's gang, saw Benny's predicament and decided that the solution was just to start singing in the hope that everyone else would join in. Fozzie, aka the Muppet, has a big square jaw like Desperate Dan's and his body is so pumped up with steroids that he can't even walk properly anymore. And I'm not sure whether it's a side-effect of the drugs or not, but poor old Fozzie doesn't seem to have two brain cells to rub together. The problems with him joining in with the singing were twofold: firstly Fozzie, being an honorary member of Densa, didn't have a clue what the words of the national anthem are, and secondly, nobody wanted to sing along with him, not even Benny who now appeared to be sulking.

'Sinne Fianna Fáil, atá na naa, na na, na naa' sang Fozzie at the top of his voice regardless.

There was a point of no return at which either a chorus of drunken voices would have droned into life or else they would never get started at all, and that moment sailed right past leaving Fozzie the only one even close to singing. He looked like a sad prick and people all over the pub started suggesting as much. Fozzie realised that he was making a fool of himself because his attempt at singing withered away to little more than muttering under his breath and his face reddened until it was the same colour as my Santa Claus hat.

Then Silky Mannix threw petrol on a dying fire by roaring a line from 'The Fairytale of New York' – 'You scumbag, you maggot, you cheap lousy faggot, happy Christmas my arse I pray God it's your last.' Whereas Fozzie's singing efforts had been met with derision, the whole pub burst into spontaneous laughter at Silky's Shane McGowan impression. But they weren't laughing at Silky of course, they were laughing at Fozzie, which was unfortunate for Silky, because Fozzie is built like the Incredible Hulk. And although he is not exactly the sharpest tool in the box, about as sharp as a ping-pong ball in fact, he knew when he was being made to look like a plonker.

Fozzie put down his pint and stretched his neck muscles by rolling his head around once, all the time staring out Silky. He cracked his knuckles and I swear I could hear the sound of bones crunching from way over by the bar where I was standing. He never took his eyes off Silky and I never took my eyes off him. I ignored the customers screaming at the bar for drink; things were about to get messy. Silky was standing about ten people away from his wife Gloria, and he was chatting to Spanner. But when Spanner saw Fozzie starting to move towards Silky, the dodgy mechanic put two or three steps between himself and his buddy. The crowd was packed too tightly to part like the Red Sea for Fozzie, but most people in his path did try to move rapidly out of his way, and those who didn't or couldn't got pushed to one side like swatted flies.

'Were you talkin about me just now?' was the challenge he threw down to a by now quite pale-looking Silky Mannix.

'Wha? No, no, I was just singin, tha's all. It's Christmas, ya know?'

'I know it's fuckin Christmas. Are ya sayin I'm bleedin thick or somethin?'

People in the vicinity stopped talking and followed Spanner's lead in taking a step back. Nobody was laughing anymore apart from a few nervous titterers. A natural circle was forming around Silky and Fozzie like they were kids fighting in a playground.

'Nobody's sayin you're thick. Are ya mad?'

'Oh, so it's fuckin mad I am now then, is it?'

'Wha? No!'

'Do ya wanna shot at the title, do ya? Well let's fuckin go man. Righ here.'

'Now look it, Fozzie, just relax the fuckin kacks there a minute,' said Silky.

'He's after callin ya a muppet,' said someone in the circle who obviously didn't want to be denied the spectacle of seeing somebody else getting punched out.

'He called ya a faggot as well,' said another helpful anonymous troublemaker in the crowd behind Silky. Silky turned around to try and identify who it was that was trying to get him killed. When he turned back around to face his nemesis, Fozzie grabbed him by the shirt with one hand while with the other he released three quick powerful punches into the smaller man's face -- BAM, BAM, BAM. When Fozzie let go of Silky's shirt, Silky went down like a sack of potatoes. Ripples of *oohs* and *aahs* and 'that'll teach that lippy cunt' emanated from the crowd. I thought that Fozzie's three blows were going to be the start and end of the night's violence showcase, but I was wrong. As it happened, things were only warming up.

Gloria let out a piercing shriek at the bar and then she hobbled through the crowd on her high-heeled boots doing a very unlikely

Florence Nightingale impression as she went to tend to her man. At that point, I could see someone else moving through the crowd at speed from the other side and I was reminded of a cartoon mole burrowing through a lawn like a torpedo. A few seconds later, Silky's son Wayne emerged from the crowd and jumped on to Fozzie's back and proceeded to try to gouge out the larger man's eyes from behind while screaming that he was going to kill him. Fozzie started to buck like a rodeo horse, trying desperately to shake off the kid on his back. But Wayne wasn't budging and so Fozzie reached back blindly over his shoulder and started clawing at his attacker's face with one hand. Fozzie got lucky and Wayne got unlucky; very unlucky.

Fozzie's forefinger found the ring at the end of Wayne's nose and he yanked hard on it like he was pulling a pin from a grenade. The ring came away in his finger as did most of the septum from Wayne's nose. At that point I closed my eyes and when I opened them again, I was running. I don't know if I even knew where I was going but I slammed Mary out of my way and I raced through the kitchen and then through the storeroom, and then I flung open the loading doors at the rear of the building, and only then could I release the breath that I didn't even know I had been holding.

The rain was coming down freely by then and it was nice. It made the air feel clean. I gulped down a few large breaths like a diver having resurfaced and I tried to maximise whatever solace I could take from being away from the punters for a little while. I was due a break so I didn't feel too bad about abandoning my colleagues. Usually at that time, I would go for a walk around the block to get a bit of fresh air but that night I didn't bother because of the rain. Instead I sat on a broken chair in the storeroom and I fantasised about a cushy job where I could sit in an office all day long and never have to deal with the public. The rain battered the cracked skylight window overhead making a sound like thunderous applause. Somewhere in the distance, I could hear the siren of an approaching ambulance.

Not for the first time that day, I could sense a strange smell flirting with my nostrils and I couldn't quite place where it was coming from. It was a vaguely familiar coppery sort of smell that stirred something in a dark corner of my mind. Something from my childhood perhaps. While tantalisingly close, the memory remained maddeningly just out of reach and so I tried to forget about it before my brain overheated. I dismissed the smell as stale beer or else something growing in the bottom of one of the bottle skips, but a nagging doubt in my mind told me that this could not be the case as I suddenly realised that the odour had been around since I had woken up that morning. I wondered if it was my aftershave or deodorant that had somehow spoiled and then I managed to forget about it again. The rain on the skylight window had a kind of soporific quality and I was just starting to doze off when Damo came into the room.

'Aw, is this where ya are, skivin off? I thought you'd gone out,' he said just as I opened my eyes.

'In this weather? Fuhged about it,' I said in the style of a New York gangster.

'Ya missed the fight. Wayne Mannix got half his nose ripped off. Fuckin blood everywhere, man.'

'No, no, I saw it all. I was servin at the time.'

'Fuckin mad it was.

'Yeah.'

'Oh by the way, your missus was in about twenty minutes ago but I told her ya were gone out. Sorry, but how was I to know ya were hidin back here?'

'Was she lookin for me?'

'No, she was lookin for Scary Mary. Course she was lookin for ya!'

'Did she say why?'

'Yeah, she was just droppin in your jacket. I left it behind the bar.'

'Nice one!' I said. That was Ashling through and through, thoughtful as ever.

'She's headin up to Johnny Fox's for her Christmas party, she tells me,' said Damo. 'Not much of a night for headin up to tha place. It's fuckin miles away.'

And it was at that exact second that the fog around my brain lifted and I could suddenly see everything all too clearly. The rain, the dark mountain road, Ashling by herself, even the faint coppery smell. How could I have been so fucking slow?

'SHIT!' I said, leaping up from the chair and giving Damo a fright in the process.

'Wha?'

'Tha's tha fuckin place up the mountains, isn't it? It's not on Dorset Street at all, is it?'

'Where?'

'Johnny Fox's!'

'Yeah, yeah, it's up the mountains somewhere I think. Wha's the story man?'

I ran towards the door that led back into the bar and then I returned and grabbed Damo by both shoulders.

'What was she wearin? Ashling, what was she wearin?'

'Eh, I dunno, I can't remember. You're freakin me out here, man. Oh no, wait, she was wearin a black coat, and a dress I think and, eh, high-heeled shoes.'

The same clothes that she had been wearing in my dream.

'SHE LOOKED VERY NICE, SO SHE DID!'

He had to shout that last bit because I had left the room before he was finished. I raced behind the bar and grabbed the phone beside the till. For a second, I couldn't remember Ashling's mobile number but then I just punched in 087 and let my fingers remember the rest.

One ring . . . I visualised her fumbling open her bag with one hand while trying to drive with the other.

Two rings . . . no answer.

Three rings . . . still no answer.

Four rings . . . *oh sweet Jesus answer the fucking phone*!

'Hi, this is Ashling here. I can't come to the phone right now but leave a message and I'll get back to you.'

'*Fuck*!' I said to nobody in particular, and then the recording beep sounded.

'Ashling, it's me. Listen, I can't explain righ now, but I have this weird feelin tha your life is in danger, serious danger. This is not a joke, I promise ya. Ring me as soon as ya get this message and in the meantime, don't walk along any windin roads in the rain. I repeat, don't walk on the fuckin road!'

I put down the phone and looked up to see Roger and Damo

staring at me as if I'd gone completely and utterly insane. I didn't waste any time explaining myself.

'Roger, somethin's come up. I have to go and find my wife.'

'This is one o the busiest nights o the year.'

'Yeah, sorry bout tha but I have to go.'

He knew that I wasn't asking for permission and he made no attempt to stop me.

'Damo, I need to borrow your car.'

'Yeah sure, no probs,' he said, handing me the keys. 'Just don't do anythin, eh . . . mad, ya know.' But I was already racing out the door at that point.

Damo's car was an ancient Toyota Crown – a huge, brown cantankerous old thing that seemed to resent not being left to rust in peace. By the time I reached the car, I was soaked to the skin. I'd forgotten my jacket but I wasn't going back for it. It was all about time now. I felt as if I was in some fucked-up, through-the-looking-glass game show where I was competing against Destiny and the Grim Reaper for my wife's life. I put the car in gear and I started driving in a mostly illegal fashion across the city. I tried to phone her again at one stage when I was stopped at traffic lights but I just got the same message. Her phone must have been on a silent setting inside her bag. I gave up on the mobile and concentrated as much as I could on the driving. Despite the frantic nature of my journey, it just simply wasn't possible to drive like Steve McQueen in the film *Bullitt*. Visibility was awful in the driving rain and time appeared to be speeding up as I crawled across the city.

I arrived at a particularly busy junction in the centre of town and while I was stopped at traffic lights, I noticed that my knuckles had turned white on the steering wheel. I tried breathing deeply in an effort to relax myself so that I could think clearly, but it wasn't easy. The rain sounded like nails being hammered into the roof of the car and the metronomic thump of the wipers was like the pendulum on a fucked clock.

Damo had left a packet of Silk Cut Purple on the dashboard. I snatched one of them and then patted myself down searching for matches. No luck. I opened the ashtray and activated the fag lighter in the car. While I was waiting for it to heat up, I sucked away on the unlit cigarette. It seemed to help my nerves a bit, but not much.

The lights turned green but my line of traffic failed to move. I pressed on the centre of the steering wheel for a few seconds, sounding the horn loudly. A few more long seconds passed with nothing happening and then finally the car at the front of the line started to move. Some fucking asshole in an SUV.

When I reached the junction, the lights turned amber and the car in front of me stopped.

'JESUS FUCKING *CHRIST*!' I roared while banging my hands on the steering wheel like a crazy man. I leaned on the horn again for about five seconds although it seemed like longer. The car in front of me was a black Volkswagon Golf GTI. Without turning around, the driver raised his left arm and gave me the finger.

That was too much for me. I flung open the car door and stepped out into the rain. I stormed up to the driver's door of the Golf and just as I went for the handle, the sole occupant punched down the locking button.

'Open this fuckin door!' I roared at him. The driver was just a kid. A boy racer whose machismo had deserted him the instant I stepped out of the car.

'Get away from me, will ya?' he squeaked.

'Ya think ya know how to fuckin drive, do ya? I'll teach ya how to fuckin drive!'

He stepped on the accelerator and broke the lights, leaving me standing on the road in the rain feeling like a spare prick. I ran back to the car and got moving again.

That was a dumb thing to do and not like me at all. I needed to get a grip on myself. The cigarette lighter popped and I jumped slightly with the fright it gave me. The unlit cigarette in my mouth was now so wet that it was beyond smoking. I threw it on the floor and grabbed a fresh one from the box. I lit it with hands that were shaking badly and then I chain-smoked it until I could feel my heartbeat begin to slow down.

Once I got to the Southside, I was heading out of town again with most of the traffic headed in the opposite direction and so I began to make more obvious progress. I even made it into fifth gear a few times. And then I was at the foot of the Dublin Mountains and driving almost steadily uphill along shitty narrow roads.

Traffic lights were scarce that far out from the city and I relished the opportunity to put my foot down a little bit. My mind started to wander. I thought about Owen and I thought about Mrs Horricks. I thought about the years that had passed since my best friend had drowned in the canal and my other best friend had died clutching her chest in her own back garden. I thought about all the times that I had beat myself up over my failure to save them and I gave myself a mental pat on the back for jumping into the ring with

Destiny on this occasion. I felt that whatever happened that night, I would at least be able to look myself in the mirror and say that I tried my best. And I must say that at that point, I definitely felt ahead in the game. I was optimistic and growing bolder by the second. The way I saw it was that Ashling would be at her most vulnerable when she emerged from the pub at the end of the night. It wasn't her style to drink and drive, but maybe the festive mood would overtake her sensibilities, causing her to stray on to the road as she made her way to the car. But just as I was coming to the conclusion that I had about four hours to spare, the sands of time ran out and the game was over.

I came around a right-hand corner and just as I was coming out of the bend, I almost slammed into the back of a car parked on the left hand side of the road. I swerved towards the centre of the road to avoid a collision and that's when I saw her. A woman in black standing in the middle of the road. She turned around and our eyes locked instantly. She held up one hand in a gesture of stop, but nothing short of a brick wall could have stopped the car in time at that stage. There was a horrible *whump* sound from the initial impact which took her legs from under her, and then she was slammed into the windscreen before being hurtled over the roof of the car and dumped on to the road behind me. I stood on the brake pedal with both feet but the wet road was like an ice rink and I skidded for about the length of a football pitch before ending up in a ditch.

When the car finally came to a stop, I didn't move a muscle. Reality had become too sudden and strange to comprehend and now time seemed to be unfolding in slow motion. There was a spiral web of cracks in the windscreen and a hole at the centre of the spiral was leaking in cold air and rain. I stared at the circular cracks and I wondered why they were circular and not straight. The effects of shock began to wash through me, dulling my senses. I noticed a dark patch of what looked like blood that was smeared across the top of the windscreen, but that didn't really register with me. The rain falling on the roof of the car was reduced to the sound of a dull patter by that point.

But then something in my brain started screaming like a smoke alarm and so I forced myself out of the car and I started walking back down the road. My legs felt like they had been filled with molten lead. One half of my brain was desperately fuelling my mind with anything other than the worst case scenario: I had hit a deer, I had hit someone other than my wife, I was at home in bed dreaming my most vivid dream to date; but the other half of my brain was able to shout louder with just a single image replayed over and over: a woman in black standing in the centre of the road; she turns around; it's the face that I love more than any other face in the world, and a fraction of a second after I see the same recognition in Ashling's eyes, I extinguish her life force from the world.

I started to run. I couldn't find her at first but then I saw a shoe on the road and I found her lying nearby on a gravel verge. She looked so exposed, so helpless and broken. A car drove past. I waved my arms frantically in its wake, trying to get the driver's attention. It didn't stop. It was only then, when I couldn't delay it any longer, that I attended to Ashling. It crossed my mind that she might have broken her back so I didn't want to move her. I lifted her head off the ground and I spoke her name. Her eyes opened slowly and she looked at me. She was bleeding from both of her ears so I knew that she was very badly hurt. Her life was like a handful of sand that was slipping away no matter how hard I tried to hold on to it. I begged her to stay with me. I begged her to hang in there and somehow I would make things all right again. She never took her eyes off me. She opened her mouth as if to speak, but before she could get a word out, a dreadful shudder went through her entire body and then she stopped moving altogether.

No longer concerned about moving her, I scooped her limp body from the ground with both arms and I held her to me as tightly as I could. Blood was in her hair. It felt like damp silk. I could smell copper again and I realised that it was the smell of blood. I let out a roar, a primal sound that came from somewhere unthinkably deep inside of me. My wife was cooling in my arms by the second and I could do nothing but drip in the rain.

After Ashling had stopped moving, I walked up and down the gravel patch by the side of the road like a man in a trance, carrying her in my arms, desperately trying to wake up. She seemed to weigh almost nothing at all. I spoke to her constantly, telling her how we were going to get through this and how she was going to be fine.

I have no idea how long that went on for but eventually I heard the sound of an engine coming up the hill and so with Ashling still in my arms, I moved until I was standing squarely in the middle of the road. After that, I closed my eyes and I prayed harder than

I've ever prayed before in my life. I prayed for a juggernaut to come tearing around the corner and knock me right out of my skin. Or if it couldn't be a juggernaut, then I would have settled for a campervan or even a HiAce van. Fuck it, I would have settled for an ice-cream van if it did the job properly. But as the noise of the engine drew closer, it sounded more like the buzz of a light aeroplane than anything else. The whole thing started to feel a bit surreal. I really had no idea what was going to happen next. I opened my eyes and resisted a cartoonish urge to tap one foot and look at my watch while I was waiting. The whole thing was taking far too long. Finally, after a little taste of eternity, a very small motorbike came around the corner, its owner wearing a luminous yellow jacket. Judging by the high-pitched whine of the engine, his bike was struggling badly against the incline of the mountain. He came to a stop in front of me with no trouble at all and then he took off his helmet, revealing himself to be an old man.

'Are ya havin a bit of trouble?' he asked while I just stared at him in disbelief. What I wanted to do was roar and scream and shout and tear my hair and kick something and shake my fists at the sky and call God a MOTHERFUCKERRRRRRRRRRR who didn't have the decency to send a juggernaut to run me down, or the balls to come down himself and face an arse-kicking from me that he would remember for the rest of eternity. But I didn't do any of those things. Instead I just stared at my sad excuse for a white knight in case he suddenly turned into the Easter Bunny and then I would know that I was dreaming. He didn't change into anything though. He just got slightly older and wetter and I knew that he couldn't help me. Nobody could.

Conversation of any description was quite simply beyond me at that point and so I turned my back on the old man and walked back to the gravel verge where I sat on the ground and held my wife's head close to my chest. The man followed me to the side of the road where he took Ashling's hand, presumably to check for a pulse.

'DON'T FUCKIN TOUCH HER!' I roared at him. I feel a bit bad about that now because he went out of his way to do the Good Samaritan routine and that was the only thing that I said to him. He must have thought that I was fucking batshit and so fair play to him for not just hopping on his bike and driving away. He flagged down the next car that came along and the driver phoned for an ambulance on his mobile. Nobody came near me until the ambulance arrived and that was fine with me.

While we were waiting, I realised that the gravel verge that I was sitting on was in fact some sort of lookout point. I raised my head and I could see the lights of the city stretched out before me all the way out to Dublin Bay. It was beautiful, like a million Christmas trees. It didn't seem right that beauty could still exist in the world after what had just happened to my wife.

The ambulance arrived and two paramedics approached me like I was a dangerous lunatic but I didn't give them any hassle. I finally let Ashling out of my arms but never out of my sight. I went with her in the ambulance to Tallaght Hospital, holding her hand and stroking her hair for most of the way. Both of the ambulance men sat up front. One of them had already pronounced her dead, and so naturally they had given up on her and I think that they were leaving me alone so that I could say my goodbyes. That was nice of them, I suppose, although how do you say goodbye to your reason for living?

See ya in the next life, kiddo; oh, and by the way, sorry about ploughing into you with the car and causing you to die like a dog on the side of the road in the rain while your ears filled with blood.

Something like that? I don't think so. I couldn't even begin to say goodbye because I couldn't accept that she was gone.

I wiped the blood from her mouth in order to add to the illusion that she was merely sleeping. It worked too well. She looked every bit as beautiful as she did when I had woken her earlier that day. I leaned over and kissed her lips because I knew that was her favourite way to wake up. But when she didn't stir, I started to shake her shoulder, saying 'Ashling, wake up, wake up, Ashling' over and over. But still she didn't move and so I began to shake her vigorously with both hands until suddenly one of her eyelids flew open like a roller blind. But there was no big brown eye staring back at me, just a glassy white orb that belonged to a creature from *Night of the Living Dead*. She was gone.

I turned her face towards the wall and I decided that it wasn't Ashling lying there after all. I didn't know where she had gone but she certainly wasn't in that ambulance. For the rest of the journey, I placed my hands over my ears and I hummed various tunes that popped into my head. And when any lucid thoughts tried to permeate my brain, I simply drowned them out by humming even louder.

I was in the middle of a stirring rendition of the national anthem when the ambulance driver threw open the back door upon our arrival at Tallaght Hospital. He looked at me with a mixture of concern and sympathy. He said something but I couldn't hear him because I had my hands over my ears and I was humming too loudly. Then the other ambulance man jumped through the double doors and started to remove the stretcher holding the body that looked remarkably like my wife's. I followed the stretcher out on to the tarmac and then a nurse appeared from nowhere and started to lead me inside. She said something to me but I paid her no attention even though I had given up on the humming by that stage.

I'm glad that the ambulance drove to Tallaght Hospital and not to the Mater where Ashling used to work because I couldn't even cope with my own shock, let alone the shock and grief of my wife's former colleagues. As it was, the news spread faster than dog shit on a running shoe, but what I didn't need at that point was people coming up to me and sympathising over the death of my wife.

The nurse led me to a cubicle and then she left me sitting on a bed with a curtain drawn around it. I tried thanking her for her kindness but no words came out of my mouth, just a kind of deflated howl. My mind was off on another planet somewhere. I started imagining the same scene as it might have unfolded at Ashling's workplace.

'Well, do you know, I am just so impressed with your dedication to your job, Nurse,' Sister Cuntface might have said. 'Not only do you come in to work on the night of that silly, silly Christmas party, but you don't even let a little thing like being dead hold you back. Well done, Nurse!'

I jumped up and puked into a vase containing two sunflowers

that was conveniently positioned on an adjacent locker. I managed to whip the flowers out first though and then afterwards I popped them back into the vase and returned it to its original place on the locker. The flowers glared at me hatefully. I glared back at them and was considering a double decapitation when a doctor and the nurse came through the curtain. They started asking me questions about who I was and how I was feeling and blah, blah, blah, blah. Their voices sounded very far away, almost as if they were coming from underwater. It was like the whole world ran on batteries, and the batteries were running out.

The sunflowers alone commanded my attention. They managed to stay in sharply defined focus while the rest of the room turned into an impressionist painting. Then, out of the blue, I could hear the sound of the singing Munchkins from *The Wizard of Oz*. 'Ding dong, the witch is dead. Which old witch? The wicked witch!' went the song. I looked around to see if maybe there was a television somewhere that had suddenly been switched on. But I didn't see any television, or a radio. What I did see was a lot more disturbing. The two sunflowers on the locker were singing and jiving away for all they were worth inside the vase. They had sprouted tiny faces since the last time I had looked and they sneered at me while singing in their high-pitched Munchkin voices. I picked up the vase like it was a hand grenade and I threw it as hard as I could over the curtain rail and out into the ward where I could hear it smashing and skidding along the floor. One or two people cried out. The nurse disappeared through the curtain only to reappear seconds later with a security man who appeared to have both the build and the brain of a Leeson Street bouncer. He wore a navy-blue blazer that didn't have a prayer of closing around his fat stomach.

'Wha the fuck do ya think you're doin?' was his opening offer of conversation. Or at least I think that's what he said, but I'm not certain as I had to kind of lip-read him because each of my ears felt stuffed with half a roll of cotton wool. Then the doctor said something to me in slow motion. I turned to look at him, but there was just a monosyllabic drone pouring out of his lips that I couldn't even begin to understand. The nurse came back through the curtain carrying medication on a metal tray which she left on a table that was suspended over the bed. She stared at me with big frightened-looking eyes. I tried to smile at her to show her that she had nothing to fear but I was distracted by a movement of the doctor who took a step closer to me while filling a syringe with something from a tiny bottle. I turned again to the nurse, seeking some reassurance, but the nurse with the frightened-looking eyes was gone. In her place stood Ashling in her nurse's uniform. And I might even have been heartened by that impossible transformation except for the fact that it wasn't Ashling as she had looked that morning, it was Ashling as she had looked in the ambulance, only worse. A lot worse. Her uniform that she had always kept so pristine was drenched in blood, and blood was still oozing from her ears and nose. One of her eyes was open and the other was closed in a freakish prolonged wink. There was no pupil in her open eye and the white part of the same eye was more pink than white. The corners of her mouth turned upwards in a sort of grotesque smile and when she parted her lips, gloopy dark red blood escaped from between her teeth and dribbled down her chin.

She held out her arms in a hug-me sort of gesture but I was more interested in getting the hell out of there. There was nowhere for me to go though and all I could do was scramble towards the headboard at the top of the bed. In my haste, I kicked the metal tray off the table and after that all hell seemed to break loose. There was a lot of noise all of a sudden and then the fat security man was pinning me to the bed while the doctor stuck a needle in me. I gave a roar at the top of my lungs that must have been heard all over the hospital. I paused only to draw breath and then I let another roar out of me. I figured that if I could shout loud enough then I might bring the world back to its senses. If I could shout loud enough then I might raise the dead.

A second later the lights went out as a meaty fist connected with my face.

I woke up in my over-soft white bed the morning after the accident. I had no idea what time it was or how I had come to be there, but the sun was high in a frosty blue sky. I could hear people talking in the living room downstairs and I listened hard to hear Ashling's voice but I couldn't. Periodic bouts of subdued murmuring were the only discernible sounds. I rolled over to her side of the bed and I pretended that she had just gone to the bathroom and when she returned, we would do spoons and have lying-down hugs until well into the afternoon. But she didn't come back. Under her pillow, my hand touched the big T-shirt that she used as a night-dress. I pulled it out and pressed it against my face and inhaled deeply. I could smell her so clearly that when I closed my eyes she was with me once again. A few hours before in that exact same spot, I had watched her wriggle while I gave her the ice-cube torture and I could see that memory so vividly, with such flawless clarity, that it made it all the more totally and utterly unbelievable that she was now gone.

I wandered downstairs just in case Ashling was about to leap out from behind the couch yelling SURPRISE! I walked into the living room and the first person that I saw was Fiona, Jack's fiancée. She certainly didn't look like someone attending a surprise party. All the colour had drained from her face and when she saw me, she put her hand over her mouth and choked back a sob and then she ran over and hugged me.

'I'm so sorry,' she kept saying in between big gulps of breath. I didn't say anything and I didn't hug her back. I think that I was afraid that any reaction from me might somehow make it even more real. Then Jack walked over and gave me an awkward hug and said 'Sorry, bro.' He didn't need to say anymore. What do you say when the right words simply don't exist? Big Damo was in the room also. He scratched his head and shuffled his feet and he reminded me of a small boy trapped in a large man's body.

I felt like I was an actor with hardly any dialogue in a really dodgy production of some play. *Waiting for Godot* perhaps, where my wife was Godot. Nobody had a clue of the right lines to say but I sensed the need of the others to fill the silence with meaningless dialogue. Jack was banging on about the first time that he met Ashling and how great she was and then Fiona started reminiscing about the time when the four of us went to Lanzarote together and my wife saved some fat man's life with the Heimlich manoeuvre. The way that piece of meat had flown out of his throat like a cork from a champagne bottle had been funny at the time, but now that particular anecdote only made me feel worse because I hadn't been able to save Ashling. I studied the pattern on my coffee mug without saying a word.

Damo threw some of his own memories into the pot without going overboard. He said that the last time he saw my wife was when she dropped my jacket into Happy's, and he said that standing there by the bar with the rain dripping off her, she still managed to look like a supermodel. Grief counselling isn't really Damo's speciality but he was doing his best, and deep down I appreciated his efforts. I caught his eye and I let my voice be heard for the first time that morning.

'Sorry about smashin up your car, Damo,' I croaked. He looked utterly horrified for a second or two before replying.

'I couldn't give a *fuck* about the bleedin car.'

He meant it too and I felt momentarily ashamed for diverting the topic of conversation away from Ashling, but I didn't want to hear other people telling me how great she was and how they were all there for me and how I was going to pull through, because I knew better than anyone how great she was, and I didn't want to pull through without her.

The next thing that I remember was a male and a female cop who called to the door saying that they were investigating a possible case of dangerous driving causing death. Jack told me afterwards that the same two cops had been at the hospital the previous night. They had told him that one of Ashling's tyres had blown out and so it seems as if she was probably trying to flag down some assistance but with the wind and the rain that night, she didn't hear or see me until it was too late. That was the explanation for my wife's role in the accident and it sounded perfectly plausible. It was slightly harder for me to explain my own involvement.

The cops asked me where I had been going the previous night and I muttered that I was on my way to save Ashling. I saw the look that passed between them but I didn't care.

'To save your wife from what exactly?' said the female cop, trying very hard not to be a hard-nosed bitch but not quite succeeding.

'To save her from being run over,' I replied in a dead monotone voice. I think that they decided at that point that my brain was obviously still porridge from the shock, or from the sedatives, or from both, so they packed up and left, but not before suggesting that I drop into the cop shop when I felt better in order to make a statement.

After the departure of our nation's finest, I tuned in and out of the strained conversation that was being carried on around me but I contributed nothing to it. I refused to let myself be drawn into the dire Greek tragedy being improvised in my living room. It didn't seem real, and it didn't seem right the way that they were talking about Ashling in the past tense.

When I felt as if I couldn't bear it any longer, I got up and went into the kitchen to make myself another mug of coffee. When I went to get the milk, I saw the message that had been left written for me in magnetic letters on the fridge door and my heart just plain stopped.

LUV U CHARLIE
TTEOTWAB
ASH

My knees turned to jelly and I slid down the cupboard doors and on to the floor where I sat with my back leaning against the cupboard under the sink. I stared at the multi-coloured plastic letters on the fridge and I allowed a little bit more of the finality of her absence to sink into my brain. I could feel the first tears begin to tip-toe down my face, and then the floodgates opened and pain flowed out of me like an undammed stream. My body was consumed by great racking sobs that threatened to overcome me. I cried with my hands over my eyes the way a kid cries. I cried until my ribcage ached. I cried until I thought something inside of me would break if I didn't stop, and then I cried some more.

After I don't know how long, I felt someone sitting down on the floor beside me. I recognised the shoes as Jack's. I knew without looking over at him that he was crying too. I put my head on his shoulder and together we wept for Ashling like a couple of schoolkids. We sat there like that, not talking, for a very long time.

I was still under sedation on Sunday evening which is why I never made it to the removal from the hospital mortuary. But the combined forces of heaven and earth could not have conspired to stop me going to the funeral. It didn't go particularly well from my point of view as I still had that punch-drunk feeling, and I probably managed to exacerbate my in-laws' grief, but I still had to be there. The funeral was one of those that rips open the wound instead of pouring balm on it, but in the circumstances that was to be expected, I suppose.

Ashling's parents did all the organising for the funeral and I met them outside the church where they shook my hand like I was carrying an infectious disease. Understandable in the circumstances, perhaps. They gave her life and I took it away again. Her father approached me at one point and asked me what exactly had happened and all I could do was shrug my shoulders and squeeze a faint rasping sound from my throat. I couldn't talk to him. I couldn't even begin to try and explain that crazy night even though I know that he deserved some sort of explanation. But the power of speech had deserted me. In fact, from the moment the emergency crew took my wife from my arms, a part of my mind shut down and the power of rational speech went with it.

I had volunteered to give the eulogy during the church part of the proceedings. It seemed like the right thing to do and besides, I wanted to tell people about the Ashling that I knew. I was never one for public speaking but I didn't feel nervous at all about saying a few words even though I had nothing prepared.

Father Harris said the mass. He's a kind old man so I have no doubt that he did a nice job and everything although I can't say for sure because my mind went into temporary shut-down mode almost as soon as he started talking. Jack nudged me in the ribs at one point during an extra long pause in the murmurings. I gazed in the direction of the altar where Father Harris was staring at me while simultaneously nodding his head in the direction of the podium. He looked like a man in a staring competition with a spasm in his neck. Then the penny dropped and I got up and walked towards the podium. When I stood behind the lectern and looked out at the congregation, it was like a cup of cold water in my face. Every single seat was filled and there were even people standing at the back. Ashling would have been so proud.

All eyes were on me. I cleared my throat and I opened my mouth. Nothing came out. I closed my eyes and I tried again. Nothing. I couldn't speak. Something had closed my throat. I stood there for a very long time opening and closing my mouth like a fish drowning on air, and with the congregation blurring in front of me as hot tears slid down my cheeks. The mourners dropped their eyes and studied their prayer books or their fingers and generally pretended not to notice. Then I felt a gentle hand on my elbow and it was Father Harris. He tried to lead me away but I pulled back towards the mike to do my dying fish impression for just a few seconds more. When he touched my arm a second time, I didn't resist and I allowed myself to be led back to my seat where, once again, I wept on to my brother's shoulder.

At the end of the ceremony, the mourners passed the front pew before leaving the church and they paused to shake my hand as they filed past. Most of them uttered the same soulless phrase – 'Sorry for your troubles'. I know that they genuinely meant to offer their sincerest condolences, so why did their words of sympathy sound so hollow? Or maybe they didn't. Maybe it was just me. I was jealous and angry. I felt as if half of the people shaking my hand would go home and watch *Sex and the City* or *The Sopranos* and by tomorrow my wife's death would be just another passing point of conversation for them. Even at that moment, outside the church, people were going about their lives: working, laughing, flirting, whatever. It was all so very, very wrong. I felt as if a black hole had opened up and sucked all that was good from the world and nobody even cared. Nobody but me.

On the day after the funeral, Jack and Damo went to the scene of the accident. Damo knocked out what was left of his windscreen and then drove his car back to Spanner's garage. Jack changed the wheel on my car and then he drove it back to Sullivan Street. I thanked him half-heartedly for his efforts and then I asked him if he wouldn't mind taking the car over to his place and leaving it there until it could be sold. I just couldn't bear to look at it in the driveway anymore. It seemed like a co-conspirator in my wife's demise; a Toyota Judas that just had to go.

Fiona later cleaned out the inside of the car and Jack sold it through the Buy and Sell magazine. The little black and gold bag that Ashling had brought with her that night was among the items retrieved from the car. Her phone was in the bag along with the leather purse that I had given her the previous Christmas. I couldn't bring myself to look through it. I knew that a passport photo of the two of us would be staring back at me through a plastic window inside the wallet and if I saw that, the cold sharp knife that I felt in my heart would be twisted just a little bit more.

In the days and weeks and months that followed, I felt a sense of loss that none of my previous experiences of death had prepared me for. I remember being amazed by the speed with which two extra-ordinarily happy lives could be turned completely on their heads. It still amazes me. I walked around in a sort of a daze and always with an ache in my stomach. People think that when you lose someone close to you, you feel pain in your heart but that's not true: you feel it in your stomach. I felt as if all of my intestines had been scooped out and cold air had been pumped in to fill the void. It's a feeling of the most dreadful emptiness and it never truly goes away.

The fact of my wife's death kept sneaking up on me from all quarters. I tried to protect myself on one side but then wham, the reality would hit me from another side like a punch in the stomach. I used to be strong but that weight on my soul was dragging me under. During the day, I could pretend to myself that there was a good possibility that Ashling at least had attained some level of peace. But at night the demons would come disguised as memories and all bets were off. My memories were like a beautiful incurable disease that was eating me alive from the inside out. I could not escape from the unbearably beautiful memory of the way we were and it was killing me.

I remembered how she would sometimes make me a cappuccino and sprinkle chocolate on the top in the shape of a heart. I remembered not being able to look at her without wanting to touch her. I remembered how she always used to say to me 'Goodnight, sweet Prince' before drifting off to sleep. I remembered waking and seeing her soft shiny hair spread around her head on the pillow like a corona. I remembered the time we were waiting for a taxi in the rain, and I asked her to wait for me while I went off to buy some cigarettes, and she said that if I didn't take too long, she would wait for me all her life. I remembered how she always seemed to know the right thing to do and then she would do it. I remembered the perfect brown freckle in the hollow of her throat and the way her eyes sparkled when she smiled. I remembered gazing into her dark eyes and thinking that I could drown in there. I remembered the perfection of her back and running my finger along her vertebrae until I reached the two dimples at the base of her spine. I remembered the tiny blonde hairs on the nape of her neck. I remembered the way she used to yawn, the way she swallowed a tablet, the way she held my hand, the way she would always give my terrible jokes at least a charity laugh, the way her hair would fall in front of her face sometimes and she would blow it out of her eyes, the way she said my name, the way she moved through a room, the way she loved me. I remembered how for all the days I was with Ashling, my life was absolutely perfect.

She is in my heart and in my bones; she is in the very depths of my being. She is my overdose, my addiction so deep that it cannot be destroyed without killing the addict too. Her face was my sun and her eyes were my stars and she is in my thoughts every minute of every day. There are a million guys out there who would have given anything for a shot at bringing her happiness, so I hope that for the short time that we had together, I at least made her half as happy as she made me.

I loved her so much and I'll always love her.

Till the end of the world and beyond.

About a week after the funeral, some junk mail arrived from the *Reader's Digest* people addressed to my wife. On the envelope it said in big garish letters – YOU MIGHT HAVE ALREADY WON ONE MILLION POUNDS! I didn't know whether to laugh or cry. It was little things like that that made it utterly inconceivable that she was dead. And now that she was gone, all of the meaningless things that happened to me in the course of a day meant even less because I had no one to share them with. Except maybe Freddy. Ashling had a small brown teddy bear named Freddy who was her second-closest friend. She kept that stuffed animal close to her all her life. It slept in the same bed as her when she was a little girl and when she got married, it was a package deal and Freddy came too. He didn't get to share her bed anymore but from his position on a shelf overhead, he still got to watch over her while she was sleeping. At first, I think he probably resented me for taking his place beside the sleeping beauty but he got over that eventually and we became great pals.

At that point in my life, I hadn't had a drink for around seven years, but after what had happened with Ashling, I think my fall off the wagon was inevitable. Nothing and nobody was going to stop me from drinking myself to death because that was the fate that I was carving out for myself. The serious drinking began in the days after the funeral. It started off purely as a social thing. People would call around to offer their sympathies and I would place a glass of whiskey in their hand even if they never touched the stuff. I poured myself a double as well of course and then I proposed a toast 'to absent friends'. I could no longer bear to even say my wife's name. Of course, nobody had the balls to say anything to me about the fact that I was drinking a lot. That was my business and I wouldn't have taken kindly to anyone interfering. And so it was in those circumstances that my days and nights began to bleed together into a big sticky puddle of crap.

I remember at one stage Spanner's wife, Donna, called around to offer her sympathies and a Tea Time Express lemon cake. She had lipstick on one of her front teeth. I don't know why I remember that but I do.

'Jesus, wha have ya been doin to your eyes?' was the first thing out of her mouth when I opened the front door.

'Cryin,' I replied matter-of-factly.

Later I caught sight of myself in the mirror and I almost smiled at the state of the face looking back at me. Sunken grey eyes peered out from a face I didn't recognise and I looked as if I had lost about two stone in weight. They wouldn't have sold me glue in a hardware shop looking like that.

With the amount of booze that I was pouring down my throat during the day, I found that I wasn't hurting quite so much by the time I passed out most evenings. On my good nights, I didn't even make it into the bedroom, passing out instead in the kitchen with my head on the table. I preferred the kitchen to the living room because I could throw up into the sink if I was caught short; I'm practical like that. No matter how hard I tried though, I could never manage to drink myself completely into oblivion because I could always feel the weight of my own sadness dragging me back to reality.

I never drank alone because fuck it, it's not like I'm an alcoholic or anything. My regular drinking partner and new best friend was Freddy the teddy. Unfortunately for him, he didn't look much better that I did. He was completely bald in places where there had once been fur and, worse than that, his nose had fallen off at some point. He was still very lovable though. My favourite thing about him was his eyes. He had big brown eyes like Ashling and he stared out unwaveringly at a world gone mad.

One of the million things that I loved about being married to Ashling was the fact that hers was the first face that I saw every morning. But after she was gone, my mornings deteriorated drastically. Freddy's noseless visage was a sorry alternative. More often than not, I would wake up feeling like my head was full of broken glass and my joints were full of sand, and then I would throw up. My life had become little more than a way of filling time between drinks. In the early stages of my attempt to drink myself to death, I spent a lot of my time continually drinking and then puking up like a bulimic alcoholic but then my liver and my brain and my stomach came to some kind of agreement and I stopped being sick. I didn't even get any serious hangovers anymore even though I spent most nights drinking until my lips went numb and my eyes rolled back in my head. Sometimes I woke up with a headache but I would just start drinking again almost immediately and that would drive it into submission. In my mind, I thought of this as chasing a hangover, but the reality is that it was the hangover that was chasing me. It would only ever catch me, though, if I stopped drinking for long enough and I was determined not to let that happen.

Ideally I was striving towards a blackout every night because on those occasions I managed to avoid that shitty time between bed and sleep when my brain would torture me with an endless spin cycle of the same corrosive memories. Sometimes the look on Ashling's face just before I crashed into her, sometimes her dying in my arms in the rain, and sometimes just the memory of the way we were. On my bad nights, I would sit on the floor in the corner with the lights off and just let the tears spill out of me.

I no longer had any interest in early morning runs, in books or films, or even in eating. Instead I smoked a lot and made myself cups of coffee that I would forget to drink. Previously I had made an effort to keep my body in shape but now weight that I couldn't afford to lose was dropping off me at an alarming rate. I wasn't alarmed though, or even concerned, and even though I usually only ate a couple of handfuls of cereal on any given day, I wasn't even hungry. It didn't occur to me to be hungry.

My diploma in Business Studies was forgotten about of course, along with all my other hopes for the future. College had once been important to me but now it meant absolutely nothing. I felt very fleeting pangs of guilt because I knew that Ashling would have wanted me to carry on with stuff like that. She would have been strong enough to carry on but I just didn't have the energy. My college career was one of the first things that got jettisoned in my post-Ashling existence and I didn't raise a finger to try and save it. I was too busy having a nervous breakdown.

I could still work a computer though and I discovered that I could buy groceries online from Tesco's with my credit card. So using that facility, I bought a thousand cigarettes and twenty-five litres of vodka without ever leaving the house. Sometime after I made the online purchase, the doorbell rang and when I opened the door, there was a kid in his early twenties standing there in a sweatshirt that had Tesco's printed on the front. I took a wild guess and figured that he was the delivery person from Tesco's arriving with my cigarettes and alcohol. Fortunately, I had moved beyond the throwing-up stage of early alcohol poisoning by then because this kid was so ugly, he's lucky that I didn't throw up on his shoes as soon as I opened the door. If a baboon had been born that ugly, it would have demanded plastic surgery.

'Are ya havin a party or wha?' he ventured as he deposited the bottles of booze on to the floor in my hallway.

'No,' I responded.

'Cos with all this fags and booze, ya could have one hell of a party.'

'Yeah,' I replied.

'Me mate Noddy has a set o decks so if you're lookin for a DJ ya know, ya could do worse. Will I give ya his number?'

'No thanks.'

'Well cheer up, for fuck's sake, it might never happen!'

That was too much for me. I gave him a shove that turned him around in the direction of the door and then I kicked him in the arse with the side of my foot. He yelped in pain and surprise and then he ran out. He didn't turn around until he was at the gate, at which point he called me a 'miserable fuckin cunt who should be in a fuckin mental asylum'. I picked up a litre bottle of Smirnoff from the box in the hall and I threw it at his head. It wasn't a bad effort given the fact that he was about thirty feet away, but I missed nonetheless. He ducked and the bottle exploded on the road. I slammed the front door and then I stormed around the house for a good half-hour until my rage had died down. Afterwards I felt a little bit bad, but only because I had wasted a full bottle of voddy on that dumb kid.

People began to worry about me. My brother arrived at the house one day accompanied by Dr Cassidy. I let them in even though I wasn't exactly thrilled to have that incompetent old bag hovering around like a bad smell.

'And how are you today?' she asked. 'Taking good care of yourself I hope?'

'I'm just fine thanks, but unfortunately my wife seems to be sufferin from a bad case o death.'

Her smiley face flickered and went out.

'Well, it's you that I've come to see really.'

'Why's tha? Are ya gonna write me a prescription for some more sleepin tablets?'

'Jack tells me that you've been very depressed lately.'

An arctic laugh escaped my lips and then I threw out another verbal dagger.

'Depressed? Gee, do ya think so? I wonder why that could be?'

'There's no need to be sarcastic,' she replied, suddenly very much on the defensive. 'I'm here to try and help you.'

I suppose that I had a lot of anger built up inside me that I didn't even know about because when Dr Cassidy pushed the wrong buttons in me, I suddenly saw red.

'I came to you for help and you gave me fuckin *sleepin tablets*,' I said in a raised voice that kept rising in volume. 'I told ya tha this was gonna happen and I begged ya to help me and you just looked at me like I was some kind o fuckin lunatic.'

'It's perfectly normal for bereaved people to look for someone to blame,' she said to Jack. That made me even angrier.

'Why are ya talkin like I'm not in the room?' I roared at her. 'I'm righ here you blind fuckin bitch.'

She stood up at that point and made her way towards the door, muttering something about how she would come back in a day or two when I had calmed down. I told her that if she ever knocked on my door again, I would cut her fucking eyes out and feed them to my neighbour's cat. I haven't seen her since so I think she got the message.

I know that Jack had only been looking out for me but still I couldn't help being pissed off with him for dragging Dr Useless into my house. He told me that I had been well out of order speaking to her like that. The fact that he was siding with her amazed and then saddened me. I gave him some leeway though because I knew that he wasn't in possession of all the facts. But he was on a roll now and so he started laying into me about how I looked like a total fucking mess and how I smelled like a week-old bag of rubbish. I poured myself a neat vodka and waited patiently for him to run out of steam.

'And another thing,' he said to me, 'you're drinkin like a fuckin fish. Wha's tha about? Ya used to never touch the stuff.'

'You figure it out, genius,' I replied. At that stage I just wanted him to go. I could feel a bastard of a headache gathering like a storm cloud behind my eyeballs.

'Look, I loved her too, ya know? She was like the sister tha I never had.'

'Yep, we all loved her. She was everybody's shinin light in the darkness and I knocked her brains out of her ears. Sorry about tha.'

'Don't do this. Please don't do this.'

'Do *what*?'

'Don't put all this fuckin blame on your shoulders. It wasn't your fault.'

'Whose fault was it then?'

'It wasn't anybody's fault. It was an accident.'

'BULLSHIT!' I shouted, standing up at the same time like a bad actor trying to add emphasis to his words. 'Who do ya think was drivin the fuckin car? It was my fault.'

I paused while I tried to think of the killer point that would finish off his argument. I couldn't think of anything to add so I just repeated myself.

'It was my fault.'

Jack stood up also and placed one of his hands on my shoulder.

'Ya don't have to go through this on your own ya know?' he said. 'Ya *can't* go through this on your own. It's too much and you're not strong enough.'

I took a large gulp of the vodka and looked at him as though he was speaking a different language.

'Are ya tryin to save me from myself, Jack?' I asked.

'Don't be an asshole,' he replied without missing a beat.

'I'm not the fuckin asshole here, Jack.'

'Hey, mind your fuckin manners, okay?'

'Mind your own fuckin business, okay?' I was raising my voice again and starting to act like a bit of a prick, so my little brother took a step back and tried once more to get through to me.

'Look, I know wha you're going through and I just want ya to know tha I'm here for ya every step o the way.'

Once again the anger rose up in me.

'Why don't ya run off and find Fiona and then run her down with your car, because then, and only then, might ya have the slightest fuckin idea of wha I'm goin through.'

'Don't be like tha. I'm just worried about ya is all. When's the last time ya set foot outside this house?'

'When's the last time ya held your wife in your arms while her life slipped away *and it was all your fault*?'

Jack sensibly ignored my sarcasm and tried to offer me some advice instead.

'It's not healthy, ya know? The thing is, ya don't have to spend every second of every day grievin over Ashling because ya think it might somehow be disrespectful to her if ya were to think about somethin else. Think about yourself for a change.'

I held my glass tightly with two hands because I knew how dangerously close I was to punching him.

'Goodbye, Jack,' I said and then I walked out into the hall. He followed me, protesting all the time that he wasn't going anywhere until he had talked some sense into me. I opened the front door and then just stood there, willing him to leave. I didn't have the energy to fight anymore. I just wanted to be left in peace. Jack saw that his argument was falling on deaf ears so he gave me a break. He said that he would call back later with Fiona and the pair of them would cook me a decent meal.

'Thanks,' I said without looking at him, and then he was gone.

I closed the door and made my way unsteadily back into the living room where I collapsed on to the couch. On the mantelpiece, there was a photograph of Ashling and me on our wedding day and I could hardly take my eyes off it. We had just walked out of the church and the picture captured her laughing and trying to avoid confetti that someone was throwing but I am staring right at the camera lens, staring at my future self slumped listlessly on the couch like a pile of coats at a party.

I retrieved our wedding album from a drawer and then I planted myself back on to the sofa. I lifted the album cover knowing all too well what I would see on the very first page. It wasn't a photo at all. It was a burgundy-coloured paper napkin stuffed down behind the cellophane that covered the page. On it, in fading biro, there was a picture of a stick man and a stick woman holding hands and with the aid of a speech bubble he was asking her to marry him. At some point Ashling had written the stick woman's response. The answer was an emphatic *YES!* in capital letters followed by an exclamation mark.

All of a sudden, gravity seemed to be turned up to ten and my body felt like it weighed about a thousand pounds. I sat absolutely still for an hour or two or three. Who the fuck knows? I was all too aware that no matter how many times the doorbell sounded or the phone rang, it would never be Ashling. She was never coming home.

I decided there and then that I didn't want any more visitors coming to the house. They distracted me from my grieving and they interfered with my drinking, so enough was enough. No more playing the patient host. I didn't consciously decide that I was going to live like a hermit but that's pretty much what happened after that. I closed myself up inside a shell in almost exactly the same way as I did after my father died, except at least then I had

Jack to keep me company. Now there was no one. I changed the phone message on my mobile to one which explained that I had taken a holiday to the west of Ireland in order to get my head together and that I would be back as soon as I was feeling better. Then I turned off my phone and threw it into one of the kitchen cupboards. I wasn't going anywhere, of course, but I was hoping that such a message might stop people bothering me every five minutes.

I felt as if all of those visitors had really taken it out of me because I found myself feeling almost constantly weary. It didn't occur to me at the time that lethargy is one of the classic symptoms of depression. Or maybe it did occur to me and I just didn't care. In any case, I pulled all the blinds, closed all the curtains, locked all the doors and disconnected the landline phone. I took off my watch and dropped it into the pedal bin in the kitchen. Time didn't matter anymore. Nothing mattered anymore. All I wanted to do was to lose myself in my memories of Ashling.

'Ya don't have to spend every second of every day grievin over Ashling because ya think it might somehow be disrespectful to her if ya were to think about somethin else.'

Jack's words were still bouncing around in my head like a laser in a hall of mirrors.

'Think about yourself for a change.'

He was right but he was wrong as well. I was thinking about myself. Whenever someone who knows you is lost, you lose a version of yourself. Those who know us make us what we are, and Ashling knew me better than anyone.

But now she was gone and my response was to retreat even

deeper into myself and into our drinks cabinet. I became a recluse inside my own home, refusing to take the chain off the door when I opened it and then, after a while, refusing to open it at all. I gave up showering and shaving altogether. What was the point? I wasn't going anywhere or planning on seeing anyone anytime soon. Besides, I just didn't have the energy. For the same reason, I didn't bother changing my clothes. I wore the same T-shirt, jeans, boxers and socks constantly, even in bed on the nights when I made it to bed.

Despite the voice message that I had left on my phone, at least once a day someone would repeatedly ring the doorbell and bang on the door and shout in my letterbox asking me was I all right and could I please open the door and saying that they only wanted to talk to me, to help me. When they went quiet, I knew it was only because they were outside the downstairs windows with their hands cupped to their eyes, trying to peer through a gap in the curtains. A couple of times, someone even jumped over the back wall and knocked on the kitchen window, but with all the curtains closed, I felt safe enough from detection. I let a collection of post build on the hall mat in an effort to give the impression that I had uprooted and left town for a while, but people still persisted in calling around. Inconsiderate considerate bastards giving me GBH of the ear hole. Why wouldn't they just let me fade out in peace?

When I was still alive after a few days of more or less non-stop drinking, I decided that I needed a little something to expedite the process and so I spent a good half an hour searching the house for any sort of prescription drugs that I could munch on while I poured vodka down my throat. All I could find was a couple of packets of contraceptive pills in Ashling's bedside locker and even though I did consider it for a second or two, they weren't what I was looking for.

'Fuck it,' I thought, resigning myself to the fact that I did not seem to be destined for a quick death. I was in quite considerable pain at that point because all of the vodka in my stomach combined with no food meant that my stomach was eating itself. I didn't care though. In fact, I almost welcomed the physical pain as it distracted me from the pain of my loss, which was also eating me alive.

Clutching a bottle of Smirnoff to my chest like a newborn babe, I went to go back downstairs. I stepped off the top step into thin air and then my other leg collapsed and I fell head over heels down the stairs. Ironically, the fact that I was so pissed probably saved my life because my body went limp during the fall and I rolled down the stairs like a beanbag. I didn't break a single bone. Unfortunately, though, the bottle in my hand broke underneath me on one of the stairs and I ended up stabbing myself in the chest. I was vaguely aware of a darting pain between my ribs but I didn't care.

Even after I had stopped moving at the bottom of the stairs, I kept on falling. Down and down, deeper and deeper into the black. I could have fought it. I know I could have. The light in the hall was right over my head as I lay there bleeding to death and I could have held on to it like a lighthouse in the storm, just to stay conscious for a little while longer. But it was late and I was tired. So very tired. My eyelids felt like they each weighed about a hundred pounds.

The light was fading. Everything was fading. I was at peace again. I was unconscious.

And not long after that, I died for the second time.

I wasn't in my body anymore. I was floating in a faraway place where the air felt incredibly thin, and yet strong enough to support my whole body. If I had a body anymore, that is. At some level, I was aware that my flesh-and-blood form was still lying in a crumpled mess at the foot of the stairs but another part of me had most definitely left the building. I was in a place that was so dark, I doubt whether the same uncontaminated pitch-blackness is even possible on earth. And yet I didn't feel anxious. All I felt was calm; a wonderful sense of calm that washed through me like a magic drug. I felt as if my whole life had been a nightmare package holiday in which everything possible had gone wrong, but now I was home again. Now I felt safe, truly safe, and I didn't need anything. I didn't need oxygen, I didn't need light, I didn't even need my body. I just needed to be.

And then I realised that I wasn't quite alone. I became aware that all around me, there were spirits or souls or whatever you want to call them. When I truly listened to the silence, I found that it wasn't quite the perfect peace that I had initially imagined it to be. There was a steady hum of voices at the bottom of the silence, but it was hard to make out at first because there was no variation in the pitch. It might just have been a ringing in my ears.

But then I could clearly make out a really bad Australian accent.

'Well, gidday, Charlene!' said a voice from behind me.

I turned around and Owen was standing there with his hands in his pockets, leaning against a huge oak tree that I recognised immediately. It was the tree that we had climbed a thousand times when we were kids playing in Rathgorman Cemetery. Owen looked exactly as I remembered but he looked different as well. There was a heightened clarity about him that reminded me of the way trees sometimes look just before a thunderstorm.

'Owen!' I said in a voice that was barely above a whisper.

'Look at you, huh!' he said. 'I leave ya alone for five minutes and suddenly you're all grown up.'

'Owen . . . is tha really you?'

'Course it's me. Don't ya recognise me? You're the one tha looks different.'

He was wearing his trademark big white runners and now he had a goofy grin on his face also.

'Sorry, Owen, this is all just very . . . weird, ya know?'

'Don't worry, ya get used to it after a while.'

'So how are ya?'

'Well, I'm dead! But hey, no biggie. I'm still doin a fuck of a lot better than you by the looks o things.'

'Whaddya mean?'

'You're cuttin off the head to cure the headache and tha's not good. Trust me, you'll be dead for long enough so don't throw away the time tha you've got just cos things got a bit fucked-up.'

He still had the body of a child but he seemed to have acquired a maturity way beyond his tender years.

'I know from where you're standin it prob'ly looks quite empty up here,' he continued, 'but there are gazillions o souls floatin about who would give anythin just to be able to walk on the earth again for an hour or two.'

'Wha's so great about walkin on the earth?'

'*What's so* . . . ? Holy mother! You must have knocked your head harder than I thought comin down those stairs. Do ya have any idea how borin omniscience gets after a while? I mean, I've practically given up watchin TV and I can't remember the last good film tha I saw or even the last decent conversation I had. Everythin is just so . . . predictable.'

'So wha do ya do?'

'People-watchin mostly. Even the dullest day in the life of the most borin trainspotter in the world is fascinatin to us cos o the element o chance.'

'Chance? But wha about omni— whatever?'

'It doesn't work in relation to people's futures cos all human beings are given the gift o free will.' Owen gave me a moment for this information to sink in and then he looked at me with raised eyebrows, probably expecting me to say something profound.

'So this whole afterlife thing is pretty overrated then, huh?'

'Oh, it's not so bad really once ya get used to it. In fact, it's wha we don't have up here that makes it kind o cool.'

'How d'ya mean?'

'Well, we don't have poverty or illness or sadness or any o those things. We don't even have death. Instead we have, and I know it sounds a bit corny, but we have love and tha's sort of enough really. The Beatles were right.'

'Holy shit! You've met John Lennon, haven't ya?'

'Dude, I've met *every*one.'

'Wha did Lennon say to ya?'

'He said "I wish I wasn't fuckin dead!" and tha's the point. Because *you* my friend, you get to make a difference. You get to change things and tha's wha's so great about walkin on the earth. Ashling had no idea how right she was when she told ya tha everyone changes the world on a daily basis just by bein in it, so don't go throwin in your cards before the game is over because I *know* tha ya can get through this.'

He flashed his goofy grin at me and suddenly he was a twelve-year-old kid again.

'And hey listen, don't feel bad about tha thing with the trolley cos as far as I'm concerned, it's all water under the canal bridge.'

He must have been reading my mind somehow. I felt as if my thoughts were being displayed on a neon sign in the place where my head used to be.

'But wha about all the things ya missed out on, ya know? Are ya gonna be twelve years old for the rest of eternity?'

'Fuck no!' he replied. 'I only look like this now cos this is how ya remember me. Time doesn't mean nothin up here. It's like a Dublin Bus timetable.'

I paused for a moment before speaking again.

'Owen, I never thought I'd say this, but are you an angel?'

'Do ya see any wings?'

'Well no, but ... is this Heaven?'

He laughed at this like I'd just said something hilarious.

'After wha I got up to as a kid, do ya think they'd let me into Heaven?'

'Then wha is this place?'

'It's not a place at all in the way tha you think about places. It's more like a state o mind.'

'Am I in my own mind? Is that it?'

'Not exactly but I don't have time to explain it to ya. Your brain is runnin out of oxygen down below, and so if ya stay here much longer, the door behind ya will close and ya won't be able to go back even if ya want to.'

'But I don't wanna go back.'

'But I want you to, Charlie,' said a new voice from behind me; the voice that I wanted to hear most of all.

I spun around and there she was, as beautiful as she had been on the day I first laid eyes on her.

'Ashling!' I said in a choked voice. I desperately wanted to hold her in my arms one more time but there was a slight problem with that because even though I could see her clearly, I couldn't see my own body and so I wasn't sure if I even had arms anymore.

'Owen's right, you know, you have to go back and you have to get on with your life.'

I completely ignored what she had just said and jumped straight to the bottom line.

'It was an accident Ash; you know it was an accident, righ? I did everythin tha I could to try and stop it happenin but I couldn't stop it. Everythin got all twisted around and I ended up makin it happen but only because I was tryin to save ya, and I tried so hard to save ya.'

'I know you did,' she said with a reassuring smile. 'But you couldn't have saved me. No one could have. It wasn't your fault.'

I would happily have walked into hell and stayed there for ever wearing petrol-soaked Y-fronts just to hear her say those words and now that she had said them, I felt as if a massive weight had been lifted off my soul.

'I miss you so much, Ashling. I don't wanna go back. Can't I stay here with you?'

'No, Charlie, it's not your time. You need to go back and you need to stop hurting yourself. When you stop struggling, you'll float to the surface.'

'But I have nothin to go back for.'

'Yes you do, believe me you do. You have a life and you have people who need you.'

'But what about what I need? I need you. Ya know tha, don't ya?'

'Go now, Charlie. There's not much time left.'

'Well if I can't stay then is there any way tha ya could come with me?'

'I'll always be with you, Charlie, you know that. Till the end of the world and beyond.'

Tears shot into my eyes and after I blinked them away, I found that I couldn't see her clearly anymore. She was still there but sort of out of focus. She was shimmering like a mirage. I turned around to look at Owen but there was nothing but deep black space behind me. I spun back around to look at Ashling but now she was gone also.

'ASHLING!' I shouted in a panic. I still had so many things that I wanted to say to her. I strained my ears for a clue as to her whereabouts but any voices that I might have heard were being drowned out by the sound of a siren that had suddenly filled the air and which was becoming louder and louder by the second. I could feel myself being pulled back into my body like a cartoon ghost being sucked up into a vacuum cleaner. Voices in the background began to filter through to my brain. They were voices that I didn't recognise and they sounded harsh and full of tension. The next sensation I became aware of was a sudden heaviness in my body as if my blood had turned to mercury and my bones to metal. My eyes opened and I could see that I was in a very different place to the one that I had just left. I was in an ambulance.

A bearded medic finished adjusting something on an oxygen cylinder and then he thrust a plastic oxygen mask over my face. Another ambulance man was standing by holding what I recognised from TV to be a defibrillator. I don't believe that I had started breathing again at that point even though I was conscious of what was going on around me. Various parts of my body seemed to be coming alive again at different times, one after another, and unfortunately my stomach seemed particularly anxious to announce its return to the land of the living. Without warning, my intestines did a back flip and suddenly the oxygen mask was full of vomit and I was choking. The ambulance men pulled the mask off immediately and turned me on to my side where I coughed up vodka and blood all over the floor of their nice clean ambulance.

'Welcome back,' said the man with the beard. 'Thought we'd lost ya there for a minute.'

IV
Zoe

There was no doubt about it, I was back. And for someone who has rarely ventured outside Dublin, I had become extraordinarily well travelled all of a sudden now that I was a veteran of not one but two round trips to the next life. In case you're wondering, by the way, it was thanks to my neighbour Tom that they found me at all. He heard me falling down the stairs and then he came knocking on my front door to investigate. When there was no answer, he looked through the letterbox and saw me lying at the foot of the stairs, and then he called an ambulance.

I'd like to be able to tell you that my most recent afterlife experience was like a huge injection of backbone that enabled me to stand up and start wading through the river of shit that I had been drowning in, but that simply wouldn't be true. It would probably be slightly more accurate to compare my latest outer body experience to a shot of heroin than to a shot of anything else because when the effects wore off, I found myself in the throes of what can only be likened to withdrawal symptoms. But even before I got to that stage, my body was in very bad shape indeed. When the ambulance men found me, they told me that my breathing had slowed to just five breaths per minute and for several minutes in the ambulance I had stopped breathing altogether. They'd had to shock me several times using the defibrillator before my heart started up again. My skin was clammy and deathly pale and I was diagnosed later as suffering from acute dehydration as well as hypothermia, both of which are apparently symptoms of alcohol poisoning. The stab wound that I inflicted upon myself with the broken bottle turned out to be a fairly minor injury compared to the damage that I could have done. They told me that I had ruptured my spleen but that was no big deal as far as I was concerned. I didn't even know that I had a spleen until I ruptured it and I found that I didn't much care either. I had other things on my mind.

My most recent visit to the next world had been such an intensely rich and beautiful experience that when I returned to my body, I was deeply traumatised. The doctors in the hospital attributed this to the shock of nearly dying but they could hardly be expected to know the truth. I didn't try and explain what I had seen to them. In fact I didn't utter a single word to anyone for several weeks after that. For the first forty-eight hours in the hospital, it would have been impossible anyway because there was a thick plastic tube attached to my mouth, similar to the ones fighter pilots use at high altitudes. And to make things even more awkward for me, I appeared to be tethered to the bed by an array of wires and suchlike that were attached to me from all angles. A hot-air balloon would have had fewer bindings than me. I know that I could simply have dropped my arm on the wires and the tubes, and my restraints would have given up their prisoner easily enough, but I honestly just didn't have the energy. I was feeling extremely weak after having eaten almost nothing during the previous ten days. There were electrodes attached to my chest by suction cups but they might as well have been chains tied around my rib cage for all the strength that I had at that point. It took just about all of my energy to manage to blink and even that hurt.

But then, in the most unlikely place, I discovered something beautiful and suddenly I was almost glad to be alive again. After my first visit to the afterlife when I was a kid, I was sure that I had brought back the gift of foresight and now I started to believe that after my most recent visit, I had somehow acquired X-ray vision. I hadn't, by the way, but I believed that I had because I found that if I stared and stared and stared at the blank wall opposite me, after a while I could make out a picture. It had been painted over with a horrible shade of pink that made me feel nauseous but I discovered that if I concentrated hard enough, then I could see right through the outer coat of paint to a mural underneath. I couldn't always see it but it was there all right and it was the most stunning painting that I've ever seen in my life. I just wanted to drink it in with my eyes with every second that I was awake because it was so beautiful.

It was a picture of a woman sitting on a low stone wall that overlooked a deserted white sandy beach and on the horizon a green ocean was clearly visible. The woman was wearing a white T-shirt and a red baseball cap. I couldn't see her face because she had her back to me but even from behind, I recognised her instantly. It was Ashling. Nobody else. I knew the contours of her body like the back of my hand. She had her hair tied up in a single dark brown plait that was threaded through the hole at the back of the baseball cap. I'd seen her wearing it like that when we went to Lanzarote. I recognised the hat too. I bought it for her. It said *beach babe* on the front and it had a picture of a cartoon woman in a bikini. She had bought me a blue and grey hat in return that said *Trust me, I'm Batman* on it. And even though I couldn't see her face, I could tell that she was sad. There was something missing from the picture and I thought that it might have been me.

And then one day while I was staring at the painting, I became aware of a distinctive smell in the room, one that was lurking amidst the sweet scent of dying flowers and the starchy, laundered smell of the sheets. After a moment, it came to me what it was. It was the smell of the ocean. And then while I was concentrating on the smell of saltwater, another of my sensory organs came back to life and suddenly I could not only smell the sea, but I could hear it as well. Very faint, but I could definitely hear it nonetheless. I focused even harder on the picture and I could see white foamy waves breaking on the shore. The picture was moving. It wasn't even a picture anymore, it was more like a vision. The whole wall had turned into a gigantic window overlooking the sea and it was so beautiful that it made me want to cry.

Without ever taking my eyes off the vision, I started to pull the suction cups from my chest, one by one, and then I pulled out my drip and the thing attached to my finger that checked my pulse. After that, I swung my legs over the side of the bed and then I tried to do a controlled fall on to the floor. It was controlled only in the sense that I chose the particular piece of floor that I fell on to and when the full weight of my body hit the tiles, white pain in its purest form shot through my nerve cells straight into my brain. Such was my concentration though that I only felt it for a second. I was still too weak to walk and so I started dragging myself along the ground towards the vision on my wall. I began crawling along on my belly like an early life-form slithering out of the sea.

I must have made quite a bit of noise because I could sense that Ashling had suddenly become aware of my presence. She started to turn around and I moved forward even quicker because I wanted to jump into the picture and sweep her into my arms. Once I was in the picture, all of my pain would be gone. She turned her face all the way around towards me before I reached the picture and at the same time I stopped dead in my tracks. I opened my mouth to scream but the only sound that came out was a tiny rasping noise that was barely audible. Ashling's beautiful brown eyes were no longer there, just gaping eye sockets that were leaking a horrible black fluid. She still had her nose and her mouth, but just barely. Rags of skin hung from a filthy yellow skull and the few remaining pockets of flesh were covered with maggots. Eventually I did manage to find my voice and then a blood-curdling scream escaped from me. And then another, and then another. When they finally got to me with the sedatives, I was curled into a ball on the floor and sobbing hysterically.

Two weeks later when I was physically well enough to leave the hospital, I was committed to St Augustine's Hospital for the mentally ill, the last stop on the loony express.

I don't know who signed what to put me in the loony bin and I don't want to know. The cold, hard truth is that it was probably the right place for me to be and because at some level I knew this to be the case, I didn't fight it. In fact, for the first few weeks I was so completely doped out of my mind on painkillers and sleeping tablets and chill pills that I did everything that was asked of me like a little lamb. In some ways it was like a holiday from myself. Not the kind of holiday that you're likely to find advertised in the window of Budget Travel, mind you, but it was what I needed at the time.

On my first day at St Augustine's, I vaguely remember somebody holding one of my arms and helping me to walk through the reception area and I have a hazy memory also of somebody giving me a welcome-to-the-loony-bin speech, except all that I heard was blah, blah, blah, blah, blah. My new room wasn't too bad even though I had to share it with someone. Seven years working in Happy's had prepared me well for the nut house but still I couldn't help noticing that my roommate had mittens taped to his hands. On that first day, I just lay on my bed with my back to him and closed my eyes. He didn't need me for conversation because he talked away to himself, or rather he screeched a lot and tried to tear spiders off his face. Hence the mittens. He would have fitted right in at Happy's on a Saturday night.

I still wasn't talking at that point, by the way. I felt that there was absolutely nothing that anyone could say to me that would make me feel any better and there was nothing that I could say to anyone to make them understand what had happened to me, and so I just decided to give up speaking altogether. The doctors who came around to chat to me seemed to regard my silence as conclusive proof that I was bonkers but I didn't care. I just ignored them and stared at the wall. I didn't see any more moving visions, incidentally. They have a tablet that cures that sort of thing, sort of like the opposite of LSD.

During the latter half of my stay at St Augustine's, the medication that I was on was gradually scaled down but while I was still on the full dosage my mind was always more lucid in the mornings because the effects of my last dose of tablets would have worn off during the night. On my first morning in the place, I looked around and tried to take in my surroundings. The sheets on my bed had been laundered so many times that they had turned from white to a weary grey and they felt abrasive and stiff. There was a window on the far side of the room that had an iron grille fixed to the outside of it. I could see dust mites floating inside cold sunrays that had penetrated the grille and I wondered how so much dust could accumulate in a place that smelled so sterile. But it really wasn't so bad.

One thing that pissed me off me though was the fact that the powers that be had placed me on suicide watch. I couldn't even take a dump without some nurse standing outside the door listening for God knows what. Maybe they thought that I was going to drown myself in the cistern. If I wanted to write anything down then I could only do so using crayons and I was forced to wear regulation loony-bin slippers as anything with shoelaces was a definite no-no. I was also denied a belt, the drawstring in my pyjama bottoms and even dental floss. It's because of this that one of my most vivid memories of the nut house consists of me shuffling along interminable corridors while trying desperately to hang on to my trousers.

At medication time, someone would come around with a

trolley full of drugs and hand me three tablets in a paper cup. I called it my happy meal as it consisted of a chill-out drug called Zercon, an anti-depressant called Xanax and a mystery tablet that was shaped like a little pink rugby ball. Everybody seemed to receive this particular tablet but I have no idea what it was for. Nobody had a clue what any of the drugs were for really. They all had names that sounded like characters from *Star Trek* but I knocked them back without a second thought. The demons inside my head were definitely toned down a couple of notches during my stay at the funny farm but I can't say with any certainty that that was because of anything that came in pill form.

Jack came to visit me almost every day. There was a recreation room with a TV and armchairs in it but neither of us wanted to spend any time there. It was full of crazy people. Instead Jack would usually hang around my room and read to me. I think he was getting his own back for all the times that I had read aloud to him when he was a little kid. In any case, he got me speaking again and I suppose I owe him one for that. One day he showed up with a copy of *The Butcher Boy* by Patrick McCabe. That's a story about a guy in a small village who slowly goes completely insane. I know that that might sound somewhat inappropriate in the circumstances but you would have to know Jack to appreciate his weird sense of humour. He started reading it aloud to me but halfway through the first chapter he broke down in tears.

'Jesus,' I said. 'Pull yourself together, man! It's not tha sad.'

His sobbing ended abruptly and he stared at me for a second as if I was part of the furniture that had suddenly come alive.

'You're talkin!' he said.

'Eh . . . yeah,' I replied.

'Does this mean tha you're better?'

'Better than what?'

'Better as in . . . well again.'

'I know wha ya mean; I'm just rippin the piss outta ya. Ya looked so miserable tha I couldn't help it.'

At that point he whacked me across the head with the book and frankly I don't blame him. But I was talking again and that was a huge step forward for me.

There were drawbacks though that accompanied my return to the speaking world and the most unfortunate one was that I was made to attend twice-weekly sessions with an in-house shrink called Dr R. Moroney MB BCH BAO DPM MRCPsych PhD. On his desk, he had a triangular block of wood with a brass nameplate attached to it and he had each and every one of those letters etched into the metal under his name. I was suspicious of him straight away, not because he was so obviously over-educated but because he felt the need to advertise this fact.

'What's up, Doc?' I said to him upon entering his office for the first time. With the return of my voice, my cockiness wasn't far behind it. The first thing that caught my attention was a life-sized human skeleton dangling from a steel holder in the corner and grinning away as if death was great fun. The doctor in contrast looked like Humpty Dumpty in a pinstriped suit. I could feel him looking me up and down while his brain tried to work out the correct textbook hole to slot me into. He had eyes like bullet holes and rectangular-shaped glasses that he never actually seemed to look through. Instead he lowered his head and peered out at me over the frames.

'Ah yes, come in, come in,' he said to me in a jovial tone that fitted him no better than his awful suit. 'Come in and sit down. I've just been reading your file. Very interesting.'

'Thanks,' I said, trying hard to override my instincts and to give him the benefit of the doubt. I sat down in a black leather chair that the good doctor had indicated was for me. It was a great chair, no doubt about it; very comfortable. Only problem was that when Dr Moron sat down opposite me, he appeared to be sitting on some sort of high stool because suddenly I had to tilt my head back just to look at him.

'So, are you settling in all right at St Augustine's?' he asked. 'Everything to your liking, I hope?'

'Eh yeah, sure, everythin's fine, Doc.'

I have always addressed doctors as 'Doc', one of my multitude of bad habits. I was hardly even conscious that I was doing it until I noticed that my interrogator appeared slightly irritated all of a sudden. He started to make a noise when he breathed that made him sound like some sort of pervert.

For a few seconds, I was a teenager again. The same insolent little fucker who had driven Doreen almost to distraction by correcting her grammar at every opportunity and the same insolent little fucker who had pushed Turkeyman over the edge with my smart mouth. I was confident that I could talk Dr Moron into such knots that he would no longer know whether he was the psychiatrist or the patient, and as tempting as it was to mess with his head, I decided not to. I knew that the smart thing to do would be to give that useless fucker only straight answers just so that I could get the hell out of there as soon as possible.

He asked me why I thought I had been admitted to St Augustine's and I told him straight up that I had killed my reason for living.

'And how do you feel about that?' he replied without missing a beat.

I felt a lot of things about that, but at that particular moment, I felt as if beating him over the head with his vainglorious name-plate would be of great therapeutic value to me. I didn't. Instead I calmly spouted a load of rubbish about how at first I was devastated, but that since arriving at St Augustine's I had realised that life must go on, and so I was going to try and make the best of my situation. He was only warming up though. He was convinced that I had *unresolved issues* and so he went on to ask me questions such as was I angry with my mother for having died while I was still so young, and was I angry with Ashling for being in the wrong place at the wrong time. He was very big on anger. But I think I displayed exemplary anger management skills by restraining myself from putting him through the window. I was only able to do this by engaging the same technique that I had used when that lunatic judge sent me away for a year. I sent ninety per cent of my mind away to a completely different place, leaving the remaining ten per cent to talk crap with the good doctor. My shrink probably just assumed that it was my medication that gave me such a sleepy look but the reality is that I had effectively hypnotised myself.

As well as my sessions with Dr Moron, I was also assigned to an addiction counsellor but my meetings with her were completely different. Her name was Lisa Brophy and she had a soft cheerful voice and amazing green eyes that sometimes contained hazel-coloured flecks, depending on the light in the room. I'm not sure what we were supposed to be talking about during the course of our sessions but I was always thinking about Ashling and so she was all that I wanted to talk about. Maybe she was my addiction and not alcohol. In any case, Lisa seemed more than happy to just let me ramble on and on about how great my wife was and how much I missed her.

I told Lisa about how Ashling loved the smell of my aftershave balm. I don't know whether she liked it because it smelled nice or because it reminded her of me, but I do know that sometimes when I was gone out, she would rub my aftershave over her own face.

I told Lisa about how Ashling used to give emotions and person-alities to inanimate objects. She wouldn't put teddy bears in plastic bags in case they suffocated. I loved that about her. I also loved the fact that she loved to read children's books. She had a load of them and her favourite was *The Little Prince*. We had talked about having kids and we had decided to wait for a year or two because we figured that we had lots of time.

I told Lisa about the time when Ashling and I were flying to Lanzarote and I asked my wife if she'd like to join the mile-high club. She didn't know what that was so I told her that it was an on-board duty-free service that offered extra-cheap deals. The next time the air hostess passed down the aisle, Ashling stopped her and asked if she had any magazines showing what the mile-high club had to offer. The dawning realisation on my wife's face that I had been winding her up was worth the cost of the holiday alone. I loved teasing her like that because I knew that she would pay me back with interest. And usually she would wait until I least expected it before exacting a playful revenge. She wouldn't forget though, that was for sure. She used to collect memories the way other people collect coins. She never forgot a face or a date, and she could remember conversations that she'd had in her childhood.

As the weeks slipped by, Lisa and I became firm friends and I began to share even more personal stuff with her. I told her about how in the weeks after Ashling's death, I had not been able to sleep at night until I rolled up a pillow like a Swiss roll and then stuck the edge of it under my ribcage so that it felt like Ashling was sticking her elbow into me. Lisa said that this reminded her of a puppy that she'd had as a child. The dog had cried all the time until her father had wrapped an old wind-up alarm clock in a T-shirt and then placed this in the basket beside the animal. The ticking of the clock sounded like its mother's heartbeat, and only then would the puppy go to sleep.

I also told her about something that happened ten days or so after the accident. Before I started buying my groceries online, I was in the off-licence section of Tesco's one day when I noticed an old lady who smelled exactly like Ashling. I don't mean she was wearing the same make-up or perfume or anything like that; I mean she smelled *exactly* like Ashling. I tapped her on the shoulder and told her that she smelled exactly like my late wife and then I asked her if she would mind if I gave her a hug. Surprisingly, the old lady didn't swing her shopping basket at my head and go running off down the aisle screaming that a madman was trying to molest her. Instead she simply placed her basket on the floor without saying a word and then beckoned me into her arms. I held her and held her until the tears were streaming down my face. I had wanted to spend the rest of my life with Ashling and it occurred to me that this is what it might have felt like if we had grown old together. When I eventually let go, the old lady was crying too. But she never uttered a single word to me. She just turned around and walked away and I never saw her again after that.

Experience has taught me that what you love, you should love all the harder because someday it will be gone. And yet it was loving Ashling too much that had driven me to the brink of madness and it was only by letting her go that I would become well again. But I wasn't sure if I could let her go. Lisa told me that I had to forgive myself but I said that I would leave it to God to forgive me; that's His business.

Jack drove me home from St Augustine's on a beautiful autumn evening. As he turned the key in my front door, I could feel a frosty apprehension in my stomach because I had no idea what was waiting for me inside. I half expected the house to be overrun with roaches after the state in which I had left the place before I went to hospital. But I need not have worried. Jack and Fiona and some of my old mates had rallied together and done a major clean-up. As soon as I stepped into the hall, I could smell fresh paint and I realised that the inside of the house had been repainted and it looked fantastic. It looked better than it did on the day that I had moved into the place. I walked into the living room and the first thing that I noticed was that the portable TV that Ashling and I had got as a wedding present was gone. In its place stood the biggest widescreen TV that I have ever seen in my life.

'A present from the lads,' said Jack when he saw my jaw hit the floor. 'We had a bit of a whiparound at Happy's and we thought ya might like this,' he said, gesturing towards the giant TV screen.

'Oh man, I don't believe this. This is just . . . wow! This must have cost a fortune.'

'Not at all,' said my brother. 'We got it off Benny Binchy for next to nothin. He said tha he found it abandoned in the car park at Powercity.'

'You're jokin?'

'Course I'm bleedin jokin. I wouldn't buy an electric toothbrush off Benny Binchy. It's all bought and paid for. I even have a receipt.'

'Thanks, Jack. I love it.'

'Fiona wanted to have a surprise party for ya when ya got home but we weren't sure if you'd be feelin up to it.'

'No, this is great, honestly. Too much in fact.'

'Damo and Gerry and the rest o them really wanted to be here so they could welcome ya back in person but now tha you're officially a crazy man, I think they were worried tha ya might chop them up with an axe or somethin just cos ya didn't like the colour o the walls.'

'Where is my axe, by the way? I've really missed it.'

'Wha?'

'Relax! I'm only messin with ya. I'm totally blown away here. This is the nicest thing tha anyone has done for me since, since . . .'

'Ah now, don't start fillin up on me,' said Jack. 'It's only a coat o paint and a telly.'

'It's a fuck of a lot more than tha and don't think tha I don't appreciate it cos this is somethin tha I definitely won't forget in a hurry.'

'Don't even mention it, bro; we're just glad to have ya back.'

'Cheers,' I said. 'Now let's go to Happy's and get totally fucked. I haven't had a proper drink in ages and I've a vodka thirst on me tha ya would not believe.'

I saw a look of horror pass over his face and the sadistic part of my brain got a big kick out of his discomfort.

'Well, eh, the thing is, I don't really think that ya should . . .'

'Ahhhhh . . . *gotcha*!'

'Well duh! I knew ya were only messin,' he lied.

'Jackie, my man, this is the new improved me and from now on nothin stronger than black coffee is gonna pass these lips.'

'Really?'

'Yeah, of course, really.'

'Not even bad language?'

'Fuck tha!' I replied and we both laughed.

My brother stayed around for an hour or so and I made us both some coffee. After he had said his goodbyes and left, I suddenly found myself alone again after spending months under the constant watch of medical personnel. It felt strange and I wasn't sure if I liked it or not. I turned on my new TV and watched half an episode of a kids' show called *Dawson's Creek*. It was about a sanctimonious kid named Dawson who was trying to shag a cute brunette named Joey. Joey is a girl, by the way, and Dawson is a boy. Eventually he got her in the sack but then he started banging on about how sacred his virginity was. The whole thing was like a big pile of putrid vomit. I felt like I needed a drink to restore the calm in my head and so, just out of idle curiosity, I got up and went into the kitchen where I opened all of the cupboards looking for a bottle of something. I kept telling myself that I was just checking to see what was there. I was on the wagon again after all and so I wasn't actually going to have a drink. I was just checking to see what was there.

I couldn't find any booze in the house so I made myself a water on the rocks instead. I went back into the living room and turned on the TV again. Not only had I now got the coolest TV in the world but Jack and the lads had hooked me up to a digital cable provider, which I'd never had before. I flicked through all my new channels before settling on some sort of awards show on a music channel. I think it might have been the Grammys and I only paused because U2 were on the screen. An award was about to be presented for Best Album. The nominees were read out and then some model in a long silver dress announced U2 as the winners. One of the losing nominees was a rap star who I had never even heard of. When the winners were announced and his name wasn't read out, he didn't even disguise how pissed off he was. He was sitting with some babe and the sentiment on her face wasn't disappointment; it was fear. She probably expected a beating from her famous boyfriend when they got home.

Then the all-conquering Irish foursome took to the stage to play a live set.

'This song is about letting go of someone that you don't really want to let go of. This is 'Kite',' said Bono and then the hauntingly beautiful opening bars of the song filled my living room. A minute later I could feel the tears streaming down my face. I wanted to watch the performance but I also didn't want to watch it because it was just so damn painful for me. I compromised and pressed the mute button. The only sound in the room after that was the sound of ice cubes knocking against the side of my glass as my hand trembled. It sounded like very gentle wind chimes. But God, how I wanted a drink at that point; a real drink. I concentrated on the silent performance as hard as I could. I was trying to lose myself in the tiny detail of the visuals in an effort to distract myself.

And then, just for a second, Ashling was there. She was in the room with me; I'm sure of it. She was sitting beside me on the couch. Nobody was touching me but I felt myself being held.

'Ashling ...' I whispered, but she was gone. She had already returned to wherever it was she had come from.

When I went into my bedroom later that evening, I didn't turn on any lights and instead I went straight to the window. It's not often that the stars make themselves visible over a big city but that night the sky looked as if it had been sprinkled with diamond dust, truly a sight to behold. I don't know much about astronomy but I saw a TV programme once which suggested that all matter came about as a result of exploding stars, and if that's true then I suppose it's equally true to say that everything is basically composed of stardust. We used to be stars and so just maybe we somehow go back to being stars after we shuffle off this mortal coil. The atoms that compose the human body are indestructible so they have to go somewhere when we die. It didn't seem all that hard to believe that Ashling was up there right at that moment, a light in the sky for all the world to see. There was a certain amount of solace in that thought and for the first time since losing my wife, I felt a flicker of peace in my soul.

It was good to be back in the so-called sane world although a part of me missed the sheer predictability of life inside a big institution. Life inside prison or life inside the loony bin feels like living inside a time capsule. You're aware that beyond the outer walls people are laughing and falling in love and getting married and doing all of those things that people do, but when you're incarcerated, no one really does anything apart from grow old and that happens so slowly that you don't even notice it. And when they finally set you free, you walk out the gates and you know that you haven't changed but everyone and everything else has. Even if only by an infinitesimally small amount, the world has evolved and you missed it, and that's what makes coming out so scary. It's not the same world as it was when you went in.

The real world can be quite a scary place at the best of times but it's even worse when you're on your own and if I've learned anything at all from my previous experiences, it's that I'm not a good candidate to be left on my own. On the two previous occasions when I found myself in such a situation, I almost cracked up and then I did crack up. After my spell at St Augustine's, I was very much aware that I needed to keep myself busy so that I wouldn't start thinking about stuff too much. I had to fill the time somehow, seeing as time was all I had left.

And so I decided to try to get my old job back at Happy's because even though I moaned about the place quite a lot, it was full of people who knew me and that seemed important all of a sudden. An equally important consideration for me was the fact that I needed a reason to get out of bed. I've always been a stubborn fucker but when I think about it now, that determination to get myself out of bed is probably my single greatest act of stubbornness. There can surely be no greater act of defiance than getting out of bed in the morning and telling yourself that you can do it, when deep down you don't really believe it.

It did cross my mind that in going back to Happy's, there was an element of moving from one asylum to another but I didn't care. I just needed to feel useful again. So I walked in and asked Roger for my job back. He said that he had taken on someone to replace me but seeing as Christmas was fast approaching, I could start back doing weekends again and build on that. Deep, deep, deep down, he's really one of the good guys.

Sometime during that first month after I left the funny farm, I got a postcard from Lisa Brophy that was so great it almost made me cry. On the front of the postcard there was a picture of a Labrador puppy in a wicker basket and beside the dog, she had drawn a picture of an old-fashioned alarm clock. But it was the message that she wrote on the back that really struck a chord with me. The instructions at the top said READ ALOUD EVERY MORNING and below that she had written: *There is beauty here, and peace. I will turn my*

*attention to the next breath, the next meal, the next laugh, the next pain,
and I will go on. I'm going to breathe in, and then I'm going to breathe
out, and then I'm going to do it again, and then I'm going to do it again.
There is still beauty in the world and it's okay to smile. It's a beautiful
day.*

I stuck the postcard to the fridge with a magnet and I re-read
it constantly.

The ghost of Ashling was everywhere in the house and everything reminded me of her. Sometimes I thought that I could smell
a trace of her perfume in the air as if she had just left the room,
and other times I would reach over in the night to pull her close
and find myself grasping thin air. All of the things that had belonged
to her now seemed colourless and lost because they were no longer
touched by her spirit and so I gave them all away. It didn't make
things any easier though. The house just felt even more empty and
echoey so I visited an estate agent's in Rathgorman Village and a
few days after that, 22 Sullivan Street was on the market.

When my estate agent phoned to say that there had been an
offer on the house, I told him that I'd take it before I'd even heard
what it was. I didn't care. He said that it wasn't a great offer and
that it was from a young married couple that were looking for their
first home. I told him to sell it to them and pass on my best wishes.
I hoped they'd have better luck in the place than I did. By that
stage, I just wanted out of there. I got in touch with a solicitor who
finalised the sale and then presented me with a big fat cheque. Even
after a chunk had been taken out to redeem my mortgage and
another chunk to pay the auctioneer and the solicitor, I was left
with a hefty sum. Over two hundred grand in fact. The property

market had gone through the roof since Ashling and I had placed our deposit on the house three years or so earlier. But the truth is, it may as well have been a cheque for two hundred euro for all the difference that it made to me. I didn't need the money and I didn't particularly want it either. My happiest memories all seemed to coincide with times when I was broke – playing Chain Gang in the dead fields of Rathgorman Cemetery with Owen and Andy and Deano and Robbie, or bunking off school and spending my days in the company of Mrs Horricks and all the books inside Rathgorman library. Or sometimes in the early part of our relationship, Ashling and I would search for money in the pockets of old clothes or down the back of the sofa and then we would send out for pizza and have a little feast in front of the TV. It wasn't much but at the same time it was everything.

I didn't put any thought into where I was going to live after the sale of my house. My priority had simply been to get out of there because it was too painful for me to stay. And so I only have myself to blame really for where I ended up living. But I don't blame myself; I blame Silky Mannix. I knew Silky because he drank in Happy's and because he is a cousin of Norman Valentine. Physically, however, they couldn't be more different. Whereas Norman is tall and blond and has eyes the same shade of blue as a pure gas flame, his cousin is about five-foot-four, bald on top, and has the eyes of a dead pig.

I bumped into Silky one day on the street and he offered to rent me a place saying that he'd heard I was almost homeless. I asked him what he had in mind and he launched into a sales pitch for a house which he said was only a few minutes' walk away from

Rathgorman Village. He went on and on about how great this place was and I told him that I'd take it just to shut him up. I know that it probably sounds idiotic to agree to live somewhere without seeing the place first, but it was convenient and I'm lazy and it was supposed to be only a temporary arrangement while I sorted myself out.

Damo helped me to move out. We filled at least ten black plastic bags full of rubbish which we then dumped in a builder's skip that was parked outside a neighbour's house five doors down. We packed the rest of my crap into the back of a van that Damo had borrowed from someone. I was only moving about a mile up the road and it took just three trips to ferry everything from one place to the next. My plan had originally been to take my new TV and a few clothes and photos and then burn the rest in a bonfire in the back garden. But when I suggested this to Damo, he told me not to be a dozy cunt all my life and then he started packing away my stuff himself. So I had to give him a hand.

After dropping off the final load at my new place, the pair of us hit a local pub (*not* Happy's!) for a well-deserved drink.

'Wha's this?' said Damo after I came back from the bar carrying a Guinness for him and a coke for me. He was gesturing towards the soft drink in my hand.

'Doctor's orders,' I said.

'Oh righ, yeah, cheers!'

He was embarrassed for having asked even though I wasn't embarrassed at all. I just wanted to be treated the same as ever.

'To absent friends,' I said, raising my coke in a cheers gesture.

'To absent friends,' said Damo, 'and happy endings.'

He downed almost half of his pint in a single gulp and then wiped his mouth with the back of his hand. The creamy part of his Guinness stuck to the glass almost all the way around, a sure sign of a great pint. I could hardly take my eyes off it.

'So when are ya startin back at the madhouse?' he asked.

'Wha?' I said, thinking that he was referring to St Augustine's.

'Happy's. When are ya startin back?'

'Oh, next Friday.'

'Well it'll be great to have ya back,' he said. 'Place hasn't been the same since ya left.'

He brought me up to date with what had been happening with most of the Happy's regulars and, unsurprisingly, nothing at all was what had been happening with most of them. The big news was that DJ Derek had been stabbed one Tuesday night on his way home after his weekly chamber of horrors gig. His injury wasn't life threatening but Roger still pulled the plug on the Tuesday night freak show which had been long past its sell-by date in any case.

But that wasn't what Damo wanted to talk about. Since we had sat down, I could tell that he had something on his mind. Whenever he is distracted, his brow furrows slightly during pauses in conversation, making him more readable than any book and a terrible poker player.

'Wha's on your mind?' I asked him after we had been chatting for a while.

'Wha?'

'Apart from pints and women, obviously, wha's on your mind? I know there's somethin so ya might as well just spit it out.'

He paused for a few seconds before replying.

'Well, there is somethin that I should prob'ly tell ya about tha I don't think ya realise.'

'Yeah?'

'The thing is, righ, ya won't like it, but you're gonna find out prob'ly sooner rather than later anyway, so I might as well tell ya.'

'Go on,' I said.

'Well, it's about your new gaff.'

'Yeaaaaah?' I said. 'Wha's wrong with it?'

'Well it's not so much the place itself, I mean, the place itself is fine, cosy an all, and near to work which is, ya know, handy like. The problem is, eh, well, have ya met your next door neighbour yet?'

'Oh fuck! Who is it? Tell me!'

'Well, eh, it's not Ned Flanders, let me put it like tha. It's definitely not Ned Flanders.'

'So who the fuck is it then?'

'Norman Valentine.'

'You're jokin me?'

'Nope.'

'ARGHHHHHHHAAAAAAHH! Fuck, Fuck, *FUCK*!'

The coke in my glass went sloshing over the side and on to my trousers.

Damo started to giggle and I threw him a dagger look. Or at least I thought it was a dagger look but whatever look was on my face, he seemed to find it hilarious. Laughter exploded out of him while he held one hand to his mouth in an effort to keep it in.

'You're jokin, righ? Tell me you're jokin.'

Damo just shook his head because he was now laughing so hard that his shoulders were bouncing up and down and he was temporarily incapable of speech.

'This is just too fuckin much,' I said, holding my head in my hands. 'I mean, fuckin hell! I don't deserve this.'

'No one deserves to live next to tha bleedin psycho,' said Damo, temporarily getting the better of his laughing fit.

'Why the fuck didn't ya tell me before? It's a bit fuckin late now to be tellin me!'

'I didn't even know meself until five minutes ago. Roger called me when ya were up at the bar and he told me tha Silky is sayin tha the other half o your gaff is rented out to Norman.'

'So wha am I gonna do?'

'Maybe ya could bake him a cake and call around with it,' said Damo and then he was off again in another fit of laughing that nearly resulted in him choking.

Technically speaking, Norman and I were actually living in the same house, which was really just Silky's old house. Silky bought an even bigger house for himself and his wife and their three offensively ugly children and then he rented out his old house as two separate homes. And how did he do that? Nothing to it really. He put in another front door on my side of the place and then he lashed up a few papier-mâché partitions and hey presto, one became two. I know that he must have been in breach of every building, fire and leasing regulation in existence and I really should have told him to stick his poxy little doll's house up his hole, but I found a reason to stay there and it was a good reason.

I moved in on a Sunday and all I wanted for my first night in the new place was a long soak in the tub to try and wash away the more recent layers of crap that had come my way. But I knew that an hour or two in the bath just wasn't going to be enough. Sometimes the grime has a way of getting under your skin. I fell asleep with a facecloth over my eyes and I have no idea how much time passed before I awoke, but when I did the water was cold. It was the voices coming through the wall that woke me. I took the facecloth from my eyes and I sat up in the bath, listening intently. Norman and his wife were fighting. I could hear both voices clearly but I couldn't picture his wife because I had never seen her. On that first night though, I had no problem hearing her cry out as Norman beat the living shit out of her.

I didn't hear how the argument started but it was blatantly obvious that Norman was going to finish it. On the other side of the partition that separated his home from mine, he sounded as if he was trying to kill a particularly nimble fly with a golf club. He started on his wife with what sounded like a few slaps before moving on to his fists, and all because she, being a 'useless fuckin cunt', couldn't get it into her thick skull how much he had done to provide for her and their kid. Accusations flew. She'd looked at some man the wrong way; she'd invited some man to look at her the wrong way; she'd signalled to some man with her eyes that she was a dirty bitch who would drop her knickers anytime, anywhere.

As Norman's rampage gathered momentum, I suddenly remembered the knife that he carried everywhere with him and I began to have genuine fears that his wife was about to get stabbed. I got up and dialled 999 from the landline in the hall, and if you're wondering why I even hesitated, well that's because around here, phone calls like that can get you killed quicker than you can say supergrass. But fuck it, I made the call anyway. I phoned 999 and when the operator asked me which emergency service I required, I asked for the fire brigade. I didn't ask for the cops because I knew they wouldn't come, or if they did it wouldn't be for a long time. If I had been living in some posh Southside suburb then they would have been on their way before I'd even put the phone down. But it didn't work that way in Rathgorman. And besides, once the cops realised that the domestic dispute was at Norman's address, they would have taken even longer to arrive. That's because if Norman killed his wife then they could lock him up for it and there would be two less Valentines in circulation, making the world a better place in their eyes.

And so I requested the fire brigade and gave Norman's address saying that there was smoke pouring out from under the front door. The operator asked for my name and I told him 'Mannix', as in Silky. He asked me for my first name but I had no idea what Silky's real name was. I tried to think of any first name but my brain refused to work quickly under pressure and I drew a blank. I pretended to have a bit of a coughing fit while I thought. Now of course I can think of a thousand male names in the blink of an eye but that's always the way. I knew that Silky's wife's first name was Gloria and my mind wouldn't let go of this so I told the operator that my first name was 'Glorious'. To their credit and to my amazement, five minutes later, the big red truck came flying up the street with sirens blaring.

I don't know whether these particular firemen had been starved of a genuine emergency for a very long time but they seemed to be mad keen for a bit of action even though a blind man could tell that my neighbour's house wasn't on fire. Two of them jumped out of the truck and started hammering on Norman's front door. They were wearing black oilskins with silver luminous stripes, and yellow helmets. I'm not sure why exactly, but they didn't look like the real thing to me. They looked like they might be actors or stripograms or giant Lego men come to life. But the shiny red truck with the big ladder on top looked almost too real.

One of the firemen who approached Norman's door was exceptionally tall whereas his colleague was definitely smaller than average. The tall one rang my neighbour's bell and hammered on the door with his hand and when no one rushed to open up, he started banging on the door with what sounded like a hammer or the back of an axe-head. There was still no response from within. I could hear Norman breaking things in his kitchen so it's quite possible that he didn't even notice the knock on his front door. Or maybe he just didn't care. In any case, the two firemen definitely heard the commotion in Norman's kitchen because the tall one escalated his hammering until it could be heard halfway down the road. Meanwhile his diminutive colleague started shouting through the letterbox: 'Are ya all right in there? Can ya come to the door or will we break it down?'

What the firemen clearly didn't appreciate was that Norman regards his property, including his women, as an extension of himself, and only a very brave or very foolish man would interfere, or threaten to interfere, with anything belonging to my psycho neighbour. But the firemen didn't know this and now one of them had well and truly lit Norman's fuse by threatening to break down the door. The clatter of breakages in the kitchen came to an abrupt halt and then I heard Norman stomping towards the front of his house. He tore open his front door and there was silence for a few seconds while each party sized up the other. Norman spoke first.

'Who did tha?' he said.

From my position at my living room window, I couldn't see the whole scene but if I had to guess, I would say that the banging on the door had damaged the paintwork or maybe even knocked a few splinters loose and that was probably what Norman was referring to.

'I had to give the door a good hard knock seein as there was no one answerin,' said the taller of the two firemen, sounding a lot less confident all of a sudden. Norman responded by head-butting him, whereupon the man dropped to the ground and stayed there clutching his face and groaning. The remaining fireman didn't take advantage of his height in order to use Norman's testicles as a punch bag. Instead he abandoned his wounded colleague and ran back to the truck. Seconds later, a brigade of firemen emerged from the truck and started descending upon my neighbour's house. Norman didn't seem at all worried by this development; in fact he seemed to be thoroughly enjoying himself. He walked halfway down his front path to meet the approaching troop and then he produced a knife from somewhere under his shirt like an evil magician.

'Do ya want some o this? Do ya? Come on, I'll take yiz all on ya bunch o fuckin faggots!' he said, stopping the approaching firemen in their tracks.

'Call the guards,' shouted one fireman to the driver who had stayed in the truck and then they all staged a tactical retreat, which was a very wise move because Norman was clearly high as a motherfucker and liable to do anything.

'Get back in your little red truck and get the fuck outta here,' he roared and then he went to go back inside. But the fireman who had been headbutted was still stranded on the doorstep, cut off from his comrades. At that point, he seemed to be trying to crawl towards the gate, doing a fair impression of Big Mickey in the process. But whereas Big Mickey might have got a pat on the head, all the fireman got was a good solid kick in the midriff from Norman's boot.

'Tha's for bleedin on my property, ya prick, ya,' said Norman and then he went inside and slammed his front door.

Five minutes later the cops arrived. A minute after that, an ambulance came screaming to a halt outside my house. And a minute after that, another cop car pulled up outside. With two cop cars, an ambulance and a fire engine outside, the street was starting to resemble a war zone. The injured fireman was loaded into the ambulance and Norman was dragged into a police car by three burly cops. Another copper came knocking on my front door and asked me whether I had witnessed the incident in which a member of the Dublin Fire Brigade had been violently assaulted. I told him that I had just woken up and hadn't seen a thing.

If only that were true. If only.

My first shift back behind the bar was hard, but the anticipation of going back turned out to be far worse than the act itself. I got through that first night somehow and it did get a lot easier after that. Most of the punters in the bar seemed afraid to talk to me because they didn't think that they could mention Ashling or the loony bin and that was all that was on their minds when they looked at me. They would tell me that it was good to see me back and that I was looking well and then quickly throw in an order for pints. I knew that it was bullshit when they said that I was looking well because I had never fully regained the weight that I lost in the weeks following my wife's death. But harmless platitudes didn't bother me. Bernie, on the other hand, did bother me.

Bernie was a Happy's regular and a part-time drug dealer on the side. He was the one who supplied Norman and his crew with all kinds of illegal substances. While I was serving him at the bar, he said that he was sorry to hear about my recent loss but then he went and ruined it by saying that it's great when people close to you die because you can behave like a fucking asshole and still get loads of sympathy. I tried to pretend to myself that he hadn't really said that and not to let him get to me but it wasn't easy. I filled my mind with thoughts of Ashling to help me get through the night. I kept thinking about how she would have wanted me to be strong and to carry on with my life. 'I'm so proud of you,' she kept repeating over and over in my mind. Or maybe she was saying it in that otherworldly place that I had visited on two occasions and somehow I could still manage to hear her.

She stopped saying it though when I stole a bottle of vodka from the cellar in Happy's at the end of that first night. I said my good-byes to everyone and then I went home and drank until I passed out. That was no big thing as far as I was concerned because in my own mind I had never really given up drink; I had just been taking a break for a while. And that first drink since leaving the loony bin tasted amazing. I remember once as a kid, I caught some sort of vomiting bug which meant that I couldn't keep anything down and on top of that I was burning up with a fever. The only sustenance that I could manage was tablespoons of cold water that my mother would give me. It was like magic water though because it tasted so good on my parched tongue and I've never sipped anything since that tasted quite so good. But the first taste of vodka on that particular night was a close second on a list of my greatest drinking experiences.

Without Ashling I felt incomplete pretty much all of the time, with or without a drink in my hand but preferably with, and so it didn't take long before I had once again embraced the voluntary madness that is drunkenness. I thought that I was clever though because I still managed to function on a marginally competent level. I continued working away at Happy's and nobody seemed to notice that I was more clumsy than usual or that my hands trembled almost constantly. Also, Jack and Fiona worked nine-to-five jobs whereas I only started work at 6 p.m. most days. The result was that they weren't around to check up on me. We usually had dinner together on Sundays but for those few hours that we shared, I became quite adept at playing the role of the teetotal saint.

You probably think that I'm a complete fucking idiot for going back on the booze, especially after my most recent afterlife experience, which I admit ought to have inspired and motivated me. But the truth is that seeing Owen and Ashling again had not made my life any easier. I had seen the light but the light hadn't seen me.

Moving house was the latest in my long list of fuck-ups. My new lodgings were terrible. They were bang in the middle of a housing estate so dodgy, some of the residents had been reduced to taking the drastic step of putting bars on their windows. Or maybe that was just part of a training programme for their inevitable incarceration. My new living quarters had two bedrooms, a TV room and a kitchen roughly the size of a coffin. But easily the worst thing about the house was the fact that the walls were so thin. I could hear everything that was going on with my new neighbours. I could hear them arguing, I could hear them shagging, I could hear what they were watching on television, I could hear them taking a piss, I could even hear bogroll being pulled from the toilet roll dispenser in their bathroom. It was enough to drive anyone to drink. And the really annoying thing about it all was the fact that I had left 22 Sullivan Street because it contained too many memories of Ashling, but the memories came with me and they continued to press down on all my other thoughts.

But I didn't sit around moaning about things. I sat around drinking instead. I did most of my serious drinking when I came home from work and I rarely got to sleep before five or six in the morning. I started getting blackouts, which were a new experience for me. I would wake up and not only could I not remember a single thing about the previous night, there were large chunks from the previous day that were also missing. It was as if my memory had just packed up and gone off on holiday. I found Lisa's postcard of the puppy and the clock on the floor one morning. It had been ripped into tiny pieces and scattered around the kitchen and I have no recollection of ever doing that. Also, I would meet people in Happy's that I had known all my life and I wouldn't be able to remember their names. That was the most frustrating part of it.

I couldn't really complain though because the purpose of my drinking was to forget; but I found that my memories of Ashling had been burned on to my brain and I couldn't stop myself from constantly replaying them no matter how hard I tried. Because I'm stubborn, though, I kept on trying and I kept on drinking.

I would crawl out of bed most days at around two or three in the afternoon and head straight for the shower. The air around me felt infected by my sense of loss and sometimes I would stand in the shower for a very long time just trying to feel clean. When I made it downstairs, I would switch on the kettle and make myself a Bloody Mary while waiting for it to boil. They have always been my favourite hangover cure although by that time I had gotten into the habit of fixing myself one for breakfast regardless of whether or not I had a hangover. I never bothered actually eating anything for breakfast and instead I satisfied myself with a Bloody Mary, a carton of orange juice and a cup of black coffee. My excessive alcohol intake left me almost constantly dehydrated, hence the orange juice. So I followed my liquid breakfast with a liquid brunch, liquid lunch and a few liquid snacks in between. I did still eat, by the way, but only because I could drink more with food in my stomach. When I got to work, I would usually help myself to a couple of toasted sandwiches and a few packets of bacon fries washed down with a sneaky double vodka and coke that I pretended was just coke. I knew that Roger had been fiddling my taxes for years and so I didn't feel too bad about helping myself to shots of his booze at every available opportunity. With all that alcohol flowing behind the bar, I could almost remember what it was like to be happy again. Almost.

After the incident with the fireman, Norman was released on bail the following day. I was a bit nervous that he might accuse me of being a rat but he never did. He thought that I was his buddy because we went back a long way and because I served him booze all the time at Happy's, but being mates with Norman is like being friends with a starving Rottweiler with toothache.

I met Norman's kid for the first time about a week or so after I moved into my new place. I had just left home and was on my way to work when I saw her. She was only about six years old but already it was obvious that she was going to break a lot of hearts. Against all the odds, Norman had produced a beautiful little girl. When I saw her that first time, she was wearing a pink headband and she was walking a small plastic horse over the tops of hedges and bushes.

I bumped into her father at around two o'clock the following morning. We were going into our respective houses at the same time so we could hardly miss each other. I was coming home from work, and Norman was, eh, coming home from where I work. He was pissed and I was pissed off that I hadn't managed to avoid him.

In a sad attempt to complete the illusion that his old house had somehow miraculously multiplied into two houses, Silky Mannix had installed a woeful excuse for a fence consisting of a chain; not a chain fence, mind you, just a chain, and a plastic one at that. And this chain supposedly divided in half the bathroom-sized square of dog shit and nettles that passed for my front lawn and Norman's. It didn't divide anything, though, because Big Mickey chewed through it a long time ago and the green plastic promptly sank into the overgrown undergrowth, never to be seen again. And even though it was undoubtedly useless, I must say that I really missed that pathetically ineffectual last line of defence from Norman because when I found myself face to face with him outside our front doors on that particular night, the only thing separating us was the smell of decaying dog turds.

'Ya know if I didn't know any better, I'd say ya were a little queer boy that followed me home,' he said with all the charm of a dead rat's asshole. He took three steps towards the non-existent fence and stood beside me. The stink of alcohol from his breath was even stronger than the stench of dog shit.

'Put it there, buddy,' he said to me, holding out his hand. 'Seein as we're gonna be neighbours now and all.'

Norman's handshake felt like a tourniquet. I tried not to wince. He put his arm around my shoulders and I didn't know whether he was going to hug me or knife me.

'How's about a real drink in my gaff instead o tha watered-down piss you've been servin me all night?' he asked.

I felt like I'd rather drink a pint of my own vomit in the company of the Grim Reaper and so I politely declined, telling Norman that

I was shattered and really had to get to bed; the working man and all that.

Norman removed his arm from my shoulders and a wintry smile crept over his face. He was definitely drunk but his eyes still looked like chips of ice, with not even a hint of bloodshot. After a beat, he spoke again.

'Ya sound like me dead fuckin granny, for Christ's sake. Wha's your bleedin problem? Do ya think you're too good to have a drink with me? Is that it? Do ya think you're better than me just cos ya have a poxy job workin as a skivvy in tha fuckin shit box?'

He was coked out of his fucking eyeballs and that made him twice as dangerous and very hard to say no to. I put my arm around his shoulders and told him how I thought a neighbourly nightcap would be the perfect way to end the night after all. I think that he decided not to kill me at that point because he grunted and turned his back on me. As he was sticking his key into his front door, Norman smiled broadly, revealing the gap between his front teeth. I think that, more than any of his other features, the gap between his front teeth was what made him look like an evil bastard. It seemed to leak evil. But it was more than just the gap itself, it was the fact that you could only see the gap when he smiled, and when he smiled, his eyes didn't close even the tiniest bit and it's impossible to give a genuine smile without closing your eyes at least a little bit. The obvious conclusion, therefore, is that all of Norman's smiles were fake.

'I'll show ya me hobby!' he said and then he disappeared through his front door. An innocent enough remark perhaps, but when Norman said it, the hairs on the back of my neck stood up like a wire brush.

As I closed the front door from the inside, Norman moved into the living room and switched on the light, sending shafts of eerie red glow spilling out into the hallway. It crossed my mind that maybe Norman's hobby was nothing scarier than amateur photography and in his enthusiasm he had turned his living room into a dark room. But no. The red light bulb was more decorative than functional. Every house usually has at least one room that has a comfortable and homely feel to it, but then again, if every yin has its yang, then your average snug little living room must have an anti-living room somewhere. And I found one. I went through the looking glass and found myself standing in my next-door neighbour's living room from hell and it was an experience that I'm not likely to forget.

Norman's anti-living room is close to what I imagine a blind, demented teenage pimp suffering from severe LSD trauma might inhabit. Over the brick fireplace, where most people hang mirrors and the like, there was a huge black and white framed poster of Robert De Niro as the boxer Jake La Motta in the film *Raging Bull*. The glass in the frame was smashed and hadn't been replaced and it wasn't difficult to figure out how it had been smashed. The picture was riddled with puncture wounds that could only have been caused by a large knife. There was an emaciated strip of silver tinsel thrown around the picture frame in a pitiful acknowledgement of the festive season. It was the only Christmas decoration on display and it almost looked as if someone was taking the piss.

There was no evidence of the existence of Norman's wife and child anywhere in the room. This was clearly not an environment where little boys made forts out of cushions and little girls played horsey with Daddy around the coffee table. This was a room that wanted to hurt you. It had wooden floors and an enormous flat-screen television in the corner. There was a filthy black leather armchair parked opposite the TV, clearly Daddy Bear's chair, and under the window there was an old couch that looked as if it might have been rescued from a burnt-out house. In the centre of the room there was a wooden coffee table, the surface of which was liberally covered with porno mags, and the only other furniture was a pair of white plastic garden chairs placed against the wall by the door.

But it wasn't the mismatched furniture that turned the room into an anti-living room; it was what was on one of the walls in particular. Glass shelves had been erected on either side of the chimneybreast and every one of the shelves was laden with knives. This, apparently, was his hobby. He must have had at least forty or fifty swords and daggers of every shape and size on display. Norman looked at me as if he had just granted me a magnificent sight to behold and was now awaiting a richly deserved bounty of plaudits to be showered upon him. I felt as if someone had pushed me into a nightmare. Personally, I wouldn't know a fish knife from a scimitar and so I didn't have a clue how to respond.

'Wow, tha's, eh, tha's some collection you've got there, Norm, very, eh, sharp.'

Norman's brow furrowed and I could see the vein in his forehead starting to bulge. Somehow I'd said the wrong thing but I had no idea how to say the right thing. There was a heavily pregnant pause during which all I could do was hazard a nervous smile.

Norman made a gun out of his fingers and then jammed it into my chest.

'Who the fuck are you callin Norm, ya fuckin Mary, ya. Me name is Norman and if ya forget it again, I'll carve it across the inside o your fuckin eyelids.'

Then he started laughing, loudly and hollowly, as if it was all a big joke really. He patted my cheek with his hand, saying, 'Don't look so bleedin worried. I'm only havin a laugh with ya, for Christ's sake.'

Good old Norm! He really missed his vocation as a stand-up comedian. From its mounting on the wall, he picked up a jagged-edged knife that was as long as my forearm and then he pretended to thrust it into my stomach, just for a laugh like.

'This one is good for carvin up assholes,' he told me.

'Really?' I said, pretending to be fascinated. I even inquired about how I might go about obtaining a few lethal-looking blades of my own but Norman just looked at me like I was dog shit on his carpet and said that they didn't hand out silverware like his to any wanker who walked in off the street. He didn't specify who 'they' were although I'm fairly sure that he wasn't referring to the good people at B&Q.

He asked me what I wanted to drink and I said that I'd have a vodka and anything, easy on the anything. Norman didn't slap his thighs, split his sides, or pause to wipe tears from his eyes after my little joke. Instead, he collapsed into the only armchair in the room.

'Pull up a chair,' he said to me, nodding towards one of the white garden chairs by the wall. As I was about to lift one of them out, Norman bellowed the name 'CHLOE!' at the top of his lungs. I turned around to face him in bewildered astonishment, becoming more and more convinced by the second that the man was dangerously unhinged.

'The service around here is fuckin terrible!' he said, flashing his creepy smile at me once more. Using the remote control, he switched on the giant television in the corner and so I faced the chair in that direction and then sat down. Norman produced a tin cigar box from his pocket and he opened it carefully. I had an inkling what the box contained and it wasn't cigars. He scanned the contents and a look of frustration crossed his face.

'Ya haven't got any o the white stuff, have ya?' he asked.

'Wha, dandruff? Are ya jokin me! I'll have ya know tha I've got hair tha the chick in the L'Oréal commercial would be proud of.'

'*Jesus,* you're some fuckin tool bag, ya know tha? I'm talkin about the Columbian marchin powder.'

'I've given it up, Norman. Doctor's orders.'

'Fuck's sake! Wha fuckin use are ya then?'

I didn't have any answer to this so I just shrugged my shoulders instead.

'Throw us over a magazine, will ya?' he said a few seconds later.

'Which one?'

'Any one.'

I picked up a publication entitled *Blade Monthly* from the coffee table and handed it to him. He placed it in his lap and started rolling a joint on it. He was crumbling a tiny block of cannabis into the rolled tobacco when there was a knock on the door. Norman said 'Come in' and then someone opened the door. I turned around to see what I took to be his wife. I had never seen her before. She was barefoot and wearing a rust-coloured dressing gown that she held closed with folded arms. She glanced at me briefly before looking away again.

'This is the guy from next door,' was how Norman introduced me. His wife wasn't introduced at all.

'He called around cos he wants to check out his new neighbours' gaff so get him a drink, for fuck's sake. I'll have a Paddy and white and our friend here wants a vodka and, eh, coke or somethin.'

'You're after wakin up your daughter,' she said. 'And I've told ya how I feel about ya smoking gear in the house.'

There was a pause. I looked over at Norman. The vein in his forehead was starting to bulge again.

'Excuse me one minute,' he said to me in a fit of uncharacteristic politeness, and then he stood up and marched across the room, taking Chloe by the crook of her elbow and leading her out into the hall. He didn't even shut the door. I heard muttered threats along the lines of, 'If I have to ask again, there'll be slaps. Is tha clear enough for ya?' Ordinarily, I think that he could best be described as a stone-cold psycho but Norman seemed to have lucid moments when he was merely a horrible human being. Half a minute later, he reappeared and planted himself back down into his wreck of an armchair.

'Tha's the missus,' he informed me unnecessarily. I felt like a man crossing a minefield wearing skis. My conversation became stilted and unnatural because every phrase out of my mouth had to first pass the censor in my head. I'd already dropped one clanger by calling my host 'Norm', and a second mistake might result in an unplanned body piercing, so vigilance was certainly the order of the day. I must have spent about five seconds just considering how I would respond to him pointing out that the woman who he seemed to treat as a twenty-four-hour waitress was in fact his wife. In the end, I just sort of grunted in reply.

'Dirty fuckin bitch,' said Norman as he sparked up the fat joint he had rolled. 'Can't let her outta me sight. If ya went into tha kitchen righ now and slapped her on the arse, she'd probably turn around and suck your fuckin knob off. She'd suck a bleedin snooker ball through a hosepipe tha one.'

'She seems, eh, very nice,' I responded. 'Ya should bring her along to Happy's sometime.'

Norman took a long drag of the joint while staring at me coldly.

'Are ya tellin me how I should treat me own wife? Think ya know better than I do wha's good for her, do ya? Maybe you should fuckin marry her then, seein as ya know fuckin everythin.'

'It was just an idea.'

'I wouldn't bring her to tha fuckin skank pit. Are ya mad? Although maybe on her birthday or somethin I might think about it. You could do the babysittin.'

An uncomfortable silence followed while I desperately tried to think of a conversational nugget that would change the course of the discussion. Eventually I broke the tension by saying 'nice picture', while staring at De Niro's lacerated body suspended over the fire-place.

'Did you fuck my wife?' said Norman.

'Wha?'

'Did you fuck my wife?' he said again.

'Course I didn't. Jesus! I only just met her, for fuck's sake.'

'You didn't fuck my wife?'

'Course I didn't fuck your wife,' I said, raising my voice slightly. Norman erupted with a big burst of hollow laughter.

'It's in the film, ya dopey fucker, ya,' he said with glee. 'The bit where he says "Did you fuck my wife?", it's in the film.'

'I thought it sounded familiar,' I said, sounding like a gobshite even to myself.

When Chloe returned a few minutes later bearing drinks, Big Mickey slunk into the room behind her. He went straight to the side of his master's chair and rested his head on the coffee table, depositing a good-sized dollop of doggy saliva on the uppermost porno mag. Chloe placed the two drinks on the table and then promptly left the room without glancing up. Big Mickey, on the other hand, only had eyes for me. He glared at me intently with his horrible black lips curled up, baring his teeth. He appeared to be growling lowly but he was outgunned by the giant television set that was blaring in the corner. Norman must have got hold of a satellite dish because he seemed to have access to about five hundred channels. After flicking through about two hundred of them, he eventually settled on some broadcast that looked like it might be the shopping channel for gun nuts. A man with bulgy eyes and a monotone voice was discussing the merits of the AK-47 assault rifle. The presenter struck me as someone who was probably bullied relentlessly at school but I found it difficult to feel any sympathy for him.

'Now tha's wha I want for fuckin Christmas!' said Norman and then he knocked back most of the whiskey in his glass in a single gulp.

'Well maybe if ya ask Santa nicely, he might sort ya out.'

'Yeah righ! I don't need nothin off tha fat cunt. I can sort meself out.'

'Hey, I'm not sayin ya can't, ya know? I mean, look at all these knives!'

'Knives are one thing, but they're not what I'd call the dog's fuckin bollox, if ya know wha I mean?'

'Eh, not really, to be honest.'

'Knives are quick and easy, and they're quiet, which I like, ya know? But they're fuckin old school, man. Worse than tha, they're like fuckin ... videotapes or somethin.'

'Ya mean they take up too much room?'

'No, ya fuckin muppet, I mean they're outta date. No one uses them anymore except bleedin bag snatchers.'

'Why are bag snatchers so keen on usin videotapes then?'

'*Jesus fuckin Christ*! When did ya get to be so bleedin stupid?'

Instead of offering me a hit of the joint, he left it resting on an ashtray and then he stood up and crossed the room. My last question was meant to be a joke but Norman was born without a sense of humour.

'Well wha are people usin then if they're not usin knives?' I asked, trying to humour him a little.

I had a feeling that I already knew the answer to that but I didn't let on. Norman was standing by the sofa near the window. He pushed it forward a few feet and then, while he was crouched behind the couch, I could hear him prising up a floorboard. When he reappeared, he was pointing a gun directly at me.

'*Wha the fuck*! Jesus, man, whaddya doin?'

'Relax, will ya, for fuck's sake. If I wanted to kill ya, you'd be dead already. I'm just showin ya me piece.'

He approached to give me a closer look at the chunky black handgun in his hand.

'Knives are for kids. This is for people who mean business,' he said and then he popped a bullet into the chamber of the gun.

'Deadly. How many, eh, bullets does it hold?'

'Fifteen in the magazine and one in the chamber. It's a Glock 22. Austria's finest. It's the same as wha the coppers use in the States.'

He pointed the gun at Big Mickey and slowly started to squeeze the trigger. He badly wanted to kill something at that point. I could sense the lust for death oozing out of every one of his pores. Big Mickey's ears stood up and he watched his master attentively with no idea that he was staring down the barrel of death.

'Is the, eh, safety on?' I inquired.

'The safety mechanism is all internal. It gets switched off when you pull the trigger.'

That didn't sound very safe to me and so I decided to make my escape before either Big Mickey or I ended up with our brains splattered against the wall.

'Listen, eh, Norman, I really should be goin,' I said as I finished off my drink in a couple of big gulps that made my eyes water.

He lowered the gun and looked at me as if he was just seeing me for the first time.

'I'm knackered, ya know? Gotta get some kip.'

'Yeah, whatever,' he replied, and then he collapsed back into his leather chair, with his gun in one hand and the joint in the other.

'I'll see ya tomorrow then prob'ly, yeah?'

Norman didn't reply. The television alone commanded his attention. I walked out of his chamber of horrors and almost literally bumped into his wife in the hallway. She had just finished doing something in the kitchen and presumably was on her way back to bed.

'Thanks for the drink and, eh, happy Christmas,' I said, realising that it was a stupid thing to say as soon as I'd said it.

'Yeah,' she replied.

I hadn't seen any Christmas tree and I hadn't seen any Christmas cards. December 25, by the look of things, wasn't a big event in Norman's house.

'I'm headin off now so I'll just let meself out.'

'Okay. Thanks for callin around at two o'clock in the mornin.'

She caught me off guard with that blast of sarcasm and I did my best to rescue the situation.

'Look, it really wasn't my idea, to be honest. Norman can be very persuasive, ya know?'

'Yeah, I know,' she replied. There was something about her eyes that reminded me of a whipped dog living in fear of its master. Even though she was acting tough, it was clearly just an act.

'Anyway, it was nice meetin ya and seein as we're gonna be neighbours and all, if ya ever need any help with anythin . . .'

'Thanks,' she said, and then she brushed past me and went up the stairs without another word.

I let myself out the front door.

December 10 2004.

Ashling's anniversary.

It was not going to be a good day for me, of that I was fairly certain. You know how sometimes you can drink loads the night before and miraculously wake up just a little bit woozy but with no real hangover? Well this wasn't one of those times. I was woken up around midday by someone hammering on my front door. I was still getting used to waking up in my new surroundings at that point and so I felt completely disorientated. On top of that, I had a pounding headache. Because I was no longer drinking every single hour that I was awake, hangovers now had a chance to catch up with me again. And they did. They caught up with a vengeance and on that particular morning there was a hammering in my head that easily rivalled the hammering on my front door. I didn't think that it was possible to have such pain and not be in the middle of a massive brain haemorrhage. But the merciless banging on my door refused to go away. I thought that someone must have died and I wished that it was me. My head felt as heavy as a sack of old pennies and my throat felt like sandpaper. I had to stop the noise before my brain exploded and so I kicked myself out of bed and pushed myself in the direction of the front door.

I've never gotten around to buying a dressing gown and so I pulled on a T-shirt and marched groggily down the stairs. My eyelids felt like they had been stapled shut. I opened the door and standing there was Chloe from next door with a screaming child in her arms. It took me a second to recognise her because it was so bright outside and my vision was trying to go double, but I knew who she was and she looked like trouble. I silently cursed myself for having opened the door at all. I was almost fully awake at this stage and conscious of the fact that I probably looked like some sort of pervert standing there in my boxers and trying to hide behind the door. But that wasn't why the child was crying. Blood was streaming down the side of her face from a wound beneath her hairline. Chloe was also obviously in some distress. She came right to the point.

'Remember ya said tha if ever I needed help with somethin . . . ?'

'Yeah,' I croaked.

'Well, I need a lift to the hospital.'

'I don't have a car.'

'Ya can take Norman's,' she said, dangling keys in front of me.

'I'm not insured,' I said pathetically. At that moment, I didn't feel capable of driving a lawnmower, never mind Norman's car.

'This is an emergency.'

I nearly said: 'So call an ambulance then,' but I didn't and I'm glad that I didn't. There are more than enough pricks already in the world without me joining their ranks. Besides, the injured kid on my doorstep hadn't asked for or wanted any of this. None of us had.

'Wait there a sec and I'll get me jacket,' I said, turning back into the hall. I ran upstairs, pulled on some tracksuit bottoms and stuffed my feet into my already-tied runners, and a minute later I was walking out the front door. Chloe and her child were now sitting in the passenger seat of Norman's ancient bronze-coloured Mercedes, the kid on her mother's lap. Chloe didn't appear to know how to drive and I wouldn't say that her husband was the type who had encouraged her to learn. As I walked around the car to the driver's door, I noticed a bumper sticker in the back window: 'Horn broken, watch for finger.' It was Norman's car all right.

Chloe handed me the keys when I was in and then we were on our way to Casualty at the Mater Hospital. The car smelled like a smoky dog kennel and it made me want to throw up. There was an ashtray hanging out of the fake wooden dashboard like a mechanical tongue and it was crammed with cigarette butts. The smell of stale smoke seemed to be competing with the smell of Big Mickey for dominance and the result was a fragrance that I suspect is not about to take the world by storm. I rolled down the window and tried to concentrate on the driving.

Chloe told me that the child had banged her head on the ground after falling off a wall. Standard run-of-the-mill childhood injury, or at least it is when it happens to other people's kids. The mother stemmed her kid's blood flow with a wad of tissues and before we'd even gone a mile up the road, the girl's wailing had died down to a steady sobbing. But even after the girl had calmed down, conversation was still difficult because there was a problem with the exhaust on Norman's car and as a result I felt like I was driving down the road inside a pneumatic drill. My hangover wasn't thanking me for the experience.

'Sounds like the exhaust is gone,' I said, trying to initiate a conversation that might alleviate the awkwardness that I alone seemed to be feeling.

'It's wha?' Chloe shouted back.

'Gone!'

'Gone where?'

'It's not gone anywhere but there's a hole in it,' I roared.

'There's a hole in the egg sauce?'

I looked over at her and I could see the corners of her mouth were turned upwards slightly in a smile. The penny dropped that she was purposely messing with my head and I smiled in spite of myself.

'Listen, I really appreciate this, ya know, and I'm, eh, I'm sorry if I was a bit rude to ya the other night, ya know?' roared Chloe.

I pulled over to the side of the road in front of a group of shops and turned off the engine.

'Don't mention it,' I roared unnecessarily now that the car was silent. 'I just have to pop in here to get somethin but I'll be back in two seconds,' and before she could say a word I jumped out of the car and ran into a pharmacy. A minute later, I ran out of the shop and into the Centra next door. When I got back to the car, I was armed with a box of Solpadeine and a two-litre bottle of water.

'Sorry bout tha,' I said, popping two big white tablets into my mouth at the same time. Chloe just stared at me like I was a raving lunatic.

'I have a bit of a headache,' I said by way of explanation.

'Aren't ya supposed to dissolve those in a glass o water?'

'Most people do, yeah,' I replied, 'but I kind o like the salty taste and the way it crackles on my tongue. Sort o like Space Dust from when I was a kid. Remember Space Dust?'

'No,' said Chloe and that was the end of that conversation. I started up the car again and we continued our journey in silence, apart from the sound of the exhaust.

A minute later when we were stopped at traffic lights, the kid on Chloe's lap turned around and looked at me with worried eyes and a quivering lip. I thought that it would be funny to give her a big frothy smile like a rabid dog, and dribble some semi-dissolved Solpadeine down my chin at the same time. So I did, but the kid didn't seem to find it very funny at all. She let a big wail out of her and then she started sobbing all over again. I wiped my chin with my sleeve and then I looked over at Chloe with what I hoped was a mixture of concern and innocence on my face. She glared back at me like I was some sort of paedophile. I shrugged my shoulders in a pretence of blamelessness and then I drove on.

At the next traffic lights, I opened the bottle of water and downed about a third of it in one go.

'Ahhhhhhhhhh,' I said, along with a big, satisfied sigh. 'If I had have known that I was gonna be this thirsty today, I would have drunk more last night.'

Chloe made a sort of a grunting sound that might have been a charity laugh. I went back to concentrating on the driving but then something shiny caught my eye. Dangling from the rear-view mirror, I noticed a tiny dagger with coloured glass encrusted into the handle. Under normal circumstances, I probably wouldn't have given it a second glance, but in Norman's car that tacky little ornament seemed to acquire the status of a miniature sword of Damocles.

'Where's Norman?' I asked out of the blue. I was finding it hard to keep him out of my thoughts all of a sudden.

'He had some business to attend to and he won't be back for a few hours.'

I had seen Norman leaving Happy's the previous night with his arm around Tanya Cox so I had a fair idea of what business he was attending to.

I stole a closer look at Chloe at the next red light. I thought that she could almost be pretty if only she would smile now and again. Tanya Cox on the other hand is a cheap, nasty skank who looks as if she applies her make-up with a garden trowel. Last night her lips were so completely covered in bright red lipstick that she looked like Hannibal the Cannibal after a main course. Lipstick like that is bound to leave its mark somewhere so I found myself wondering whether Chloe knew the score regarding her husband's away fixtures. I figured she must.

But it wasn't lost on me that while Norman was off shagging his mistress somewhere, there I was, running errands for his missus, looking after his kid, and driving his car, and we had only been neighbours for about five minutes. I couldn't help but get the feeling that being neighbours with Norman was going to be a full-time job.

But once I was a bit more awake and the Solpadeine started to kick in, I honestly didn't mind helping out his wife and kid. It made me feel good, in fact, or at least it gave me a feeling of not being a completely useless bastard. And that was nice for a little while. Anything that would break the cycle, even for just a few minutes, was very good indeed because I was starting to feel a lot like a clock in an empty house – still functioning but totally pointless.

'Wha's her name?' I asked Chloe, while nodding towards the little girl.

'Zoe,' shouted her mother over the noise of the car.

'Chloe and Zoe? Are ya jokin me?'

But she didn't look like she was joking.

'Not tha there's anythin wrong with Chloe and Zoe,' I added quickly, backtracking like a maniac. 'I mean, Jesus no. It's just tha, the way they rhyme an everythin; it's kind o funny.'

'Funny weird or funny ha ha?'

'Funny ha ha. No, not Funny ha ha, I mean funny weird. Well no, I don't mean tha like your names are weird or nothin. It's just a bit unusual, tha's all.'

The phrase, *When you're in a hole, stop digging*, flashed across my mind in giant neon letters but it was a little late for that. I stole another glance at Chloe. She was staring straight out the front windscreen a little too intensely and she made no further effort to respond to the stupidity pouring out of the hole in my face.

As we approached the hospital, the noise in the car was accompanied by the sound of an ambulance blaring its siren directly behind us. Zoe turned around and looked at it through the back window and then she asked why the letters on the front of the ambulance were written backwards. Grateful for an opportunity to show that I could say something without sounding like a complete idiot, I explained to her that they write the word 'ambulance' in mirror writing so that drivers in front can read it in their rear-view mirrors.

'Yeah, it's good tha ya know,' piped up Chloe. 'Cos otherwise ya might be wonderin what the big white van was with the flashin lights and the sirens.'

I was definitely impressed with the quality of her sarcasm. Even though she had married Norman, she clearly wasn't stupid. But while I was thinking those thoughts, the moment passed in which

I might have responded with a witticism of my own. She probably thought that I was some kind of dry shite who doesn't even get sarcasm. But fuck it, I had other things on my mind like Norman and sleep and alcohol and hangovers and Ashling. Always Ashling. The Mater Hospital was my wife's old workplace and we were almost there. I could feel a tightening sensation in my chest which was a clue that an anxiety attack might be in the post but I ignored it and concentrated on the driving instead.

When we finally reached the hospital, we sat in a row of yellow plastic seats in the waiting area. It didn't appear to be particularly busy although I knew that we were still guaranteed a couple of hours waiting around. I wondered why they hadn't erected a TV to keep the punters amused but there wasn't anything like that. There was a mural that took up the entire wall opposite from where we were sitting. It wasn't as distracting as a TV might have been but it wasn't bad. It showed Santa and his sleigh flying over the Ha'penny Bridge. The only problem was that there was a woman with heroin eyes and a hacking cough leaning against the picture looking as though she was getting ready to puke all over it. I tried not to look at her and checked out some of the people sitting down instead. Further along the row that we were sitting in, there was a guy and a girl wearing dinner-dance outfits. They both looked about eighteen and they both looked exhausted. There was no obvious injury to either of them and so I wondered what they were doing there. Maybe they were waiting for someone. She had been awake when I came in but when I looked over again, she was sleeping with her head on her partner's shoulder, her arms wrapped around his waist. In a different setting, they might have looked almost beautiful but in the casualty waiting area it looked all wrong. Somewhere behind us, there was a man with one shoe sleeping across three of the seats. I wondered how long he had been waiting. He looked as if birds had been pecking at his face.

We had only just arrived when Chloe started urging me to go home, saying that she was going to phone Norman and tell him to come in and collect her and Zoe. I didn't leave, though, and she didn't phone her husband. Instead the three of us waited together. I thought that having come this far, I might as well see it through to the end. I'm no hero though and probably not even much of a gentleman because it certainly wasn't for purely unselfish reasons that I stayed. I enjoyed some female company for a change and fuck it, it wasn't as if I had anything better to be doing.

But then wouldn't you know it, just when I was least expecting it, I fell madly in love all over again. There were no thunderbolts and lightning this time, no fumbling chat-up lines or stolen glances. This was a completely different kind of love. This was a straight in, no messing – *I am so impossibly cute that you cannot fail to love me and I will love you back if you buy me sweets* – kind of love.

I asked Zoe who her friend was and that's how I got introduced to a stuffed panda named Tiny. Tiny had a white belly and a black head and limbs. I suggested that he might be a polar bear who didn't like to wash his face or paws and she seemed to think that this was quite funny. The sound of a child laughing was a sound that I hadn't heard in a long, long time. Maybe not since I'd been a kid myself. Zoe and I got on so well so quickly in fact that I didn't feel in the least bit awkward or uncomfortable in asking her if she was married or if she had a boyfriend. She sat on the chair with her feet swinging beneath her and told me that she wasn't married and didn't like boys. I think she liked me though. She said that her favourite food was chips and sometimes her mother let her make Rice Krispie buns, and that was her second-favourite food. She also informed me that she had asked Santa to bring her new clothes for her dolly and a pair of glitter shoes. I have absolutely no idea what glitter shoes are (shoes with glitter on them perhaps? Just a wild guess!), but the sheer modesty of the child's Christmas list made me want to run out and buy her half of Smyth's toy shop. I would have done it too but I think her father might have strongly disapproved and I was too pathetic to risk pissing him off. When I asked her how Santa would know where she lived, she looked at me for a few seconds with a kind of *how did you get this far in life when you obviously have no brain whatsoever?* expression on her face.

'Because he's magic!'

Because he's magic. Simple as that. I had a fleeting vision of Norman lounging in his swivel armchair dressed in a grubby Santa Claus outfit and throwing random knives at an angel on top of a Christmas tree. Then Zoe beckoned me closer with her finger so that she could whisper in my ear.

'I asked him as well to bring a new necklace for my mammy because daddy broke the old one and she was sad.'

I gave her a conspiratorial wink while, on the inside, yearning ran through me like a cramp. I couldn't help thinking that Zoe would have been far better off with acute appendicitis or even a broken leg because then she would have been admitted to the children's ward, the walls of which are covered with Disney characters around this time of year. Also, I knew from Ashling that the hospital received tons of donations of toys at Christmas and these were then distributed amongst the kids on Christmas day. So if her timing had been a little different, or her injury a little worse, then I think Zoe might have done a lot better than glitter shoes and dolls' clothes.

Chloe politely pretended not to listen while I chatted to her daughter but I'm sure she heard every word even though her face was giving nothing away. I asked her if she wanted a coffee and she replied 'That would be nice' without even looking at me. As I stood up to go and get the coffee, Zoe asked her mother if she could come with me. Chloe thought about it for a second or two but then she told her daughter to stay where she was. Norman's wife seemed to be a lot less trusting than his kid.

I went off and found some vending machines around the corner. I may as well admit at this point that I did have an ulterior motive in focusing my energy on Zoe. Obviously she was a great kid, and worth every ounce of my attention, but the sight of all those nurses wearing the same uniform that I had seen my wife wearing a thousand times was starting to drive me crazy. I couldn't handle looking at them anymore but they seemed to be everywhere.

I bought a Twix and a carton of orange juice for Zoe from one machine and then I got the coffees from another. As I was trying to figure out the best way to carry all the items at the same time, I felt a tap on my shoulder. I looked down and behind me at the same time. I could see the white shoes and stockings of a nurse and I felt my heart do a little somersault in my chest. I turned around to find myself face to face with a former colleague of my wife's. She was suspiciously tall for a woman and had about half a cement mixer's worth of make-up on her face, probably to try to make her look more feminine. It wasn't working.

'Hi,' she offered by way of an opening.

'Oh, hi!' I offered in return, and just a shade too enthusiastically considering I had only met her once before and I couldn't remember a single thing about her.

'I'm Paula!'

'Yeah, I remember,' I lied. 'You used to work with Ashling, didn't ya?' I added for the sake of saying something.

'Yeah,' she said softly and then she shifted her gaze on to the floor in a gesture of quiet respect. Just when I thought that she wasn't going to speak again, she looked up and said, 'We all still miss her terribly, ya know? The place just isn't the same without her. If there's anything I can do, anything at all ...'

'Ya can help me carry tha coffee to the seats over there,' I replied, nodding towards the second cup of coffee that was still in the machine. She picked up the hot drink and walked along beside me.

'So what brings you here?' she asked, now with an unmistakable chill in her voice.

'My neighbour's kid fell off a wall and banged her head. We're worried she might have a concussion or somethin.'

When we reached Norman's wife and child, I introduced Paula to them and then I collapsed back into a plastic chair. Chloe and Paula started nattering away to each other but I didn't even pretend to be listening. Instead I just stared straight ahead of me at whatever happened to be in my field of vision. I could see a doctor with a stethoscope around his neck and a clipboard in his hand waiting for a lift. He kept pressing the button over and over again as if that was somehow going to make it arrive faster. He didn't seem all that bright for a doctor. I took a sip of the coffee. It tasted like battery acid but I didn't care. I glanced to my right and I could see Paula doing a cursory examination of Zoe's head. I heard her saying that she would see if she could get the doctor to see us next and then she left, not acknowledging me in the slightest as she walked past.

'Good work, Batman!' said Chloe, nudging me gently in the midriff at the same time. A shiver travelled the length of my spine and then bounced back again, reverberating throughout my body.

'Wha did you say?' I asked her in a voice that sounded small and distant. I thought that it was possible, at least, that because it was the day that it was, I might have simply misheard her.

'Good work, Batman,' repeated Chloe. 'Ya know, from the old TV series.'

I felt the colour drain from my face and at the same time I could feel a constriction in my chest, as if a hand had reached inside me and was squeezing my heart. I don't think Chloe even noticed. She was too busy helping Zoe pierce the juice carton with a plastic straw. I stood up and mumbled something about going out to get some air. When I got to the hospital porch, I leaned against the wall and then I slid down it and sat on the ground. A couple of smokers in dressing gowns gave me concerned looks but they weren't sufficiently concerned to inquire whether I was all right. Pricks. I could have been in the middle of a fucking coronary right there in the hospital and nobody would have given a shit.

But the truth is that the lack of attention suited me fine. Maybe the fact that three innocent little words from someone could reduce me to a quivering lump of jelly makes me a pathetically weak individual, but that's the way it was. In any case, I'm fairly sure that Chloe's echoing of one of my wife's favourite phrases was only part of the problem. The other part was the hospital itself. I felt as if I had made a dreadful mistake in going there. It was too much, too soon. Far too much. Just being in the same building where I knew my wife had spent hundreds of waking hours seemed to set me back weeks and weeks in the healing process, if there really is such a process. I felt like a recovering alcoholic who makes the fatal error of convincing himself that he is doing so well, he can handle one quick short. But now the damage was done and I felt as if I needed a drink, a real drink, more than I had ever needed anything in my life before.

I stood up and tried to decide what to do, but the decision had already been made by the noisy craving in my head. From the front door of the hospital, I could see the sign of a pub across the street. It was called *Madigan's* or *Mulligan's*, I can't remember which, but it had a circular Guinness sign dangling from a crossbeam. I could almost hear the place calling to me like a Siren enticing a ship on to the rocks and it was a call that I found impossible to resist.

I marched across the road and through the double doors of the pub with scarcely another thought about Chloe and Zoe. I sat at the bar and ordered the raw materials for a drink that I invented myself, and which I christened the tequila submarine. The barman was an old guy with a face like a rotten turnip but he was still able to line up a pint of Budweiser and a shot of tequila in front of me. Normally, I would never order Budweiser because it looks and tastes like something squeezed out of a mop, but I find that with the extra zing offered by a dash of tequila, it's a lot more drinkable. I dropped the shot glass into the pint where it plunged to the bottom like a depth charge and then I downed the whole concoction in one. Almost immediately, the demons in my soul were subdued but they were still there, nonetheless. I ordered a double Jameson with a pint of Guinness as a chaser. After I knocked back the double Jemmie in one, the barman was staring at me like I was a complete madman so I just smiled at him and said, 'Trust me, I'm Batman,' and then I winked at him. Fuck it, I'd done my time in the nut house so I figured that I was more entitled than anyone to act a little bit crazy if I felt like it. Besides, I didn't give a shit what he thought as long as he kept lining up the drinks in front of me.

I was on about my third or fourth pint-and-a-short combination when I heard the double doors opening and closing, and a few seconds after that, I became aware of someone standing inside the door who wasn't making any attempt to approach the bar. I lurched my head to one side and I saw Chloe and Zoe standing there, hand in hand.

'Heeeeeeyyyyyyyyyyy!' I said, swinging the rest of my body around on the stool to face them. They made no attempt to approach me.

'I need the keys o the car. Ya never gave them back,' said Chloe in a tone which gave me the feeling that she wasn't about to join me for a drink, not if this was the last oasis on a desert planet and I was the last man in the universe.

'How did ya know where to find me?' I asked, trying very hard not to slur my words and overcompensating slightly, with the result that I sounded like someone speaking to a novice lip-reader.

'I guessed,' said Chloe.

'It was a good guess,' I replied. I shifted my head down a notch to look at Zoe. For some reason, it felt easier to move my head than to move my eyes.

'How ya doin kiddo?' I inquired.

'Fine,' she answered, giving me an unsure smile as she did so. I could see a dressing on the side of her head, and on her chest she had a sticker showing a picture of a teddy bear on crutches.

'Her name's Zoe, remember?' said her mother. 'And she wants to go home, so can ya gimme the keys so we can leave, please?'

'But you can't drive and I might be slightly over the limit at this stage.'

'Just gimme the keys,' said Chloe, taking a few steps towards me with her upturned palm held out in front of her.

'Okaaaaay!' I said with a look on my face that implied she was making a big mistake. I dropped Norman's car keys into her hand.

'We're headin back now so if ya wanna lift, now's your chance.'

'But I haven't finished me drink,' I replied.

'Suit yourself,' she said and then almost immediately she turned and headed out the door with Zoe.

'Would ya like a drink before ya go?' I called after her. She either didn't hear me or else chose to ignore me. Probably the latter. I looked at the barman and he was staring at me again.

'Wha the fuck are you lookin at?' I said to him. And then I ordered another pint and a short.

The next thing that I can remember is waking up on the pavement in an alley by the side of the pub. The sun was long gone and my head was thumping once again. I propped myself up into a sitting position and tried to get my bearings. There was a pool of vomit near where I lay on the ground and my tracksuit bottoms were covered in a dark, suspicious-looking stain. It wasn't exactly my finest hour. Cars were whizzing by on the road perpendicular to the alley. They all had their headlights on and I thought they had a futuristic look about them. Then I heard a taxi driver brake suddenly and shout out his window:

'Wake up, for fuck's sake, ya dozy cunt, ya!'

For a moment I was sure he was talking to me, but he wasn't. He was talking to a pedestrian who had crossed the road in front of him. I stood up and immediately white lights swirled around my head like extra-bright fireflies. I had to lean against the wall until they disappeared. When I felt as if I could walk, I staggered towards the main road where I managed to hail a taxi. I sat in the back with the window rolled all the way down and I concentrated on not being sick. I hoped the driver wouldn't say anything about how badly I smelled but he didn't seem to notice. The thought crossed my mind that once upon a time, the most beautiful girl in the world had fallen madly in love with me, and now I was practically indistinguishable from a drug addict living on the streets.

I couldn't wait to get home so that I could have another drink.

I woke up the next day feeling even worse than usual. The memory of how I had abandoned Chloe and Zoe in the hospital came back to me in little pieces and each piece made me squirm further and further under the duvet until I was almost under the bed. And then another thought struck me: I had completely forgotten to show up for work the previous evening and so I had let down Roger as well. But he wasn't foremost on my list of concerns. My mind kept flicking back to thoughts about Chloe. I knew that I owed her an apology and I was too nice a person to avoid doing the right thing. I wasn't looking forward to it though.

I decided to go for a walk in the park to try and clear my head. It was Baltic outside and so I wrapped up well in my scarf and jacket. I didn't bother with gloves. Gloves reminded me of my roommate in the loony bin with the mittens taped to his hands, but that wasn't the reason why I didn't bother with them. It was just too damn hard to smoke while wearing gloves.

The park, incidentally, is really just a euphemism for a bumpy grass hill with a bandstand at the bottom. The bandstand had been there since I was a kid and I had vague childhood memories of bands actually playing in it, but those days are gone. Long gone. Nowadays it's a hangout for smack heads and skateboarders with the occasional paedophile or flasher also dropping in from time to time. But I still liked to go there all the same. I liked to sit and watch people passing by so that I could imagine what their lives might be like. My father once told me that if you look at anybody for long enough you can see their humanity but I still haven't decided whether or not I agree with him.

I was sitting on a bench and lighting a cigarette when I saw Chloe Valentine approaching with a shopping bag in each hand. She saw me at around the same time that I saw her but whereas I stayed looking at her, she looked away almost instantly. Then she looked at me again about two seconds later and pretended that she was seeing me for the first time that day even though we had locked eyes a moment before.

I stood up while she was still a few steps away from me and she stopped in front of me.

'Hey, Chloe, how's it goin?' I said, injecting an air of fake joviality into my speech.

'Fine,' she replied, without the slightest hint of joviality, fake or otherwise. She was wearing a sweatshirt with something written on it. I tried to see what it said out of curiosity but she saw me looking and without a doubt she thought that I was looking at her breasts. Bad start. Again.

'How's Zoe today?' I asked. 'Any better?'

'Oh, ya know, she'll live. She needed five stitches but the doctor doesn't think there'll be any scar. Not a big one anyway. What about you, how's your head?'

'Whatcha mean?'

'I mean how's your head. Do ya have a hangover?'

'Ah no, sure I only had a couple o pints.'

Chloe made no reply to my blatant lie and instead she turned her head towards the bandstand. 'NATALIE LYONS TAKES IT UP THE ARSE!' was painted in huge red letters across the concrete back wall of the structure. There was an awkward silence that was becoming increasingly more awkward as the seconds ticked by. Chloe turned back towards me but she didn't say anything. She was waiting for me to apologise. It was obvious. Now was my chance. It was now or never.

'Good old Nat'lie Lyons!' I said while nodding in the direction of the bandstand.

'I should be gettin back,' Chloe said and then she threw a token smile my way and walked away. I paused for a few seconds and then I went after her, desperate to try and retrieve the situation.

'Ya know, eh, it's funny tha I ran into ya cos I'd just been thinkin about ya.'

'Yeah?' she said. She didn't stop walking and so I walked along beside her. 'Wha were ya thinkin?'

'Well I was thinkin that, eh, well, tha I owe ya an apology.'

'For wha?'

'Ya know! For leavin ya in the hospital and headin off to the pub.'

'It's a free country. If ya wanna go to the pub then ya can go to the pub.'

She was being as nice as possible about it and I felt hugely grateful for that.

'No, it was a shitty thing to do. I should have stuck around.'

'It's fine, honestly. Don't worry about it.'

And that was that. I was off the hook and it had been easy. I tried to win back some more brownie points by offering to carry her bags. She let me carry one of them. It was a ten-minute walk back to the street where we lived and we chatted all the way home.

'Where's Norman?' I asked as we turned on to our street.

'He had to see a man about a horse,' said Chloe. 'Do ya wanna come in for a cup o coffee?'

'Eh, yeah, sure,' I replied and then I followed her into her house.

We went into the kitchen and she put away the groceries while waiting for the kettle to boil. It was my first time inside Norman's kitchen but it was more Chloe than the surroundings that held my attention. Her hair was scraped back in a ponytail which emphasised the strong bones in her face. She was wearing an old pair of jeans and a sweatshirt that had been washed too many times but she still looked great. She had a great figure and a great ass that I couldn't help but notice. It didn't make any sense that Norman would repeatedly cheat on this woman but I had given up trying to understand him.

There was a crayon drawing stuck to the wall over the table. A spiky yellow sun shone down on a man who had big rectangular feet and sausage fingers. He also had teeth like piano keys and a smile that literally went from ear to ear. Beside him there was a four-legged cloud shape that might have represented a dog.

'Very nice,' I said while looking at the picture. 'Did you do this?'

'Yeah,' said Chloe. 'I've been goin to art classes for five years now and the teacher says tha I have a real talent for it. She says that my inner child really comes through in my paintins.'

'But this is done in crayon.'

'Yeah, it's, eh, one of my early works,' she said as she placed a steaming cup of coffee on the table in front of me. I helped myself to milk and sugar.

'Are ya into art?' she asked and then she sat down opposite me and leaned back against the wall. I thought at that point that she might have been flirting with me but I wasn't sure. I kind of hoped that she was. We had a proper conversation after that, a proper grown-up conversation. And it wasn't about art. Once she dared to trust me a little bit she told me all kinds of things. She told me about how when she was sixteen, Norman had made her pregnant and then two years later they were married. I asked her whether

255

she had any regrets and she said that sometimes she wonders how her life might have been different but then she looks at Zoe and it's as if nothing else matters. Chloe was lonely and clearly dying to talk to someone. She didn't seem to have any friends and I could only imagine that that was because Norman had driven them all away. If he remained the dominant presence in her life then there would be no one to encourage her to stand up to him and he would have total control.

After I finished my coffee, she asked me if I wanted another cup and I heard myself saying that I would love one. But I didn't want coffee; I just wanted to talk to her. I wanted to try and understand her and maybe even help her if I could. Maybe I wanted something more as well, but I'm not sure. In any case, Chloe talked and I listened and it wasn't long before I lost all track of time and I completely forgot that I didn't have a real drink in my hand. I felt like she had cast a spell on me and I didn't want it to be broken.

But then . . .

DING DONG, DING DONG, DING DONG.

It was only the sound of the doorbell but to me it sounded like the Gestapo banging down the door.

'OH FUCK!' I said. 'Is tha Norman? It is, isn't it? JESUS CHRIST! It's Norman or else one o his lunatic friends and here we are drinkin bleedin *coffee* together. SHIT!'

I was thinking about Lefty and how Norman had beaten him unconscious with his own artificial leg after he got too close to Norman's mistress. But even if I was somehow able to re-live that moment in my neighbour's kitchen a thousand times over, I don't think that I could possibly be any less cool than I was on that day.

And I completely blew my hand regarding the fact that I was thinking not-so-innocent thoughts about Chloe.

'No, I really don't think that it's Norman, or Jesus Christ, or any o Norman's lunatic friends. I recognise the ring,' and with that she went to open the front door. A few seconds later, Zoe breezed into the kitchen, followed by her mother. I was mortified at my reaction to the doorbell and so I focused on Zoe so that I wouldn't have to look at her mother.

'Hey, Zoe, how's it goin?' I said, genuinely pleased to see her.

'Fine,' she replied, smiling bashfully. In her burgundy school uniform, her little white blouse with its buttercup collar, her knee-high socks and her Harry Potter backpack, she looked like an angel.

'How was school?'

'Fine.'

'Wha did ya do today then?'

'We did em ... lots o things.'

She moved to pour herself a glass of milk from the fridge and then she sat down beside me at the kitchen table like we were old pals. Her drinking glass had a picture of Bart Simpson printed on one side of it.

'Did ya get any homework?'

'Mmmm, yeah. I mean no.'

She stared at me in that way that children can stare right into someone's eyes without feeling uncomfortable and without trying to communicate anything through the look. I smiled at her milk moustache and she smiled back.

'My friend Rebecca has a rabbit, a white one, and she says tha

I can come over and see it whenever I want. Ma, can I go over to Rebecca's house?'

'Not right now, Zo. Your dinner will be ready soon.'

'Wha's for dinner?'

'Dung beetles and carrots,' replied her mother.

'URGHHHHHHHH!' She grimaced at me in exaggerated disgust and I shook my head to indicate that it wasn't true.

'Do ya like *The Simpsons* Zoe?'

'Yeah.'

'Which character do ya like the best in it?'

'Errm, Bart. He's so bold. "Eat my shorts," he says. "Eat my shorts".'

Chloe and I laughed at the child's attempt to impersonate Bart Simpson's voice and Zoe laughed too, delighted with herself, and then she repeated the remark several more times with diminishing success. After that we played a game. We took turns doing impressions of people while the other two guessed who it was supposed to be. It wasn't very sophisticated but it was a lot of fun. Characters from *Sesame Street* featured heavily. Chloe asked me if I wanted to stay for dinner but I declined. I didn't want to overstay my welcome and I wasn't all that mad about dung beetles and carrots in any case.

That night, the dreams started up again.

Sometimes I felt as if I had a ghostly TV screen inside my head that broadcast grey snow for ninety-nine per cent of the time but then sometimes when I was asleep, my internal channel changer flicked to channel 13 whereupon I was forced to watch snuff movies starring the people that I loved the most. I knew from experience that the dreams would become more frequent as the present caught up with the future and, similarly, the signal in my head would get stronger and the images slightly clearer as somebody's time ran out. But I was losing whatever it was that gave me access to such terrible visions. The dreams that I'd had about Owen had contained clear and distinct images almost from the very beginning, whereas my dreams about Mrs Horricks were never quite as lucid. My dreams about Ashling had been somewhat fragmented initially, and even by the end there was nothing like the same level of detail that I'd had in my other two sets of nightmares. This latest dream episode was barely there at all. But it *was* there and I still saw far more than I would ever have wished to see in a thousand lifetimes.

I spent most of my post-Ashling existence as a prisoner in my own mind, evicted from the world. I killed my wife, the only woman that I've ever truly loved, and that has cast a shadow that will always be with me, even on my good days. There is no closure for something like that. Sometimes I find myself standing in the super-market or in the park or wherever, and I get a horrible queasy feeling in my stomach, sort of like vertigo. But it's not a fear of falling as such; it's a fear of somehow having to crawl my way through every day of the rest of my life knowing that I will never see Ashling ever again.

Death held absolutely no fear for me and so if the premonitions had started up again featuring my own violent death as the main event, then I probably would have woken up laughing. I would have danced out of bed and gone running down the street shouting good morning to everyone like Ebenezer Scrooge on Christmas Day. I have experienced both heaven and hell in this life and so the next life doesn't scare me at all.

Or why could I not have foreseen the death of someone I didn't like, or a complete stranger? There had to be thousands of complete strangers dying every day, tens of thousands even, so why couldn't I have just anticipated some stranger going head over heels down a well, say, or electrocuting themselves in the bath? I would still be having disturbing dreams, of course, but I'm sure I could have gotten used to them. Anything would have been preferable to repeatedly witnessing the suffering of the people that I cared about most.

My latest set of precognitive dreams featured Zoe in the starring role. I never thought that I would fall in love again after Ashling but it was impossible not to love Zoe. I loved her bright blue eyes that had not been dulled by age or disappointment. I loved her skin that was so fine and perfect that it seemed to have no pores at all. I loved her hair that felt as soft as a puppy dog's ear. I loved the frown of concentration firmly etched upon her face as she coloured in pictures at the kitchen table. I loved her because she gave me something that I thought I would never have again. She gave me the will to live. In fact she gave me something even more than that. She gave me the possibility of atonement. If I could save Zoe then just maybe I could forgive myself for the deaths I'd caused.

But saving her was never going to be easy because my dreams about Zoe were hardly even worthy of being called dreams. What I saw more closely resembled a single snapshot that would appear suddenly and completely out of context whilst I was in the middle of dreaming about something else entirely. The image was always preceded by music – brash, ugly notes that were instantly recognisable as the melody of 'Teddy Bears' Picnic' without the words. I didn't need to hear the words though because I knew them already.

> *If you go down to the woods today*
> *You're sure of a big surprise.*
> *If you go down to the woods today*
> *You'd better go in disguise.*

This is supposedly a song for little kids to enjoy and yet when I listened to it in my head, there was an unmistakable air of foreboding lurking in the lyrics. For me it conjured up the image of a violent paedophile waiting behind a tree with a hammer in one hand and his exposed cock in the other. There's a verse in the middle, for instance, that goes like this . . .

> *If you go down to the woods today*
> *You'd better not go alone.*
> *It's lovely down in the woods today*
> *But safer to stay at home.*

Need I say more? But the bogeyman in my latest dream wasn't hiding behind any tree in the woods; he wasn't even outdoors. In my dream, Zoe was indoors and there wasn't a tree or a patch of woodland in sight. And although I could make out some things with a certain amount of clarity, there wasn't enough detail to determine the exact location of where the dream was set.

It began in Happy's though and it started off featuring Ashling as the star. My wife had been appearing in my dreams almost every night anyway so that in itself was nothing new. This particular batch of nightmares began with her sitting at a table in Happy's with her two friends on the night we met. And like most dreams it was built on the foundations of memory because there were a lot of accurate details in there. She was wearing the cream-coloured jumper and silver chain that she had been wearing that night and her incandescent beauty made it impossible to focus on anything else. She leaned back and laughed at something and then she tucked a loose strand of hair behind her ear in the way that she used to. I wanted to go to her and whisper something in her ear. I wanted to tell her to get up and get out of the pub before she met me and sealed her fate. But in the dream I had no voice. I was rooted to the spot and all I could do was watch. And then right on cue, the guy wearing the rucksack appeared and knocked over the drinks on the table. A minor scene followed during which Ashling reached underneath the table and began trying to retrieve her bag. As she did so, her cheek almost touched the tabletop. I was watching her from an overhead position when that damn melody started playing, and then, everything changed.

Having been completely focused on my wife with her head almost on the table, there was a flash of light and then *boom*; the bar stools and the drinks and the punters all disappeared and, where Ashling had been, there was now a little girl. It took me a second to realise that it was Zoe. Her head was resting sideways on the tabletop and instead of drinking glasses and bottles, there were painting materials strewn around her. We weren't in Happy's anymore. The child looked almost like she could be sleeping except for one small but very significant detail – she was lying in a pool of her own blood. Her skull appeared to have suffered a recent major injury because blood was pumping out of a hole in her head and creeping towards the edge of the tabletop. It was an image more horrible than I could ever have imagined and that fact along with the ever-increasing frequency with which it appeared in my dreams left me in no doubt that I was seeing snapshots of the future.

I had to save her. I simply had to. This time there could be no fuck-ups because Zoe was the only light that I had left in a world that had turned cold and dark. But then I had another thought. What if I was playing into the hands of some unseen and anonymous force? My mistake with Owen and Mrs Horrick and Ashling had been my attempt to intervene and alter their destinies. In trying to save them, I ended up being the agent of their doom and I couldn't let that happen again. My dilemma therefore was whether or not I should even attempt to change Zoe's fate as I had seen it. I was adamant in my own mind that if God wanted Zoe dead then this time He would have to do His own dirty work because I would have no part in it. I loved that kid way too much to ever want to hurt her and I simply wasn't capable of causing injuries like that to a child, even by accident. Norman, on the other hand, seemed capable of almost anything. He was the one that I feared most for Zoe's sake because even though I was the one who had spent time in a mental hospital, Norman Valentine was just a full moon away from being criminally insane.

After I failed to show up for work on the night of Ashling's anniversary, Roger gave me an official warning and a tension crept in between us after that. I'm the first to admit that I deserved a kick up the arse but I thought that Roger went a bit overboard when he was telling me off. He said that he wasn't 'running a charity for drunken psychos' even though the continued presence of Norman and his gang seemed to suggest otherwise.

A week or so after I got the warning from Roger, there was a particularly nasty fight at Happy's and that was the catalyst that led to me leaving the place for good. The main fight of the night was all over in a couple of seconds because Norman was twice the weight of his opponent. But he didn't care about fighting within his own weight division and that night he picked on a featherweight – Tanya Cox, his occasional girlfriend who can't weigh more than about eight stone without her make-up.

It all started because Norman was sucking the face off Michelle O' Regan in one of the snugs. It's always been my view that sex, unlike justice, should not be seen to be done but Norman looked as if he might just drain his spuds right there on the couch in front of all the punters. But because he's such a classy guy, at the last minute he took her into the jacks and fucked her in a cubicle. Tanya arrived in the pub with her friend Kelly just as Norman and Michelle were emerging from the toilets and she knew the score straight away. Norman meanwhile had returned to sit with his cronies. He had already lost all interest in Michelle after he had taken what he wanted from her and she now looked on the verge of tears. I saw her sidling towards the door, trying to look like she was in control when the truth is that she was just a kid, trying not to look scared.

As it turned out, though, it was Tanya that Michelle should have been scared of that night. Before she reached the front door, Tanya caught up with her and walloped her across the face while screaming at her that she was 'nothin but a dirty fuckin slut'. Norman and his mates looked on and laughed but that just seemed to enrage Tanya even more because she stormed up to Norman, picked up his pint and then emptied it into his crotch. Hats off to her gutsy gesture but it wasn't worth it. Norman isn't worth it. After his Guinness ended up seeping into his underpants, most of the people at his table broke into a chorus of 'oooooOOOH!' like school kids when one of them is summoned to go and see the headmaster. I'd been around Norman's gang long enough to know that one of their ten commandments was that you don't mess with a man's Guinness and Tanya had just taken a dump on that sacred dictum.

The penalty was quick and severe. Norman didn't fly off the handle as you might have expected. Instead he just smiled his gap-tooth smile as if it was all a bit of a laugh really and then he beckoned Tanya to lean down towards him as if he was about to whisper undying love to her. Tanya's head of steam had cleared by then leaving her head full of air once again, and so she complied with Norman's request and leaned in towards her lover. She was half-smiling herself by now, probably thinking that Norman was going to respond to her great gag by pulling her on to his soaked lap and squeezing her tits and telling her that she was going to have to suck all that spilt Guinness out of his crotch. But that's not what happened.

As soon as she was within range, Norman struck like a cobra and bit off her earlobe. I didn't see this happen directly but what I did see was just as disturbing. I heard a loud piercing scream and I looked up to see Tanya with both of her hands over her right ear and a bright red liquid pumping out from between her fingers and streaming down her forearms. I looked at Norman just in time to see him spitting a lump of human flesh on to the ground. Blood was dribbling down his chin and he wiped it away with the back of his hand. He was actually smiling, I'm sure of it. But he had gone too far even by his standards. The rest of his table stared at him aghast. They wanted to be hard men and pretend that they approved but the look on their faces told a different story.

I shouted at Scary Mary to call an ambulance and then I grabbed a handful of tea-towels and ran to help Tanya. She was still screaming. She would pause only long enough to draw breath and then she would start screaming again.

'Shut the fuck up and take it like a man,' roared Norman, making no sense whatsoever.

'Jesus Christ, a big fuckin song and dance over nothin,' said Benny Binchy, looking as if he was about to puke.

I reached Tanya just in time to catch her. She collapsed into my arms in a dead faint, probably after seeing huge drops of her own blood dripping on to the carpet. I wrapped a towel around her head and it began to turn red almost immediately.

Tanya's best friend is a rat-faced girl named Kelly Reilly and she was there also. Kelly is all loopy earrings and sovereign rings and she has a face that only a pimp could love. But she's a good kid all the same. We each grabbed one of Tanya's arms and carried her outside. The fresh air revived her a bit and thankfully she didn't start screaming again. She made a sort of whimpering sound instead and that was almost as bad. I told her not to worry, that the ambulance was on its way and that she was going to be just fine. But she didn't look fine. All of the colour had drained from her face and she looked like she had been dead for about a week.

'Tha prick! Tha fuckin animal!' was the only speech that Kelly seemed capable of. She continually muttered the two phrases to herself, constantly varying the intonation like an actor rehearsing lines.

The ambulance arrived a few minutes later and Kelly and Tanya were bundled into the back of it. Roger came out of the pub carrying Tanya's earlobe on a beer mat. It didn't look much like an earlobe anymore. It looked more like a ketchup-covered chip that someone had stood on. Roger gave it to one of the ambulance guys who packed it in ice and then Tanya and Kelly were sped off to the hospital.

I didn't go back inside the pub. I lit a cigarette and then I just walked away. I heard Roger shouting after me that there were punters that needed to be served and to get my arse back behind the bar but I kept on walking and I didn't look back. I had reached my limit and I was just fucking sick of it; sick of all the posing and the attitude and the violence. My days working in Happy's were over and this time there would be no going back.

I went home and took a bath. For company, I was enjoying the pleasure of five generations of McCabe's finest malt whiskey. Maybe it was drinking down all of those generations that had left me feeling so old all of a sudden. I knocked back a few more shots and then made a submarine out of my glass.

I was already a bit pissed when Damo phoned me. As usual he came straight to the point.

'Wha the fuck happened to you tonight?'

I didn't mince my words either.

'Listen, Damo, you've been great and all but I've had it with tha fuckin job. It's not therapeutic anymore, it's just a gigantic head-fuck and I'm not goin back.'

'Wha?'

'It's no big thing, ya know, and it doesn't mean tha I'm crazy or nothin but I just can't do it anymore. Everythin about tha place wrecks me head.'

'Well tha's nice, tha is!'

'No, I don't mean you. I just mean ... well, ya know yourself ... *everything*. Except you. I was only doin it cos it was sort o therapy for me, ya know, gettin outta the house an all, but I don't need any more therapy. I'm grand.'

'I see,' he said, even though I knew he didn't.

'C'mon, Damo, don't gimme a hard time over this. It's nothin personal. You of all people should understand why I don't wanna work there anymore. It's got more loonies than the fuckin nut house.'

We talked for a while longer and by the time I put down the phone, I think I had convinced him that I was doing the right thing.

I can be very convincing sometimes. I took another swig of Mr McCabe's finest malt whiskey and then I sank my head beneath the surface whilst holding the bottle triumphantly aloft like the sword of King Arthur.

I was awoken the next day by two cops knocking on my front door. Good old Roger must have given them my address. They asked if they could come in and so I let them. It simply wouldn't do to leave our nation's finest standing on the doorstep like a couple of Jehovah's Witnesses. They said that they were investigating 'a very serious assault that had occurred between the hours of midnight and 1 a.m. in The Jolly Roger public house.' I asked whether they meant the thing with Tanya Cox and they said that they did. In the conversation that followed, I pretended to be as helpful as possible while at the same time telling them nothing. I said that unfortunately I had been in the cellar changing a keg at the time of the incident and so I hadn't seen a thing.

I thought that they might just leave after that but they didn't. Instead they started asking me questions about Norman. I admitted that I knew who he was because I had to. The fucker practically lived in Happy's and when he wasn't there, he was living next door to me. They asked me whether I had seen him in Happy's the previous night. I told them that with Christmas approaching, every night in the pub was extra busy and so I couldn't be sure. Then one of them asked me whether my guide dog was allowed inside the pub while I was working. The other one cracked up laughing at this as if it was the funniest thing he had ever heard in his life. I pretended to laugh as well as if it was all a big joke really and we were all in on it together. The cops stopped laughing immediately and glared at me.

'Do ya think this is funny? Wasting police time is a serious offence, ya know?' said the comedian cop. I pretended to be slightly offended at the suggestion that I was being anything less than a star witness but they knew that I was fucking with them.

'At what time did Norman Valentine enter the pub?' said the dopey-looking straight man in an accent as thick as the shite on his father's wellies. He now had his notebook and pencil out and he looked like he meant business. Actually, he looked like someone getting ready to buy heifers at a fair but I guessed that it was the best stab at gravitas that he could muster.

'Eh, I'm not too sure, to be honest. Like I said, it was busy, so I didn't see much o Norman, or Tanya, but I would say tha it was definitely some time before midnight.'

The guards looked at each other and then back at me.

'What have we got here, then, a comedian, is it?' said the comedian cop. 'Norman Valentine is about to be arrested for a Section 3 Assault. Do you have any idea how serious that is?'

'Eh, very serious?' I ventured.

'There's a girl runnin around with half o one o her ears missin where Norman's after takin a bite outta her,' said the bog warrior sidekick. I think that I was supposed to look horrified by this revelation but instead, and I know this is bad, all I could do was bite the inside of my cheeks in an effort not to laugh. I pretended to have a coughing fit in order to release some of the laughter welling up inside me. When

I finally made eye contact with the cops once again, I must have been still smirking because something seemed to snap in the comedian cop.

'I think that we've heard enough of your smart talk, mister, but don't you worry, Garda Geelan and myself will be keepin a very close eye on you from now on,' said the comedian cop and then both of them started moving towards the door. At that point, I just thought *fuck it* and gave up all pretence of being helpful.

'All the best then, Garda, eh ... Geebag was it?' I said to the bog warrior. He followed his colleague into the hall, pretending not to hear me.

'Next time you're callin round, give me a bit o notice and I'll have a pot o tea and some jaffa cakes waitin for yiz, and then afterwards ya can beat a confession outta me with the poker from the fireplace. Would ya like tha?'

There was a loud bang as the cops slammed the front door behind them on their way out. I knew straight away that I'd probably live to regret that little performance but for the next minute or so anyway, it seemed worth it.

After leaving my place, the two wonder cops waded through the knee-high foliage that passes for my front lawn and then they started banging on Norman's front door. I think that Garda Geebag might have stepped in a Big Mickey dog turd landmine because I heard him cry out and when I looked out the window, he was either wiping his shoe in the long grass or else he was pawing the ground like a bull about to charge. Maybe he fancied himself as a human battering ram although he never got to prove himself in that department because Norman opened the door.

'Ah, wha the fuck do youse want?' he said, sounding genuinely surprised that the cops were at his door. The comedian cop came right to the point and in doing so, he fucked me from a height.

'Your next door neighbour has been most cooperative in telling us all about the assault you committed in the Jolly Roger public house last night, and we're now arresting you for an offence under Section 3 of the Non-Fatal Offences Against the Person Act 1997. You don't have to say anything but I must warn you that anything you do say may be used against you in evidence.'

Garda Geebag then stepped forward and snapped the cuffs on Norman.

Norman didn't go mad like you might expect. In fact, he went like a pussycat. But when he was halfway down the driveway en route to the patrol car, he turned and he stared straight at me through my living room window. The look that he gave me said more than a torrent of violent expletives. It was a look that made my blood turn cold.

A few days later, I was on my way back from the newsagent's and the off licence when I met Chloe by the front gate we shared. She had her back to me as she was pushing an empty wheelie bin in from the kerb. She was still wearing her dressing gown and that made me smile as it was already well into the afternoon. Obviously we had quite a few things in common.

'Need any help there?' I said, trying to do the neighbourly thing and probably managing to sound like a chauvinist pig in the process.

No response. She didn't even raise her head to look at me

though she definitely heard me. I walked past her and went inside but I was feeling a bit miffed. I made myself a Bloody Mary and tried not to think about what had just happened but the snub kept pushing its way to the front of my mind. How dare she fucking ignore me when I probably saved her life by calling the fire brigade that night when Norman was on the verge of slicing her up.

How dare she fucking ignore me after I went out of my way to drive her and her kid to the hospital.

How dare she fucking ignore me after I apologised to her and carried her shopping home and listened to her stories.

How dare she fucking ignore me after making me care about her.

I wanted to just have a few beers and forget all about her but my blood was up and I was getting angrier by the minute. The only possible explanation for her ignoring me was that she thought that I had grassed on her husband. But I hadn't grassed on anyone and so, not for the first time, I felt like an innocent man wrongly accused and that kind of injustice drives me crazy. So before I could cool off, I got up and marched next door to put her straight about a few things.

I rang the bell and when there was no answer within about thirty seconds, I started banging the letterbox on the off-chance that the bell was broken. Eventually I heard Chloe shuffle up to the front door and open it a couple of inches. She took one peep at me through the crack and then she closed it again. I was about to start hammering on the door like a lunatic when it was re-opened. She had only closed it in order to take off the chain.

When I could see her properly, all of my hot-headed indignation evaporated in an instant. The woman's face had all the colours of the rainbow in it but none of the charm. Before the cops had taken Norman away and while I was most likely passed out, Chloe's husband had left her a little present to remind her of him. One of her cheekbones was signposted with an angry purple bruise that looked like an ink stain. Her left eye was encircled by a spectrum of black, yellow and brown bruising and the white part of the same eye had a drop of red suspended in it, like a frozen bloody tear. There was a Band-Aid concealing a further injury just above her left eyebrow, and to complete the oil painting, she had a split lip that was still showing traces of dried blood. She looked as if she had been ram-raiding on a scooter the night before.

'Oh I don't fuckin believe this!' I said in perhaps not the most tactful choice of words.

'Whaddya want?' she replied, making me feel about as welcome as a family of cockroaches living in my underwear drawer. I did some fast thinking and tried my best to improvise.

'I just thought tha ... ya know ... I wanted to see if there was anythin tha I could do, now tha you're eh ... I mean, now tha your husband is eh ...'

She stared at me just long enough to make me feel extremely uncomfortable and then she spoke.

'Ya must be feelin guilty about gettin my husband arrested then.'

'Wha are ya talkin about? He bit off someone's ear, for fuck's sake. He got himself arrested.'

Another pause while she weighed up this information and then she sighed heavily and asked me if I wanted to come in. I didn't, but I couldn't very well not go in without looking like an ignorant fucker and I felt a bit guilty as well for having so badly misconstrued the situation earlier on, and so I followed her inside. We went into the kitchen and I sat at the table while she filled the kettle. The tabletop was littered with spent lottery scratchcards.

'Ya didn't win the lottery then?' I volunteered as an icebreaker.

'Wha do you think?' she replied. The lottery was obviously a conversational cul-de-sac so I tried a different approach.

'How's Zoe?'

'She's great. She's due to have her stitches out in another fortnight and I've never once heard her complain. She really is a great kid, considerin.'

I didn't know whether she meant considering her father is in prison or considering her father is a violent psychopath but I'm fairly sure that there was some reference to Norman in that statement.

'And, eh, how are ya keepin yourself?' My pathetic attempt at small talk made me wince on the inside as soon as the words left my mouth.

'Well, I've had better days, to be honest,' replied Chloe, not punishing me for my stupid question. 'Wha about you? Are ya still a ragin alcoholic?' she added, suddenly very much punishing me for my stupid question.

'Wha?' was the best response that I could come up with while I figured out my bearings.

'Look, don't worry about it. It's none of my business if ya wanna drink yourself to death. Go for it, ya know, if tha's wha you're into. I just think tha it might be a bit of a shame cos ya seem like a nice enough bloke.'

'Wha are ya talkin about?' I replied, now on the defensive.

'I mean I don't know ya or nothin but I'm just sayin, like, the way ya brought Zoe to the hospital and all, I thought tha was fairly sound.'

'No, no, wha are ya talkin about sayin I'm an alcoholic?'

'Well ya are, aren't ya?'

'No. I just like a drink is all. Same as lots o people. I wouldn't say tha I have an alcohol problem at all.'

'Sure ya do. Two hands and only one mouth.'

I responded to that last remark with a charity laugh, or a charity snort to be precise but I have to admit that the 'raging alcoholic' tag had left me on the ropes for a few seconds. I've been called a lot of things in my time but never an alcoholic, never mind a *raging alcoholic*. It's a term that just doesn't seem to fit me, even if it does. I've always considered alcoholics to be people like Paddy McKenna who fell off the motorway flyover when he was drunk, not people like me who until very recently managed to hold down a job. The way I see it, Paddy was an alco not because of the amount of alcohol that he drank but rather because of what he drank, and he drank everything: meths, turps, aftershave, silver polish, weed-killer, paint remover, Tipp-Ex thinner, cough mixture, nasal decongestant, Windolene, varnish, washing-up liquid . . . whatever. He didn't give a fuck. I, on the other hand, am that bit more choosy. I wouldn't drink washing-up liquid no matter how gasping for a drink I was.

'If ya would prefer a beer instead of tha, ya only have to ask,' said Chloe, placing a cup of coffee in front of me and then joining me at the table. I considered getting all indignant at that point but then I decided that I just couldn't be arsed pretending. She had seen the state that I ended up in on the day that I drove her to the hospital and after that, she wouldn't exactly need to be Sherlock Holmes to figure out that I was more than a little fond of the sauce. There were other clues as well that were all too obvious. As soon as she had opened her front door, she had probably smelled the booze on my breath from the previous night. Also, about a week previously, Norman had staggered home pissed one night and knocked over my wheelie bin, not his one of course, just mine. And when I looked out at around 2 p.m. the next day, our common front garden was flooded with empty cans and bottles, all the contents of my bin. Those bastard bin men had just ignored it, so I went out and cleared up the mess myself as best I could. But the likelihood was that Chloe had seen the contents of my bin and knew the score.

'Maybe I'll have one after,' I said, 'but only if you'll have one with me.'

That definitely sounded as if I was coming on to her a little and I was surprised at myself because I hadn't intended to flirt with her.

'Fair enough. It's Norman's booze anyway but seein as he's not here, we may as well put it to good use.'

She was easy to talk to. There was no doubt about that. She had a straight-to-the-bone brand of honesty mixed with a sharp wit and that made her very good company. But underneath it all she was obviously a damaged human being. I got the impression that on some miserable secret level, she believed that her life was what she deserved.

After the coffee, she poured me two fingers of whiskey and didn't offer any choice of mixer. That was fine with me. She had another cup of coffee. That was fine with me also. It wasn't even lunchtime yet, and one raging alcoholic in the room was more than enough.

'So have ya heard from Norman at all?' I asked. She replied with a shrug of her shoulders. Her hands were clamped together like a padlock in her lap.

'Is he gettin on all right?'

Chloe paused for a second too long before replying, during which time I got the impression that she was trying to figure out whether I might have been taking the piss.

'He's in Cloverhill Prison.' She paused and gave me another suspicious look. 'So I suppose he's not gettin on all tha great.'

'Have ya been to visit him?'

'Not in Cloverhill no, but I saw him in court yesterday. He was refused bail because he hadn't bothered showin up for a couple o court dates in the past.'

'They wouldn't give him bail? Ah, now here, tha's a fuckin disgrace,' I said, trying hard not to show how happy I was to hear this news. 'He must o been well pissed off.'

'Ya could say tha, yeah. It took about four prison officers to drag him back down to the holdin cells after the judge remanded him in custody. And even with the cuffs on him he was kickin and bitin and spittin at anyone within reach. He was like a man possessed, he was.'

'Really?' I said, swallowing a big mouthful of whiskey and remembering the look that he had given me as the cops led him away.

'He's prob'ly just goin mad cos he hates bein apart from you and Zoe so much.' Now I really was taking the piss because Norman is about as sensitive as a toilet seat. Chloe just laughed though.

'Yeah righ. I'm sure he's cryin his eyes out up there in prison cos he has no one to wait on him hand and foot.'

There was an awkward silence for a few seconds, during which I knocked back the rest of the whiskey. There were a lot of things that I thought needed to be said, but I really didn't think that I was the man for the job. It wasn't my business and it wasn't my problem. I tried convincing myself that Chloe would not thank me for interfering in her marriage and that I would probably only make her feel even worse by getting involved. Then I thought about Ashling and those lies in my head dropped away like scales from my eyes. If my wife had seen Chloe's battered and bruised face for even half a second, she would have tried to help her any way she could and so for what it was worth I decided to throw my oar in. I thought that, if nothing else, I could perhaps offer her friendship.

'Listen, eh, maybe ya should get someone to have a look at your face, ya know? Not tha there's anythin wrong with your face, I just mean tha, ya know, it looks like ya got a bit of a knock there, and, eh, ya might have a concussion or somethin.'

My feeble expression of concern was about as helpful as throwing a ping-pong ball to a drowning man and almost immediately I wished that I had kept my mouth shut. Chloe just stared straight ahead. She knew that I knew how she had been injured even though I had spent the previous couple of weeks tiptoeing around my half of the house, afraid to even swing the fridge door shut lest I be heard. I figured that if the Valentines couldn't hear me, then they would assume that I couldn't hear them, thereby fortifying my magic invisible force field.

'I'm fine,' was her eventual tight-lipped response. I waited while

279

our mutual sense of awkwardness rose to even higher levels and then I leapt over the line even further, venturing completely out of my depth into somebody else's business.

'Why don't ya leave him?' I asked.

If brevity is the soul of wit, then Chloe's reply was very witty indeed: 'Because he'd kill me.'

Fair enough. I didn't press the matter any further. I didn't get the chance. Chloe threw the spotlight right back on to me: 'Why don't ya stop drinkin?'

I didn't have an answer on the tip of my tongue in the way that she had to my last question and so I gave myself time to try and find the right words. I knew that I wasn't going to lie. I'm not sure why exactly but the kitchen in Norman's house at that moment felt like a bullshit-free zone in the way that the visitors' hall at St Pat's had been. I think that the reason might have been because Chloe's beat-up face looked like an SOS signal to the world. Her injuries emanated a kind of brutal honesty in that she could not pretend that she was in anything like a happy marriage while her face screamed the truth. She had no mask that she could hide behind and so I dropped all pretensions of being a teetotalling saint and decided to take off my own mask.

'I can't,' was my eventual response. 'I need it to help me forget.' And with that, I poured myself another shot of Norman's whiskey.

'To forget wha?'

'Tha I killed my wife.'

If Chloe was shocked by this revelation, she didn't show it. In fact, her reaction was one that the world poker champion would have been proud of.

'I didn't know ya were married,' she said.

'I was, but my wife died. It was an accident . . . sort of . . . with the car.'

'"An accident . . . sort of"?'

'It *was* an accident but I knew it was gonna happen and I was drivin the car.'

'I'm sorry.'

'So am I,' I replied, and then with embarrassing speed, tears filled up my eyes and spilled down my cheeks. But I didn't turn away or pretend to have something in my eye. I was in the bullshit-free zone and so I just let it happen.

'You must have loved her very much,' said Chloe, deducing as much from my tears.

'Yeah,' I croaked by way of reply. But Norman's wife didn't look as if she was going to let me off the hook that easily. She stared at me expectantly and a part of me wanted to talk to her. A part of me wanted to at least try and make her understand even though I doubted that I ever could. And so before I really knew what I was saying, words started pouring out of my mouth.

'She was directly responsible for all the best things in my life, but it was more than tha. She was like oxygen to me. She kept my heart beatin and my lungs pumpin just by knowin tha she was a part of my life; but it was more than tha as well. She wasn't just a part of my life, it was like she was a part of me. She was my soul-mate and I loved her with every ounce o life in my body.'

'Wow!' said Chloe. She was staring at me with big sad eyes and hanging on every word I said. 'Lucky you,' she added.

'Sorry?'

'Most people go through their entire lives without ever knowin a love like tha, so when ya think about it tha way, you're really one o the lucky ones,' and with that she reached over and gave one of my hands a quick squeeze. I looked her in the eye and I saw her smile properly for the first time and even with the bruises on her face, in that instant she looked quite beautiful. She had perfect teeth and dimples like God's thumbprints.

'I just wish I could have saved her,' I said with teardrops escaping from both my eyes at the same time. I lifted up my T-shirt and dried my face with it, briefly exposing my belly as I did so. Chloe didn't seem to mind. I said a silent prayer that the next phrase out of her mouth wouldn't be a soulless platitude and she didn't disappoint.

'Tell me wha it's like to meet your soulmate,' she asked, 'if ya wanna talk about it, tha is.'

'No, no, it's fine, honest. I like talkin about it . . . I think.'

I paused to consider what I might say next because I had no idea, but then the words started to flow once again.

'This might sound a little bit weird but when I was a kid, I really wanted to be one half o twins because I thought tha twins were so cool. And I wanted it so much tha I dreamed up this fantasy in my head about how I really was a twin only I had somehow become separated at birth from my other half. But I wasn't completely cut off because sometimes I felt as if some of the random thoughts in my head were really my twin sendin me telepathic messages, but I could never get any proper two-way communication goin. It was a bit like gettin text messages on a mobile tha has no credit left on it. Deep down, I knew tha it was all bullshit but I enjoyed pretendin to meself all the same. It was sort of a beautiful lie.'

'Like Santa Claus?'

'Wha are ya sayin? Ya don't believe in Santa Claus?'

'No, no, course I do.'

'Good. Anyway, the first time tha I saw Ashling, it was sort o like comin face to face with my lost twin. It was a surprise to me o course tha she was female, but fuck it, as soon as I saw her there was this connection like a tractor beam, so wha was I gonna do? Send her back with a note sayin "attachments missing"? Not in a hundred million years. She was beautiful!'

'Don't take this the wrong way or nothin, but ya have to admit tha tha does sound a tiny bit incestuous.'

'Jesus, is tha the way it comes across because it wasn't like tha at all. It was the greatest, most natural thing in the world because I felt so ... loved when we were together. I felt like her heart would split in two if the world fucked me up, ya know? And tha gave me the strength to make sure tha the world didn't fuck me up.'

'Sounds amazin,' said Chloe.

'Did ya ever read those *Asterix* comic books when ya were a kid?' I asked after a short pause.

'Eh, no, sorry. Can't say tha I did.'

'Well they were about a tiny French village tha had resisted being conquered by the entire Roman army, and the villagers were able to do this because one o them was Getafix the druid, and whenever the need arose, he would cook up a magic potion tha would turn Asterix and his fellow villagers into supermen who could then take on the world if necessary, and win.'

'I wouldn't mind some o tha potion,' said Chloe.

'Who wouldn't? But the point is tha Ashling was sort o like my magic potion.'

Chloe nodded her head slowly but I could tell from her furrowed brow that she wasn't really getting it so I tried explaining myself a bit better.

'This might sound a little corny but the thing is, she believed in me. She believed in me more than I ever believed in meself and tha gave me amazin strength ... superhuman strength almost. I don't mean tha I could lift buses or nothin, but I did walk around with a feelin tha I was sort o invincible and tha I could do anythin. And now tha she's gone, I feel like I can hardly tie my shoelaces in the mornin. And so I do whatever I have to in order to make it through another day.'

With that, I picked up my glass and dumped the remainder of the contents into my mouth and then I walked over and placed the empty container in the sink. I paused for a few moments with my head bowed and my back to Chloe. I was doing my silent crying trick again while fresh teardrops collected on the end of my chin in one big drop that hung there in a gravity-defying feat.

I heard Chloe follow me over to the sink and then I felt her hand on my shoulder. I turned around but I could no longer look her in the eye. There was too much honesty in the room and I suddenly felt very exposed.

'It's okay to cry,' she said. But it didn't feel okay to me and that was the problem. It was all so embarrassing. I closed both my eyes tightly but it didn't make any difference as a few more of my tears squeezed their way into the world regardless.

'I just miss her so much,' I offered by way of explanation.

'I know ya do,' said Chloe, taking hold of one of my hands again, only this time, she didn't let go.

'I never imagined or wanted a future without her,' I said.

Chloe gave my hand a little squeeze and what happened after that was pure instinct on my part. I threw my arms around her and clung on like a drowning person. I held her so tightly that I could feel the vibrations of her heart beating in her chest and all the time I kept saying *I'm sorry, I'm sorry, I'm sorry*, over and over again. Chloe was holding me almost as tightly, and she kept repeating *it's okay, it's okay*, while making a circular movement with one of her hands on my back. I wanted to stay like that for ever. Getting that close to another person felt like a highly effective form of pain relief and I could sense that Chloe felt the same.

Long after the time when an embrace like that should have ended, we were still there in Norman's kitchen, clinging to each other as if our lives depended on it. My chin was resting on the top of her head and my arms were joined around the small of her back. She was the same height as Ashling had been and the perfect height for hugging. I smelled her hair and it smelled like coconut. I could feel the swell of her breasts beneath her dressing gown and I felt something stirring in me downstairs. I found myself wondering what she would look like naked.

It was Chloe who spoke first from that position but she made no effort to withdraw from my arms.

'Ya know, unless you're gonna ask me to dance or somethin, ya have to admit tha this is startin to feel a bit weird, don't ya think?'

'You're prob'ly righ,' I replied.

'So do ya wanna dance?'

'Trust me, ya don't wanna see me dance.'

I am a terrible dancer but there is one dance that I can hold my own at, a dance that I used to do with Ashling and one that we called the walk-around-slowly dance. Basically, two people embrace and then walk around slowly in a sort of a circle and that's all there is to it. But I was afraid to do the walk-around-slowly dance with Norman's wife because I knew that I would be thinking about my own wife and that wouldn't be fair to Chloe.

'I used to love dancin but I hardly ever get the chance anymore,' she said.

I didn't want to have a conversation about dancing and so I changed the subject completely. 'Chloe?'

'Yeah?'

'Remember when I drove you and Zoe to the hospital?'

'Uh-huh.'

'How did ya get home in the end?'

'I drove.'

'I thought ya said ya couldn't drive.'

'No, I never said tha.'

'Then why did ya need me to drive ya there?'

'I didn't.'

I paused for a moment to try and make sense of this information but it didn't add up.

'So why did ya ask me?'

Now it was Chloe's turn to pause.

'I just thought tha ... it would be nice if ya were there to keep me company.'

'But why?'

'Because you're not Norman; you're so not Norman.'

'I hope tha's not the best compliment ya can think of.'

'And ya have a cute bum,' she added.

'Tha's okay then. So do you.'

'Really?'

'Really. And ya have an even nicer pair of . . . eyes.'

She smiled again and then buried her face in my shoulder. Drunk with confession or maybe just drunk, I think that I might have kissed the top of her head at that point but I'm not sure. If I did then I suppose that it was me who took the next step into something more than platonic, or maybe we had already gone sailing over that line. It doesn't really matter. But shortly after that, I thought at first that I might have been imagining it but then I was sure; she was peppering the hollow of my throat with tiny kisses. I willed her not to stop but she did. She stopped and moved her head back so that she could look up at me. I looked into her eyes and I saw the loneliest person in the world staring back at me. After that, my heart just sort of melted and we dissolved into each other. Our mouths locked on to each other like two halves of a rugby scrum coming together while our hands raced over each other's bodies as if frantically searching for something. I pulled apart the belt on her dressing gown with my left hand and then I slipped the same hand under her gown and around her waist. Now there was only a thin cotton nightdress separating me from her smooth white skin, and God how I wanted to touch that skin. I slipped my other hand under her gown and caressed her back, while all the time we explored each other's mouths with fervour.

'Wait a sec, I'm sorry,' said Chloe when her lips eventually broke away from mine. 'I'm not sure if I can do this.'

'Oh, em, yeah. Look, *I'm* sorry. I didn't mean to, eh . . .'

'I'm not sure if I can do this because I've got a sore lip.'

'Oh *right*! Of course. Sorry!'

'I've got a sore neck as well but maybe you could kiss it better.'

With that she leaned her head back and I kissed her exposed throat and then her neck and then her shoulder. At that moment, I wasn't thinking about Ashling or where I would get my next drink from; I was thinking about Chloe and every cell in my body suddenly felt alive and electrified. A few minutes later, I felt her fingers interlocking with mine and then without saying a word, she led me upstairs to what was obviously the bedroom that she shared with her husband. She sat down on the double bed and I sat down beside her. There was a chest of drawers in front of us and on it stood a framed photograph of Norman and Chloe on their wedding day; Norman with a big cheesy grin on his face as if he had never raised a hand to a woman in his life. For about ten seconds, we sat there like a couple of awkward teenagers not knowing what to do next, and then Chloe reached over and took my hand.

'We don't have to do this if ya don't want to,' she said.

'I know,' I replied, 'but I do want to.'

'It feels sort o righ, doesn't it?'

And I had to agree with her. It did feel right. It felt so right, in fact, that it would have felt like a crime against nature to get up and walk out of the house at that point. So I took her in my arms and I pulled her close and I remembered what it felt like to be whole again.

When I returned to my half of Silky's house later that afternoon, there was a brand new ache inside of me that seemed to be centred somewhere in my stomach. At first I thought that it might just be my body crying out for me to feed it but even after a plate of my legendary scrambled eggs and toast I could still feel the ache nagging away inside me. It had something to do with Chloe, that much was obvious even though I couldn't say for sure what I was feeling. It wasn't guilt; I knew that much. Since the accident, I had become so well acquainted with guilt that it was now almost like an old friend of mine. It didn't seem like the beginnings of love either, although I was slightly less sure about that.

I had already fallen for Zoe because kids are so easy to love. She conned me right into it. Maybe in another time and another place, her mother and I could have been perfect for each other but at that particular moment, the timing felt all wrong. I cracked open a beer and sat at my kitchen table with all these thoughts flying around in my head. And then I remembered a discussion that I'd had once with a Jamaican guy called Royston Deloquart who used to deliver kegs to Happy's. His name was Royston but everyone called him Roy and in return, he called everyone *my friend*. He had a voice that that you could gravel the driveway with and he used it to preach his own armchair philosophies at every opportunity. One of his theories was that the timing of a person's life is never a random accident, and therefore everyone comes along at a time that is best suited to them. By way of example, he named people like Shakespeare, Hitler, Elvis, Bill Gates and Jesus, and maybe there was something in what he was saying because, let's face it, if Jesus came along now, he'd be fucked for the lack of capital punishment.

Unless, of course, he ended up in America and somehow managed to get himself on death row in which case the universal symbol of Catholicism might have been the electric chair, which I can't really see catching on somehow.

But it was the memory of that particular discussion with Royston Deloquart that made me question whether the timing of my liaison with Chloe was really as bad as I had thought at first. It crossed my mind that, just maybe, what had happened between us was all part of some greater plan. But when I thought about it some more, I realised that there was a flaw in Roy's theory which meant that I couldn't possibly take it seriously. Of course I only realised the flaw about two years too late but that's always the way with killer points in a discussion; they're never there when you need them. The flaw as I saw it was that there could have been loads of people born with the talents of Shakespeare, Hitler, Elvis, and so on, but they just never came to prominence because they were born in the wrong era, and so I arrived back at my original conclusion which was that the timing of me and Chloe getting together really was terrible.

I was still thinking about Norman's wife when my thoughts were interrupted by the sound of the phone ringing. I went to the hall and picked up the receiver warily.

'Hello,' I said.

'Hey fucko, guess who!' came the unmistakable voice of Norman through the earpiece. It was a voice that reminded me of razor blades wrapped up in a silk handkerchief. I immediately felt my pulse quicken and my blood turn a shade cooler. He knew. Somehow he knew and now he was ringing to tell me what he was going to do to me just so that I would continually shit myself until he actually caught up with me.

'Norman, how's it goin? I thought ya were in prison,' I said, trying hard to suppress the tremble in my voice.

'I am, thanks to you, and now I've only got a few minutes so I'm gonna make this quick. I know tha ya talked to the cops about me . . .'

'Ah, now here, Norman, I never said . . .'

'SHUT UP! JUST SHUT THE FUCK UP! I'll talk and you listen, righ?'

'Eh . . .'

'*RIGHT*?'

'Yeah sure, whatever.'

'Ya know, I ought to cut your fuckin bollox off for grassin me up, but seein as we go back a long way and all, I've thought of a way how ya might still get outta this with your nads intact.'

That's when I realised that he had no idea that I was after sleeping with his wife. He was pissed off but not that pissed off, so I knew that this was about something else entirely. I found myself holding my breath in silent dread of what he might say next.

'Well if there's anythin I can do to help . . .' I offered.

'Oh there's somethin ya can do, aw righ, and ya will do it. I've put in an application for High Court bail tha's gonna be heard on Monday and I need you to go surety for me.'

'Wha's a surety?'

'It's a piece o fuckin piss, tha's what it is. All ya have to do is tell the judge tha you'll pay a certain amount of money if I don't turn up for me next court date. Ya don't even have to do nothin;

just say tha ya wanna be me surety and then show him a statement or somethin so they know you've got money.'

'Why don't ya get Chloe to do it?'

I said this not because I was trying to pass the buck but because
she seemed like the obvious choice in the circumstances.

'Because she doesn't even have a fuckin bank account and I know
you have wads o cash after sellin tha gaff o yours.'

'Ah now, I wouldn't say tha I've wads o cash, Norman. I had to
pay off me mortgage on the last place outta ...'

'SHUT THE FUCK UP YOU WHINEY FUCKIN CUNT! I'm
not wastin all me call credits listenin to you lyin to me, so just
fuckin tell me ... are ya gonna go surety for me or not?'

It didn't matter whether or not I went surety for him, or whether
or not I had grassed him up, or even whether or not I had slept
with his wife, because it was quite obvious that Norman had plans
for me just as soon as he got out of prison. I could sense bad
thoughts breeding in his head like maggots in a cadaver.

There was a pause of about three seconds during which I felt
like I was having a staring match down the phone line with Norman.
It was me who blinked first.

'Yeah, sure, course I will, cos like ya said, we go back a long way
and all. But just for the record, I want ya to know tha I didn't ...'

'My solicitor's name is Alex Meehan. He's in the phone book.
Give him a ring and find out when ya have to go to court.'

And then he hung up on me.

I poured myself a shot of whiskey to steady my nerves and then
I went back into the hall where there was a telephone directory
under the phone. I found Alex Meehan & Co. easily enough and

I gave them a call. The person who answered the phone said that all the solicitors were in court. I told her that it was an emergency and so she put me through to someone who said he was an apprentice but who probably just made the tea for all I knew. But he seemed to know all about Norman Valentine without having to consult any file and so I believed that he knew what he was talking about.

I told him that I had agreed to be Norman's surety and he told me that there would be a bail application made on Monday. I already knew that but he also told me that I wasn't required to go to court until the following Wednesday because it would take two days for the court order to be prepared. He asked for my name and address so that the guards could run a check on me and he told me to show up in the Bridewell District Court on the following Wednesday and to bring a bank statement with me. I asked him if there was any chance that Norman could get out before the following Wednesday and the apprentice told me that there was very little chance of Norman getting bail at all. This was because he had committed his latest offence while he was on bail for assaulting the fireman, and so the guards would most likely object to him getting bail again. I felt a little bit better after hearing that. I had absolutely no intention of going to the district court and entering into a bond to be Norman's surety. No fucking way. The only reason that I had phoned up Norman's solicitor was to find out when that lunatic might be released.

That was a Friday and so I figured that I probably had at least five days before Norman killed me. I figured that to be the worst-case scenario. And when I failed to show up in court to be his surety, he wouldn't get bail until he could get someone else to act as his guarantor and that was bound to take at least another few days to sort out. The best-case scenario would of course be if he was denied bail altogether. If that happened, then he would have to remain in custody until his trial and if the justice system worked even a little bit, he would surely go down for three or four years. But I focused on being ready to deal with the worst-case scenario. I really had no idea if Norman would get bail or not but I knew that I definitely didn't want him living next door to me again and beating the crap out of Chloe every time he felt pissed off about something. Whether I liked it or not, things had changed and I couldn't go on pretending to be deaf and dumb.

I went for a walk to do some thinking. I had a lot to think about. I had kissed the mouth that had kissed the mouth of Norman Valentine. I had slept with the wife of a stone-cold lunatic who already wanted to kill me for entirely unrelated reasons. But the threat of Norman's revenge didn't scare me as much as it should have because I found that my thoughts kept drifting back to Chloe. I tried to remember as many details as I could about what had happened between us because I wanted to prove to myself that it had in fact happened and wasn't just something that I had dreamed up.

I didn't see her again until the Sunday of that week, two days later. I agonised over whether or not to call around on the Saturday but eventually I reached a point where I was just too pissed to go anywhere. The next day I hated myself for not being more decisive and at the same time I decided that nothing was going to stop me from meeting up with Chloe that day. I needed to eat first though and so I force-fed myself a box of some convenience crap that I nuked in the microwave. It was hard to tell where the cardboard ended and the meal began but I didn't care. I ate in silence at the kitchen table and as soon as I was finished, I put something in a bag for Zoe and then I marched next door with a steely determination. I had to ring twice before Chloe opened the door with obvious trepidation.

'Oh, em, hi!' she said. She was turning her wedding ring round and round on her finger and for a second it looked doubtful whether she was even going to ask me inside, but then she opened the door wider and I followed her into the kitchen. Zoe was hosting a doll picnic on the floor. Although mind you, it was a doll picnic that a stuffed panda appeared to have gatecrashed. When she saw me, a big smile broke out on her face.

'She's mad into those dolls,' said her mother. 'I just can't get her away from them.'

'Well I'm glad tha she's here cos it's Zoe tha I've come to see really.'

Chloe blinked once and in that blink I thought I saw a flicker of disappointment.

'You want to see me?' asked Zoe, pointing at herself as she did so in case there was any confusion.

'Sure,' I said. 'I brought ya somethin,' and with that I gave her Freddy the teddy. Zoe took him out of the bag that he was in and then she stared at my wife's teddy bear as if he was something miraculous.

'He's very old and he needs someone to look after him but he's very special as well and tha's why I couldn't hand him over to just anyone. But I have a feelin tha he'll be very happy here. I've told him all about Tiny and I think they're gonna be great friends.'

Zoe gave Freddy a big hug and I thought at that moment that I would give my life for that kid if it came down to it.

'Wha do ya say?' said her mother, looking sternly at the child.

'Thank you,' said Zoe shyly but without ever taking her eyes off me.

'He can join in the picnic,' she added and then she sat Freddy down next to Tiny on the floor and placed a plastic cup and saucer in front of him. *If you go down to the woods today* . . . sang a little voice inside my head. I pushed it quickly out of mind and said something that surprised even me.

'Anyone wanna come to the zoo?'

'The zoo?' said Chloe.

'The *zoo*?' said her daughter. 'Wha's the zoo?'

'It's great, you'll love it. They have real pandas there, and real bears too.'

'And rabbits? Do they have rabbits?'

'Oh yeah. They got more animals than Noah. Whaddya say, Chloe?'

'Well, em, she's never been to the zoo and it would be a treat for her I suppose. When were ya thinkin o goin?'

'Well, no time like the present, so how about now?'

And that's how we ended up taking Norman's car and heading off to the zoo for the day. And it was great, really, really great. We walked around and saw all the animals and we ate ice cream and then we ate fish and chips in the restaurant. Anyone watching us would have thought that we were a regular happy little family on a day out. And that's kind of what it felt like as well. It was a feeling that I thought I could get used to. My favourite part of the whole day was when we were standing by the monkey cage, and Zoe slipped her hand into mine and looked up at me with those trusting eyes. I think that it was probably at that exact moment that I knew what I was going to do.

I was going to run away.

That night, there was a variation to my usual dream about Zoe. This particular nightmare was set in the front room of Norman's house where he kept all of his knives. In the dream, I was sitting on the couch beneath the window and my hands were tied behind my back. There was something stuffed into my mouth that made me want to gag and I was sore all over. I knew that Norman was in the room because I could hear his voice but at first I couldn't see him. Then I noticed something different about the *Raging Bull* poster that was hanging over the mantelpiece. It was the same black and white photo of a boxer facing the camera in a fighting stance only now Norman's head was where De Niro's should have been. And that wasn't the only thing that was different. The picture looked a lot more real than it had any right to and that was because in my dream it was real. In fact, not only was it real, it was moving. Norman was dancing from foot to foot and punching the air while saying *Did you fuck my wife?* over and over again. After a while he stopped and he turned slowly towards me. He looked me right in the eye and then he began to sing:

If you go down to the woods today
You'd better not go alone.
It's lovely down in the woods today
But safer to stay at home.

The last time that I had seen a picture on a wall come to life, I had been admitted to the loony bin very soon afterwards but this experience felt very different to my previous one. This time, my vision was in the context of a dream, whereas when I saw the moving picture of Ashling on the wall in front of me, a tiny part of my brain remained aware that my mind was taking a break from a reality that had become simply unbearable. But now it seemed as if an alternative reality was being thrust upon me and it was entirely beyond my control to do anything about it.

Admittedly I had stopped taking all of my prescription drugs. I had been prescribed a daily fistful of pills that included anti-hallucinogens. I stopped taking them because I could never remember to do so and also because they came with a severe warning never to mix them with alcohol. To my credit, I never did take them with alcohol; I never took them at all in fact but I don't believe that my dream was in any way related to me not taking my medicine. Don't ask how I know this but the dream was something that came from outside me, broadcast directly into my brain. Its origin did not lie in my subconscious. I may be screwed up but I'm not that screwed up.

In the dream, I tried to cry out but I couldn't do so because there was something in my mouth. My breathing became shallow and fast and suddenly I was roasting all over. I felt like I was suffocating. I started shaking my head from side to side and that's when I woke up. One corner of the pillow was stuffed into my mouth, stifling a scream.

Something terrible was going to happen and soon. Of that I was certain and I knew that I had to do something. I had been wrestling with a dilemma about whether it might in fact be best if I just didn't get involved, but I found it impossible to stand back and do nothing simply because I'd had bad experiences in the past. The bottom line was that Zoe and her mother needed me and I can't tell you how good it felt to be needed again. It was like a warm breeze on a dying fire.

I threw on some clothes and, as I did so, the coppery smell of blood filled my nostrils. I knew from bitter experience exactly what that meant. Today was the day. It may as well have been painted in blood on my bedroom walls.

I raced out of the house and started banging on Chloe's front door. When she didn't answer within five seconds, I became convinced that I was already too late. But then I heard the kitchen door opening and someone walking the length of the hallway. Chloe opened the door tentatively and looked at me with concern.

'Are ya aw righ?' I said.

'Yeah. Why wouldn't I be?' she replied.

'Wha about Zoe? Where is she?'

'She's havin a nap. Wha's wrong?'

'Can I come in?'

'Sure.'

I stepped into the hallway and then I gave her a hug that lifted her off the ground. I didn't want to let go but eventually I had to release her.

'Wow, now tha's the sort o hello tha I could get used to,' she said.

'Can I see Zoe?' I asked.

'Eh, okay,' said her mother and then she took my hand and led me upstairs. We paused together in the doorway of the sleeping child's room and looked in. She was lying under a single sheet and she had managed to get one arm around both Tiny and Freddy while the thumb of her other hand was in her mouth. There were cartoon rabbits on her pyjamas. Her chest was going up and down as she breathed and there was no sign of any head wound whatsoever. I could quite easily have cried with relief when I saw that she wasn't hurt. The child looked so beautiful that just the sight of her almost gave me a pain in my heart.

'I'm so glad tha you're both okay,' I said to Chloe who was standing in front of me and then I slipped my arms around her waist and gave her a squeeze. She turned around and kissed me on the mouth. It was a lingering kiss that turned into a snog. For the second time, Chloe took me into her bedroom and we made love. Afterwards we lay side by side together for a long time. The anguish induced by my most recent dream hadn't completely melted away and I still had work to do.

'Listen, eh, Chloe, I think I should tell ya tha I'm leavin.'

'Wha?' she replied.

'I'm gettin outta here. This estate, Rathgorman, Dublin, everythin! I can't stand it anymore.'

'Where are ya goin?' she asked quietly.

'I dunno. London prob'ly.'

'You're runnin away?'

'Too bleedin righ I am.'

'Why?'

'I need to start again somewhere completely new. There are too many bad memories for me in this city and it's wearin me down. I feel miserable pretty much all the time and tha's not the real me, ya know? I'm sick and tired o bein sick and tired.'

There was a pause for a few seconds while she absorbed this information and then she spoke again.

'Wha about me? I thought tha you and me ... ya know?'

'I feel the same, ya know I do. And tha's why I want ya to come with me. Both o yiz.'

'Wha? Me and Norman?'

She was joking of course and a part of me loved her for that.

'No, you and Zoe.'

'Wha about Norman?'

'In the circumstances, I think it would prob'ly be best if he didn't come.'

'No, I mean ... wha about Norman?'

'Wha about him? He doesn't deserve ya. Or Zoe. You'd be better off without him.'

'Yeah but ... ya don't know wha he's like. He'll come after us and he'll kill me. He'll kill both of us.'

'By the time he gets out we'll be long gone and he'll never find us. We won't leave any forwardin address and he won't be arsed leavin the country to look for us.'

'Yeah but London ... it's a different country an everythin.'

'Good. It'll be a new start for both of us then. For all three of us. And don't worry about money, I've got more than enough to get us up an runnin until I can get another bar job.'

'Wha about Zoe? I can't just pull her outta school and drag her off to England.'

'Sure ya can,' I replied. 'Think about wha's best for her.'

'Maybe she needs her da.'

'Maybe she does but look at it this way ... do ya really think she needs to see her da bringin drugs into the house and layin into you whenever he gets pissed off about somethin? Do ya think tha's not gonna fuck her up when she gets older?'

I might have crossed a line by saying that. Chloe stiffened slightly and a flash of anger passed across her face but it was only for a second. I felt that she was very slowly coming around to the idea. The real difficulty was that after years of being married to Norman, almost all of her self-esteem had been eroded and so she couldn't understand why I would want to be with her. She didn't say anything for a little while and then she went straight to the bottom line.

'Why would ya want to run off with me?' she asked.

'Because ya make me smile and tha's an amazin thing at this point in my life.'

'But look at me ... I'm damaged goods.'

'Don't ever say tha. *Ever*! We're all damaged goods and besides, it's me who should be askin you why would ya possibly want to run off with me. I've been in prison and I've been in the loony bin and I've got more baggage than bleedin Ryanair, so I'm not exactly catch o the day, ya know?'

'Sorry.'

'You've got nothin to apologise for,' I said.

'Love means never havin to say you're sorry, righ?'

'Well, I wouldn't go tha far! We hardly know each other.'

She looked at me in exaggerated disgust, forcing me to back down.

'I'm only messin with ya! Ya know I am. Why is it only you tha gets to crack the funnies around here?'

'Because I'm the smart one.'

'Well then prove it and come away with me.'

'I'll think about it. How's tha?'

'Well I hope tha you're a quick thinker because I'm leavin in a few hours.'

'Wha? Why?'

'Things are gonna go bad around here, very bad, and soon. I don't mean between me and you, I just mean ... well, don't ask me to explain cos I can't righ now but I know tha we have to get outta here as soon as possible.'

'Are ya serious?'

'I've never been more serious about anythin in me life.'

'I don't know wha to do.'

'Okay, well let me help ya. There's a voice inside ya tha only you can hear, righ? And ya should listen to what it says.'

'It says "kill all the whores!"'

'Wha?'

'Joke!'

If she kept making jokes like that then I was seriously in danger of falling in love with her.

'I think we should do this, Chloe. I really do. I'm not sayin tha I can cure your life or nothin but I just think tha we could be good for each other. And ya know tha I'm completely nuts about your kid.'

'She is a great kid.'

'She's perfect and no offence but I think she deserves better than this.'

'How can I not take offence at tha?'

'Come on, Chloe, I'm not criticisin, I'm just sayin . . . this is not as good as it gets, ya know? Sometimes you've just got to say *fuck it* and take a chance.'

'I know tha.'

'Well then ya should reach out and grab somethin better when it comes along.'

'How do I know tha you won't leave me high and dry? I could end up homeless and broke in a foreign country.'

'I won't ever let tha happen, I promise ya, and I never break a promise. Ya have to believe in somethin, ya know, and I'm askin ya to believe in me.'

'Tha's a lot to ask.'

'Yeah, I know.'

She didn't say anything for a minute or so and I knew well enough when to stay quiet. Eventually Chloe broke the silence.

'Ya said tha ya never break a promise.'

'Never.'

'Well I won't go anywhere with ya unless ya promise me sincerely tha you'll clean up your act.'

'If tha's wha it takes to get ya on tha plane, then I promise I'll stop drinkin.'

'Do ya mean it?'

'Cross my heart. Now will ya come with me or wha?'

'Aw righ then, just this once.'

'Yeah?'

'Yeah.'

'Woohoo!'

For the first time since Ashling's passing, I actually felt happy. Walking on air happy. I kissed her and hugged her and then I kissed her again. I jumped up and started pulling on my clothes. I told Chloe that we would have Christmas dinner in the Ritz Hotel and that Zoe could have whatever she wanted out of the biggest toy shop we could find. That wasn't bribery, by the way, as Chloe had already agreed to come with me, but ideas were coming into my head thick and fast now and they all sounded great. We could take a carriage around Hyde Park or go to a West End show. We could check out the museums and the art galleries or even just feed the pigeons in Trafalgar Square. I had never been to London. I had been hardly anywhere in fact and now it felt as if the whole world was on the verge of opening up to me.

But we still had some way to go before all our troubles were behind us. I knew that I would be a lot less anxious when we were safely on the plane and I told Chloe as much. I told her to start throwing what she regarded as essential into a bag because we were leaving as soon as possible. How long does it take to pack up your life into one or two suitcases? I had no idea but while Chloe was busy doing just that, I decided to walk into Rathgorman Village in order to buy the plane tickets from the local travel agent. I was so excited that I almost got run down crossing the street. I jumped back out of the path of a filthy white van and it was such a near miss that the driver didn't even have time to blow his horn. I had narrowly escaped death or serious injury and I found that I cared. I had regained the will to live and somewhere along the way I started believing that everything was going to turn out okay.

I was wrong.

When I got back to the house about an hour later, the curtains were closed in the sitting room and the front door was slightly ajar so I had a bad feeling straight away. My heartbeat moved up a gear and my palms began to sweat. I gave the door a little shove and it swung all the way inwards in a silent arc.

'Chloe?' I called into a very empty-looking house. There was no reply. There was no sound of any kind, in fact, just an uncomfortable silence that hung in the air. I feared the worst. I had fucked up. I had left them alone at a time when they needed me the most and now they might be dead already. And even if they were still alive, I knew that they were in trouble. Norman-sized trouble. Every nerve ending in my body was screaming at me to turn around and walk away.

But then I thought *fuck it* and stepped over the threshold and into the hallway. There were only two people left in the entire world who needed me and so walking out on them when they needed me the most simply wasn't an option. If there was even a one in a million chance that I could save them then I knew that I would take those odds and play the game. Besides, I had grown intensely weary of crawling through life on my hands and knees and it felt good to stand up again. It was time to show some character.

Even though I had announced my presence by calling out Chloe's name, I still tried to be as quiet as possible when I entered the house so as not to alert any intruders. Zoe's coat was hanging by the hood from the end of the banister and I knew that her mother wouldn't have let her leave the house without it so I figured that she was either still in the house or else she had been taken away in a hurry. The kitchen door was open and I had a quick glance inside. From what I could see the room appeared to be empty unless someone was crouched down behind the counter. The sitting-room door was closed. I paused in front of the closed door and listened as hard as I could but the strident thumping of my own heart made it impossible to hear anything. My heart felt like a wild animal inside my chest, struggling to escape. I held my breath and folded my arms and tried again to hear something. I became convinced that there was someone on the other side of the door listening intently for sounds outside the room. I was about to knock on the door or call out again when I heard a noise from within. It wasn't much of a noise but it upped the ante considerably on the tension that I was already feeling. The noise that I had heard wasn't quite a groan; it sounded more like a sort of a muffled cry and it scared the hell out of me.

I abandoned my position by the sitting-room door and I sneaked into the kitchen. I walked over to the sink and drew a knife from a triangular block of wood that lay on the counter. The knife that I chose had a big don't-fuck-with-me blade on it and it looked quite capable of stopping an elephant in its tracks. I went back to the sitting room and paused once again by the door while I considered my options. Someone was inside Norman's chamber of horrors.

I was sure of it. I considered kicking in the door and barging in NYPD-style, but the chances were that whoever was in the room was already aware that I was creeping around the house, and so the element of surprise might backfire as I was the one who was likely to be surprised the most. I bent down and tried to look through the keyhole but the key was in the lock on the inside and so I couldn't see anything.

I pulled down the handle of the door very slowly with one hand while brandishing the carving knife with the other. The door opened a crack and I could see Chloe sitting on the couch by the far wall. She lifted her head as the door opened and I could see that she had black tape plastered over the lower half of her face and her hands appeared to be tied behind her back. As soon as she saw me, she started making guttural noises and gesturing with her eyes and with her head. I instinctively took a step into the room to go to help her and almost as soon as I started to move I realised what she had been trying to tell me – there was someone behind the door.

I just had time to register Norman stepping out from behind the open door before he locked his free hand on to the handle of my knife, crushing my hand in the process. After that he let go of my right wrist and with his right arm he smashed his elbow into my face. His elbow felt like it had been carved out of solid granite and contact with it felt like being hit with a sledgehammer. There was a sort of crunching sound as my nose broke in several different places and at the same time I felt my mouth filling up with blood.

But Norman was only getting warmed up. He leaned forward and headbutted me full in the face and that was even more painful than the blow from his elbow. My vision exploded into a burst of white stars and at the same time I felt my knees go weak. Norman still had a grip of my right hand, the hand in which I was holding the knife, but I might as well have been holding a bunch of flowers at that point for all the difference it made when it came to defending myself. With his free hand, Norman grabbed my left hand by the wrist so that he was now holding both of my hands and then he pulled me forward suddenly and forcefully on to his raised knee. I think he was aiming for my testicles but my stomach took most of the impact. He let go of my hands and I immediately collapsed to the ground.

After a few seconds, I opened my eyes. I was lying on the varnished floorboards and everything seemed to have turned pink. A blood vessel must have burst inside one of my eyes and the result was that I was seeing the world through a rose-coloured filter. I blinked once and when I opened my eyes again I could see within touching distance a pair of little feet wearing little pink shoes. Norman's daughter had the best seat in the house to see her father beat the living shit out of me. I wanted to tell her to look away but I couldn't and so I concentrated on her feet instead. There were tiny butterflies sewn around the top of each of her socks and they reminded me of a time when I was a kid and my mother was showing me how to draw a butterfly. I was very young, younger than Zoe, and I was sitting at the kitchen table watching my ma closely as she drew beautifully symmetrical butterfly wings. When it came to be my turn, I held the crayon using all of my stubby little fingers while she guided my hand over the paper. I remembered the feel of her hand on mine and the kindness in her eyes.

And then Norman's boot crashed into my kidneys.

'THIS ...' he yelled, 'IS FOR GRASSIN ME UP, YA JUDAS FUCKIN CUNT, YA!' He said it slowly in order to give himself time to punctuate the remark with five or six good solid kicks into various parts of my body. I had no doubt in my mind at that point that Norman was going to beat me to death but what really bothered me was the fact that Zoe was going to witness my demise and might even have been about to follow me prematurely into the next life.

'AND *THIS* IS FOR TRYIN IT ON WITH MY WIFE,' roared Norman and with that he planted his final kick into my head.

The world turned black.

I don't know for how long I was out but it was the taste and smell of my own sock that brought me back to this world. I woke up sitting beside Chloe on the sofa and with my hands bound behind my back with what felt like tape. My feet were similarly bound and Norman was trying to cram one of my socks into my mouth. I tried to spit it out but before I could he wrapped black tape over my mouth and around my head. My stomach started to gag and I felt a stab of agony from what was probably several broken ribs. But far more worrying than that was the fact that I now felt like I was going to vomit and my mouth was taped shut. The sock in my mouth became sodden by the sudden rush of syrupy liquids trying to escape from me but nothing was able to pass in or out of my mouth. I would have given anything at that point just to be able to spit but I couldn't.

I bit down hard on the sock and breathed heavily through my nose. Survival now was all about trying to remain as calm as possible because any element of panic would surely result in me drowning in my own fluids. I picked a spot on the floor and I concentrated hard on it. I thought about the message on Lisa's postcard and I recited it over and over in my head: *I'm going to breathe in, and then I'm going to breathe out, and then I'm going to do it again, and then I'm going to do it again.* I don't think that she meant it to be taken quite so literally but I found that having something to concentrate on calmed my mind and suppressed the urge to be sick at the same time.

'Are ya aw righ there, petal?' said Norman, grabbing my hair and pulling my head back so that I was staring right into his face. His gun was tucked down the front of his jeans and he had a jagged-edged hunting knife in one of his hands. He stroked my cheek with the flat of the blade as he spoke to me.

'Ya looked like ya were gonna puke there for a minute. Ya must o had a bad pint or somethin. Maybe one o those pints o fuckin piss that ya spend your life pullin in Happy's, you pathetic fuckin loser.'

He let go of my hair and my head fell back to looking at the floor.

'Wha about you, sweetheart?' Norman said to his wife. 'Would ya like a glass o water or somethin? Or wha about your man's cock in your mouth? Would ya like tha? Cos after I cut it off, tha's where it's goin.'

I tried to ignore that last comment of Norman's but it wasn't easy. If he was trying to scare me then he had succeeded. I was scared shitless.

I was wearing a short leather jacket and now Norman pulled it open using his knife. He reached into my inside pocket and pulled out the paper pouch containing tickets that the travel agent had given me. Now I was even more worried because the tickets were undeniable proof that I had intended to run off to London with that lunatic's wife and daughter.

'Goin somewhere?' said Norman as he thumbed through the tickets. I risked a glance at Chloe. She was visibly trembling while staring at the wall. I touched her thigh with my thigh in an attempt to try and comfort her but she didn't respond.

'London!' said Norman. 'Very nice. I've always wanted to go to London. But hang on a minute, I don't see any ticket here for me. There must be some mistake. Let's see now, we have a ticket for you, a ticket for this slutty bitch here, and a ticket for Zoe. Where's my ticket, huh?'

I looked straight ahead and did my best to ignore him but that just seemed to piss him off even more.

'Look at me when I'm talkin to ya,' he said, grabbing me by the throat. 'It's only fuckin manners.'

I looked at him and he stared back at me with a sort of leer on his face.

'Maybe ya thought tha I wouldn't be able to go cos ya put me in fuckin prison but I asked Santa for bail without a surety and the old cunt sorted me out early. And now I come home *to this*?'

He punched me hard in the face and I fell into Chloe's lap. My cheek had been cut open by one of his rings and now I could feel warm blood flowing down my face. Norman pulled me back to an upright position by my hair before he started talking again.

'Ya know I have to say I'm surprised,' he said. 'I always thought ya were a faggot and now I find tha ya were plannin on runnin off with me wife and kid. Do I look like the sort o man who would just let tha happen? Do I? Cos I'm not.'

He threw his knife forcefully at the floor where it jammed into the floorboards with an ominous *thunk* sound and then he ripped up the three tickets right in front of my face.

I tested the strength of the binding on my wrists but they were securely bound. I looked over at Zoe. She was still standing in the same place and she looked as if she had been hypnotised or some-thing. I tried to give her a reassuring smile but it wasn't possible with the tape over my mouth.

'I've heard about sick cunts like you,' said Norman as he pulled his gun from his waistband. 'Ya go around lookin for a woman who already has kids and then when ya find one, ya pretend tha you're interested in her when all ya really wanna do is ride the hole off the kids. Does tha sound familiar at all? Cos ya can't expect me to believe tha you're runnin off with this stupid bitch for any other reason.'

He waved the gun around as he spoke. I wondered whether he was going to kill us using the knife or the gun but as it turned out, Norman had something else in mind entirely.

'Did ya ever see tha film *Reservoir Dogs*?' he said. It didn't seem to bother him that all of his questions had become rhetorical seeing as Chloe and I were gagged.

'Great film,' he said. 'I was thinkin about it on me way over here and it gave me an idea for somethin.' He stuck the gun back into his waistband and then he reached down by the side of the TV and pulled out a five-gallon can of petrol. He held it up with a big shit-eating grin on his face like a woman selling washing powder in a sixties television commercial. Then he unscrewed the cap and started throwing petrol over Chloe and me. As far as I know, petrol can be used as an antiseptic but I had serious doubts that Norman's actions were intended for any medicinal purposes.

'There's this great scene in *Reservoir Dogs* where one o the guys pours petrol all over this cop tha he has tied up, and then he cuts the guy's ear off. It's fuckin brilliant.'

Norman put the petrol can on the ground and then he sat down in his favourite black armchair.

'The electrics in this place are a fuckin joke. I mean look at this . . .'

He picked up the flex of an electric heater and I could see that it was slightly frayed near the plug end. Norman ripped the insulation back a few inches until the coloured wires were clearly visible.

'Stuff like this is an accident just waitin to happen,' he said. 'It's a fuckin deathtrap, I'm tellin ya. Liable to burn this whole fuckin dump to the ground. And no one wants to get burned alive, do they? I've heard it said tha it's one o the worst ways to go cos it's not quick, and ya can bet your last fuckin euro that it will hurt in ways tha ya didn't even believe were possible. Still, though, couldn't happen to a nicer couple.'

Norman started rummaging through his pockets searching for something.

'Ya haven't got a light, have ya?' he asked. I ignored him and kept staring at a spot on the ground. Norman got up and retrieved a lighter from the mantelpiece.

'Any last words . . . ? No?'

Zoe was still in the room standing by the door. If her mother and I were to be burned alive, I simply couldn't bear for the child to witness such an appalling spectacle and so I started writhing furiously and making all the noise that I could. Chloe did likewise.

'Daddy . . .' said Zoe hoarsely. I think that Norman had completely forgotten that his daughter was in the room because he looked surprised when he turned around and saw her standing there.

'Kids, wha? Always lookin for attention,' he said. 'Don't go away now cos I'll be righ back,' and then he took Zoe by the hand and led her out of the room.

Norman had no sooner disappeared through the door when I set about trying to free myself. I leaned forward with enough momentum to get me on my feet for a few seconds and then I slid my hands down behind me so that they were at the back of my knees when I sat down again. From that position, I could reach down and pull off the tape that was holding my shins together. Norman had wrapped the tape around the outside of my jeans and so fortunately it wasn't too difficult to undo the binding.

As soon as my legs were free, I stood up again and returned my hands to their original position behind my back so that I could walk. The action of standing up made me feel dizzy and light-headed and I had to wait a few seconds for the sensation to pass. Once I knew that I wasn't going to faint, I walked over to the door where I could hear Norman talking to Zoe in the kitchen. He was setting her to work with some paints and a colouring book. I closed the door as softly as I possibly could by using my hands to gently pull the handle down and release it again once the door was closed. I discovered that the easiest way to do this was not with my back to the door but by leaning towards it with my hip and manipulating the lever from a sort of sideways position.

A closed door in itself wasn't likely to do Chloe or me much good. Now I had to lock it. Crucially for such a manoeuvre, the key was in the lock on the inside but when I went to turn it, it was stuck. By jiggling it up and down though I managed to get some movement in the mechanism and I locked the door. But only at a price because Norman heard me. A second later, his footsteps came charging back from the kitchen and then the handle on the door flew down as he tried to open it. When he found that it was locked, he started thumping on the door.

'OPEN THIS DOOR! OPEN THIS DOOR RIGH NOW AND MAYBE I WON'T FUCKIN BURN YA,' he roared.

I knew that the door wasn't going to hold him for very long and I had only bought us a couple of minutes at best. My priority at that point was to get my hands free and for that I would need something sharp. I looked around the room but I didn't have to look very hard. My eyes immediately fell upon the knife that Norman had left jammed into a floorboard near the coffee table. With a fresh surge of adrenaline racing through my body, I hobbled over and dropped to my knees beside it.

'LITTLE PIG, LITTLE PIG, LET ME COME IN!' shouted Norman in a change of tack.

The knife was sticking into the floor at around a forty-five degree angle. I got myself into a position so that the handle was pointing away from my back and then I slipped my hands over the butt end of the knife without touching it.

'OR I'LL HUFF, AND I'LL PUFF,' roared Norman as he started kicking the door.

I needed the knife to remain stuck solidly into the ground or I was in big trouble but fortunately it seemed to be holding. My task was made much more difficult by the fact that I was absolutely shitting myself. There was a crash of splintering wood and then one of Norman's boots came through a bottom panel in the door.

'HEEEEEEEEEEERE'S JOHNNY!' he yelled with insane glee.

If my hands had been tied with rope then I might have had a serious problem but that wasn't the case. The blade was razor-sharp and the tape that was binding me melted away almost as soon as the cutting edge touched it. When the tape had been cut right through, I yanked my wrists apart and then I ripped the gag off my mouth and pulled out the sock. The sound of splintering wood got louder as Norman kicked his way through the door. He was almost in the room.

I yanked the knife out of the floor and then I ran to free Chloe. My plan was for us to escape out the window and then call the cops from a safe distance. Chloe leaned forward and held her wrists apart, making the tape taut so that I could easily slice though her bindings. Once her hands were free, I immediately set to work on her legs and I had just cut through the final piece of tape when Norman gave the door an almighty kick, sending what was left of it crashing against the wall.

'C'mon!' I shouted to Chloe, pulling her up by the arm. I then jumped over the back of the couch and began trying to open the window. Before I could get it open, though, I felt a hand clamping on to a huge fistful of my hair and then I was thrown back into the centre of the room.

'No more fuckin around!' said Norman. 'It's payback time. Bye bye, fucko!'

He raised his gun and pointed it directly at my chest. Everything had been happening so fast up to that point but now it felt as if time had slowed down dramatically. I stared into Norman's icy blue eyes and any glimmer of compassion or sanity that might have once been there had now well and truly disappeared. Nothing was going to stop him from firing the gun. I switched my gaze to his trigger finger and I concentrated hard on it. As soon as I saw that finger move, I was going to dive to my left and hopefully dodge the bullet.

While I was staring down the barrel of death, my life didn't flash in front of my eyes in the way that I had always heard it would. Instead something else happened. I started to hear that melody. The notes were grating and harsh, exactly as they had been in my dream. I thought they might have existed only inside my head but then I realised that *If you go down to the woods today* was coming from a passing ice-cream van out on the street. The sound of the music sent an image of Zoe flashing through my brain and it was the vision of her slumped over a table with blood pouring from a hole in her head. My nostrils filled with the scent of blood and suddenly, all of the pieces of the puzzle came together in my head and it became blindingly obvious what was going to happen next. Just as Norman fired, I would leap out of the way and the bullet would pass through the wall and then straight through Zoe's head as she sat in the kitchen working with her crayons.

But it would only happen if I allowed it to happen. If I didn't jump out of the way then maybe I could somehow catch the bullet with my body and Zoe would be saved. I closed my eyes and I held my breath and I braced myself for what would surely be the end. I heard an agonised cry and I thought that maybe I was having some sort of out of body experience because I was pretty sure that the sound hadn't come from me. But the cry hadn't come from me. It had come from Norman. I opened my eyes and I saw Chloe standing behind him. She had taken the knife that I had used to cut her bindings and she had plunged it between her husband's shoulder blades.

Norman's eyes were wide open with the shock of the cold metal being driven into him. He fell to his knees and he started gasping for a breath that he wasn't quite able to catch. Chloe looked terrified and in deep shock. I started walking towards her. I wanted to hold her in my arms and tell her that everything was going to be all right. She had saved my life and I was going to spend the rest of my days showing her just how grateful I was for that. I think that I might have fallen in love with her at that exact moment because my heart felt as if it was floating up through my chest. I wanted so badly to hold her and I knew that when I did, I would never let her go. I opened my arms to embrace her but in the blink of an eye, the world faded away from me and she was gone.

The last face that I saw in the world was Chloe's before the sound of a gunshot filled the room and the lights went out.

Have you ever been in a place that is so dark, it looks exactly the same whether your eyes are open or closed? Well when I opened my eyes, I found myself in such a place. A blanket of darkness had descended over the living room and I couldn't see anything. Although that's not strictly true because the living room wasn't even there anymore. There was just that now familiar black velvet space all around me. My body had become weightless and I seemed to be floating gently on a cushion of nothing at all. The tension and the ugliness of the scene inside Norman's house melted away and I felt as if I was being reborn. Relief flowed through every cell in my body and in no time at all, I found that all of the disappointments and regrets of my life had been purged from me. Where there had been despair, there was now hope. And where there had been uncertainty, there was now only knowledge. An abundance of knowledge.

Once, as a child, I had felt that same powerful surge of enlightenment and afterwards I had regretted that while I was in that place of infinite knowledge, I had considered only the past and not the future. I would not make the same mistake twice.

I reached out with my mind and suddenly, as if by magic, I was standing by the side of a grave surrounded by mourners. I spotted Chloe dressed all in black and fumbling in her bag to retrieve a packet of disposable tissues. She was not so much crying as sobbing profusely, and I could tell that she was making some of the other mourners feel inadequate regarding their own displays of grief. The peace of mind that I had finally achieved was in serious danger of being snatched away again with the realisation that despite my best efforts, I had failed to save the one last beautiful thing in my life.

Zoe was dead.

It was obvious from the flood of tears pouring from her mother and from the weight of sorrow hanging over the group. Saving Zoe would have given a meaning and a purpose to my life but I hadn't even been able to do that. Once again, I had failed.

I couldn't bear to watch her mother's pain and so I switched my focus to some of the other mourners standing around the grave. Jack was there and Fiona was beside him. She was also crying. I could see Damo, Scary Mary and Roger all looking suitably sombre. Good of them to turn up. In the second row of graveside mourners, I spotted Silky Mannix and his wife Gloria, Spanner and Donna, Tanya Cox, DJ Derek, Kelly Reilly and half a dozen or so other Happy's regulars. My old neighbour Tom was also in attendance, standing behind Lisa Brophy, my addiction counsellor. I paused to consider what on earth they were doing there as Lisa especially couldn't possibly have known the Valentines. As I scanned the mourners again, I realised that everyone standing around the grave was connected to me in some way and so finally the penny dropped that this wasn't a service for Zoe after all. I was attending my own funeral.

I quickly switched my attention back to Chloe and once again I reached out with my mind, only this time I pushed even further. I reached inside of her, searching for information about Zoe. It wasn't hard to do. Her mother had not brought her to my funeral because she had attended her father's funeral the day before and Chloe didn't want to upset the child any more than was absolutely necessary. At that exact moment, the little girl was at her grandmother's house eating a Penguin chocolate bar and managing to get quite a bit of it on her face. Later her granny will show her how to make a sponge cake and Zoe will get her first taste of cake mixture when she licks it from the spatula. It was enough to fill my heart with joy and I had to pull back from the image because the sheer wonder of such perfect beauty threatened to overwhelm me.

The realisation that Norman was also dead gave me no pleasure at all. Without a doubt, he was an appalling human being and even though he ended my life in the world as you know it, I don't hold that against him. I really don't. He did take my life from me but the truth is that there are worse things than dying and thankfully I won't have to deal with any of those things ever again. And so rather than thinking of Norman as the man who killed me, I think of him as the man who set me free.

There are plenty of things that I will miss of course. I'll miss drinking a cold beer and stopping to eat curry chips on the way home from the pub. I'll miss the captivating magic of a great film and the way my favourite rock songs could give me a rush of adrenaline. I'll miss the smell of a coal fire and watching television in bed underneath two duvets on freezing winter nights. I'll miss long hot showers and Sunday newspapers. I'll miss reading about the fascinating weirdoes who write in to the problem page of the *Star*. But most of all, I'll miss Chloe and Zoe and all of the other people who I loved and left behind. But I don't feel sad about that because I didn't really leave them. They're still with me and I'm still with them. And that won't ever change. The world can be a wonderful place full of mystery and beauty, but I'm headed for somewhere even better.

On the back of the wrapper of the Penguin chocolate bar that Zoe was eating at the time of my funeral, there were three lines of writing stating as follows: 'Funny Fact 5: In 1969, Neil Armstrong and Buzz Aldrin walked on the surface of the moon and the footprints that they made are still there.'

I'll tell you a far more impressive fact though – everyone who walks upon this earth leaves behind a footprint that will always be there. That's because the human spirit endures beyond your last breath. It will endure beyond the last person who will ever live in this world and it will endure when the earth is no more and the sun has burnt itself out. There is a goodness inside all of us, even Norman, and that is what prevails when everything else has turned to dust. And if we nurture that goodness while we are still alive, then we leave a bigger footprint and an even stronger sense of us lingers after we have moved on.

If you remember nothing else after reading my story, remember that. I'm signing off now because I have a date with my wife and I think she's been waiting long enough. But feel free to look me up whenever you drop by, because I can assure you, someday you will. You can bet your life on it.

Acknowledgments

This book would be no more than a sad little pile of unread sentences languishing in a drawer somewhere were it not for the labours and expertise of the following people, to whom I shall be forever indebted:

To Kate Weinberg for rescuing me from the slush pile;

To my agent Gillon Aitken for saying *yes* when no one else would, and taking me on this amazing adventure;

To Matthew Hamilton, my first editor, for his inspired suggestions and brilliant critiques;

To Ciara Doorley, my Irish editor, for her unwavering belief in this book even after I had given up on it;

To Jocasta Hamilton, my English editor, for her wonderfully infectious enthusiasm and for making me an offer that I couldn't refuse!

To Justine Taylor, my copy-editor, for a beautiful final polish;

To the superb team at Sceptre for being so great at what they do;

To Breda Purdue and everybody at Hodder Headline Ireland for being equally great and such a pleasure to work with;

To Karen Gillece for her publishing insights and friendship;

To Aisling Ryan, Paili Meek and Cathal McGreal for their encouragement and assistance with the early drafts;

To my friends and family for all their support and good wishes;
And finally to Rita, for sharing her life with me and making every
day magical.